BAD CRUSH

Rebecca Jenshak

Cover Design by Emily Wittig Designs
Formatting by Jersey Girl Design
Editing by Edits in Blue and Ellie McLove at My Brother's Editor

ALSO BY
REBECCA JENSHAK

Campus Nights Series

Secret Puck

Bad Crush

Smart Jocks Series

The Assist

The Fadeaway

The Tip-Off

The Fake

The Pass

Standalone Novels

Slapshot

Jilted Jock

Sweet Spot

Electric Blue Love

PLAYLIST

"Crush" by Tessa Violet
"Stuck in the Middle" by Tai Verdes
"Play Date" by Melanie Martinez
"Righteous" by Juice WRLD
"Supalonely" by BENEE feat. Gus Dapperton
"Dropout" by OMB Bloodbath feat. Maxo Kream
"Dear Society" by Madison Beer
"Like This" by 2KBABY feat. Marshmello
"I'm Ready" by Sam Smith feat. Demi Lovato
"Rooting For You" by Alessia Cara
"Superpower" by Adam Lambert
"Satellite" by Lena
"Remember Me" by Dove Cameron feat. BIA
"Queen of Broken Hearts" by blackbear
"Your Body" by Christina Aguilera
"Drinks" by Cyn
"Oh My God" by Alec Benjamin
"Bad Boy" by Juice WRLD feat. Young Thug
"So Pretty" by Reyanna Maria
"Boyshit" by Madison Beer
"Side Effects" by Carlie Hanson
"Holiday" by Lil Nas X
"Stupid" by Tate McRae
"Alone In My Car" by Niki Demar
"Fuck My Friends" by Eddie Benjamin
"If I Hated You" by Fletcher
"Break My Heart" by Dua Lipa
"Crush" by Jennifer Paige

Chapter One

REAGAN

CANCER, TODAY YOU MIGHT FEEL OVERWHELMED. GET OVER IT. SERIOUSLY, EVERYONE IS OVERWHELMED THESE DAYS. DON'T STRESS OR MAKE ANY MAJOR DECISIONS. PRACTICE SELF-CARE, MEDITATE, AND RESERVE ENERGY FOR EXCITING THINGS COMING LATER THIS WEEK. YOU'VE GOT THIS!

Few things are scarier than that moment when you wake up hungover and the events of the night before wash over you with sober clarity. My stomach twists and turns, and it isn't the bottle of wine I consumed late last night with Ginny. Though, it probably isn't helping. Neither is the lack of sleep. We drank, laughed, crafted elaborate and daring plans, as one does when they're drunk, until our late night crept into the very early hours of the morning.

I sit up in my bed and squeeze my eyes closed. My head pounds.

Flakes of gold glitter dot my bedspread. Construction paper and markers are tossed haphazardly around the floor and on my desk. Several prototypes have also been discarded around the room. Hearts of varying sizes in six different shades of red. It's like the Valentine's Day card aisle and a Michael's store had a baby, and that baby threw up all over my room. Never underestimate the ingenuity of two girls after a bottle of wine.

Oh no. No, no, no, no.

No more online dating. At least the guy from last night hadn't been fifteen years older than his profile stated. What can I say? My standards are low, expectations even lower, thanks to several dates that ranged from boring to flat-out cringe-worthy. I'm giving up on dating, focusing on my friendships or whatever cliché thing people say when they cannot go on one more bad date. Besides, my friends kick ass. Case in point, last night. Ginny is always a blast, but after another failed date, my friend really came through for me, showing up within the hour ready to console me with wine and ice cream.

I really should have known better than to get out of bed yesterday. My horoscope said I should look for the good in the worst situations. The good of last night's date—well, I'll figure that out when my head stops throbbing.

The apartment is quiet as I walk out of my room to the kitchen. My roommate Dakota is already at class. If she'd been around last night, she would have stopped us. Damn her busy schedule this semester, working and taking eighteen credits. She's the rational one in our friendship trio. Ginny is the optimist, I'm the dreamer, and Dakota is our dose of reality.

I find my phone buried in the couch cushions and call Ginny. I need a little of that optimism right now.

"Good morning," she answers. Her voice is scratchy and less bubbly than normal.

"Are you at the guys' apartment?" I peek out of the front door across the breezeway to our neighbor's door.

"No. I went back to my dorm when Heath left for conditioning this morning."

I check the time. "How long before it's over?"

"They should be finishing up now. Sometimes they go a little over. Why?"

"Why? Seriously, why?"

"Uhh..."

"The note," I whisper-screech.

She's still silent on the other end. Maybe I dreamed the whole thing. Nope, I'm not that lucky.

"I wrote Adam a letter last night. Heart-shaped and covered in glitter. Ringing any bells yet?"

"Ooooh. I forgot about that," she says like I didn't just tell her about my most embarrassing moment in recent memory. "I mean, I remember now, but I'd completely forgotten. What did he say?"

"I don't know. I haven't seen him. I'm hoping that he hasn't found it. If he has, I'm moving and changing my name." My skin goes clammy, and I take several deep breaths through my nose.

"So dramatic."

Seriously, I don't think she understands how bad this is. I just told a man I like him via a drunken craft project. Nothing makes a man fall harder than a homemade secret admirer letter. *Groan.*

"I'm going over there to grab it before he comes back."

"Why? I thought you were ready to tell him how you feel."

"Do you really think a red heart cut out of construction paper with glitter is the way I should do that?"

She giggles. "We were going for fun and heartfelt. My brother is a romantic."

"He's also a twenty-one-year-old man. I don't think bedazzling the sentiment was my best-laid plan."

"I think it's sweet."

"Well, when I decide to tell you how much I like you, I'll keep that in mind."

"I prefer chocolates."

"Helpful."

"What if he's already seen it?" she asks.

"Then I'll send a postcard when I get settled in my new town. I have to go."

"Relax. If he saw it, then he finally knows, and if not, then we'll figure out another way to tell him. You *have* to tell him."

"Promise me you'll never let me craft for a man again."

"I can't promise that. Two glasses of wine and my judgment goes right out the window."

"Again, helpful."

She laughs into the phone. "Text me and let me know how it goes."

After saying our goodbyes, I toss my phone back on the couch and cross over to the apartment where Adam, Heath, and Rhett live. I try the door, finding it thankfully open.

The living room is empty and quiet as I rush toward Adam's room. Their apartment has a similar setup to mine and Dakota's place with bedrooms on either side of the living area. Heath and Rhett are on one side and Adam on the other. I glance over my shoulder toward the hallway that leads to the other bedrooms to make sure Heath or Rhett aren't home.

As I get near the closed bathroom door, I hear the shower

going. *Crap!* He's here.

My heart races as I hurry into Adam's room. His scent temporarily stops me in my tracks. Old Spice deodorant and Calvin Klein cologne. I'm not some sort of creeper; it's just that he's worn both as long as I've known him. There are always at least two different scents of the deodorant on the vanity in the bathroom right next to the cologne, Obsession, which stuck with me for obvious reasons.

The next thing that causes me to freeze is his bed. His white sheets are rumpled, covers thrown back. My imagination runs away from me creating vivid and amazing scenarios that include the two of us wrapped up in those sheets. Sweaty, but like that glowy, dewy look, not gross sweat.

My crush on Adam knows no respectability. For the past two years, I've had it bad for my neighbor. He's just… everything. Smart and sweet, caring, protective.

He could easily be a conceited jerk. I mean the guy is seriously hot. He's the captain of the Valley University hockey team, and he's ridiculously smart. Like straight As, premed smart. But he's not conceited or a jerk. Sure, he's a bit of a playboy. He jumps from girl to girl, but not the same way his friends do. Adam is a relationship guy. He goes all-in with every girl. Those relationships just don't seem to last very long. He was with his last girlfriend for just over three months.

Three very long, heartbreaking months. For me, at least.

Giving my head a shake, I scan the room for the note. We slid it through the crack at the bottom of the door sometime very early this morning. A vision of Ginny and me on all fours, giggling and shushing one another, as we pushed my heart-shaped confession through to the other side makes me wince. *What the hell was I thinking?*

I find myself on all fours again, desperately searching for it. A trail of glitter leads me toward the bed, and I reach under it, feeling around. I pull out a dirty sock which I fling toward the hamper, and then the letter. Score!

Oh, dear lord. The nightmare version did not do it justice. It's huge and gaudy. The heart is lopsided, one side bigger than the other. My normally neat penmanship is sloppy. I have a vague recollection of acknowledging that and saying it was my passion that couldn't be contained in a tidy manner.

ADAM,
MY HEART IS YOURS.
REAGAN

With another groan, I fold it three times until it fits in my palm. That line isn't even good enough for a Hallmark greeting card. No more wine. Ever.

"Reagan?" Adam's deep voice washes over me.

I'm still on my knees. Quickly, I scramble to my feet and force a smile. I start to speak, but the wall of naked man in front of me renders me speechless.

Fresh out of the shower with only a towel around his waist, he's straight out of every woman's fantasy. At six-foot-three, two hundred and fifteen pounds (yes, I've memorized his height and weight from the hockey roster because, hello, mad crush over here), every delicious inch of him is chiseled. Jaw, chest, abs, and—I'm only guessing on this one—ass.

Water drips from his dark blond hair. My gaze follows a slow trickle that dips between the valley of his pecs, down his six-pack, and then is absorbed into the white terrycloth that hangs just below his waist. Cockblocked. Me and you both little water droplet. What I wouldn't give to be a bead of water on his–

"Reagan? Is everything okay?"

"Yeah. Perfect." My voice is tight and squeaky. Sweat beads on my forehead and between my boobs. Not the glowy sweat I was imagining happening in this room either.

One side of his mouth pulls up. His smile is my undoing every time. He doesn't do it often. Not that he isn't a happy guy, but Adam is serious and controlled. Even when he's having a good time his smiles and laughs are few.

Growing up like I did, his determination and the values he lives by speak to me in a way that I can't describe. It's as sexy as those rare smiles.

"What were you doing under my bed?" Hazel eyes narrow, taking in the scene.

"Oh, I…" My fist closes around the paper. "I was looking for my scrunchie. I let Ginny borrow it. I thought it might be in here."

"A scrunchie?"

"Like a hair tie. For my hair," I add dumbly and then comb my fingers through the tangly locks.

"Like the one on your wrist." He points.

Right, because why would I be looking for a scrunchie when I have one? Hiding my arm behind my back, I smile. "It's my good luck scrunchie. It's black and has little gold stars on it."

"I haven't seen it, but I'll keep an eye out."

"Thanks. That'd be great."

We're in an awkward stare-off.

"Anything else?" His hands go to his waist. He's literally waiting for me to leave so he can get naked.

Move your feet! Flee! Go! Don't say another word!

Unfortunately, my brain works in slow motion when Adam is nearby. Obviously, he's gorgeous, but it isn't his looks that make me dumb. It's just him. My crush is out of control. I've built him up so much over the years; no one can compare. Not even him. That's partly why I haven't told him. The other reason is far too self-deprecating to admit, even to myself.

"Nope. All good," I say finally. I lift a hand and salute him. A salute? Seriously?

"You've got a little..." He stops speaking and steps forward. His hand grazes my cheek. With a thumb, he strokes my skin. I melt into his touch. My eyes flutter closed. Sweet, sweet nirvana.

"What is this? Glitter?" he asks.

"Hmmm?"

His hand falls away, and I open my eyes to his finger in front of my face with a dot of gold. He's so close I could lick the water droplets off his neck. I refrain.

"Oh, yeah. I was crafting last night."

"Crafting, huh? Well, whatever you did, it must have been fun. Ginny was a mess this morning. Hungover as shit." Adam moves past me and digs in his dresser. He pulls out jeans and a gray T-shirt, then socks and black boxer briefs.

Right. A mess. Like me. I'm suddenly acutely aware that I haven't washed my face or brushed my teeth yet this morning. My standard sleep attire is shorts and a T-shirt, so I'm not exactly undressed, but I sure feel naked and unworthy standing here.

I'm still gawking too, which is about to get uncomfortable as he reaches for his towel again. "Are you sure you're okay? You're acting weird."

"I'm good. All good." My voice lowers like I'm some sort of suave dude. I wave him off, and the red heart falls from my hand and tumbles like a weed toward his feet.

He picks it up and looks over the red square. "Some of your crafting? What is it?"

He starts to unfold it, but I snatch it from his hands. "It was a rough concept of an idea that didn't really work out."

"If you did it, I'm sure it's great."

The compliment warms my insides. Everything he says is so perfect. "Thanks, Adam. I should..." I motion with my head. *Leave before I make this any more uncomfortable.*

One of those rare smiles tips up his lips. "Later, Reagan."

I hustle out of the apartment and back to the safety of my own. Dakota's back from class and standing in the kitchen throwing ingredients into the blender for a smoothie. The same one every day. Chocolate protein powder and a scoop of peanut butter. She adds peanut butter to everything, buys it in bulk. I've had so many peanut butter sandwiches since we started rooming together freshmen year; I can't even look at a jar of Jif anymore.

"Where have you been looking like that?" She waves a peanut butter-covered spoon in my direction. "And without shoes."

"Retrieving a secret admirer letter." I run a hand over my messy hair again and then use my scrunchie to pull my hair back. Where is that black and gold scrunchie anyway? It isn't exactly lucky, but it is my favorite, and I haven't seen it in weeks.

"Oh." Her brows lift. "Sounds like I missed an interesting night."

"You have no idea."

Chapter Two

ADAM

I'm broken.

A hot girl is sitting on my lap and the only thing I can think about is how her bony ass is digging into my thigh. I try to adjust to find a more comfortable position without tossing her off my lap. She turns and smiles at me, bats her lashes.

She's pretty—stunning blue eyes, a cute pixie haircut that few girls could pull off. My gaze drops to take in the skintight dress that molds to her curves and stops mid-thigh. Nope, nothing. I feel nothing. I really am broken.

Being single isn't my jam. Sure, it's fun hanging out and drinking, flirting, but it all feels so shallow. I flirt with a purpose—to get a girlfriend. And the one in my lap isn't really my type.

"Hey," she says for about the tenth time. That's all she says. One word, repeated. I can't tell if it's some sort of private joke we're supposed to be sharing or if it's the only thought floating in her head.

"Hey," I parrot back. I don't get the game, but I play along.

She smiles and shifts, digging her tailbone into my thigh. Fuck, that hurts worse than taking a stick to the face. At least the latter is over quickly instead of this constant, unrelenting jab.

I'm not this guy, sitting around with a random girl I'm not interested in draped over me. Which is kind of the point lately. Whatever I've been doing isn't working. Four different girlfriends in less than a year. That sounds like a lot, even to my own ears. I like being in a relationship, but I can admit that something needs to change. Maybe shallow interactions are exactly what I need right now.

The door to our apartment opens and our neighbors, Dakota and Reagan, step through. It's just a small party tonight, but the living room is crowded.

"Hey guys," Dakota says. She marches right in like she owns the place and motions for Maverick to move over so she can sit between him and Rhett.

Maverick's dog, Charli, lifts her head from where she lies on the floor at his feet.

"Hey, pretty girl," Dakota talks soft and sweet, highly un-Dakota like, to the dog.

Reagan is more hesitant and polite than her roommate. She waves and scans the room, smiling at everyone and presumably looking for a place to sit.

The only empty seat is next to me. I pull bony ass girl, Leah, higher up on my leg to make room and find some relief from her tailbone too.

"We've got room over here," I say to Reagan. "Have a seat."

She meets my gaze and then drops hers to the floor as she squeezes past us and sits as far away as she can. We've known each other for two years, but Reagan is sort of shy. I say sort of because

I've seen her come out of her shell lots of time with Ginny and Dakota, but any time I've tried to talk to her, she's quiet and hard to get to know. I always found it ironic how timid she is in person because on stage, she's vibrant and alive.

"Did you find your scrunchie?" I ask.

"What's that?" She leans closer to hear me. Honey blonde hair falls over her shoulder and tickles my arm.

"Did you find your lucky scrunchie?"

"No, but it's not a big deal. I'm sure it will turn up." She gets an embarrassed look on her face and pulls back.

She has no reason to be embarrassed, though. I know how possessive girls can be about their shit. Finding her in my room, searching under the bed for a scrunchie my sister borrowed—not even the weirdest example I can come up with. Once, Ginny had a meltdown, complete with tears, when I borrowed her concealer. I was seventeen, and it was prom night—I needed a little extra coverage hiding a zit in the middle of my forehead. Anyway, Ginny caught me with her makeup and she flailed and screamed, *"It's discontinued. That's the last tube!"* Then she didn't talk to me for three days.

"I tore my room apart this afternoon looking for it."

"You did?" Her eyes, brown with light flecks, lock on mine and hold. Her lips pull higher, and her dimples come out to play.

Leah shifts, making it harder for me to see Reagan. "I didn't find it. Found some odd things, but no black scrunchie with gold stars."

"What kind of odd things?"

"I think I might embarrass myself if I divulge too much." I inch closer.

"Well, now you have to tell me."

I shake my head. "Oh no. You wouldn't share your bad artwork with me. Speaking of, I keep finding more glitter in my room. I went to class with it all over my face."

"I'm sorry." Reagan smiles shyly again and a small laugh escapes her lips.

"It's cool. I—"

"Hey," Leah snaps at her, cutting me off. "Find someone else to hit on. I was here first."

I guess she does know more words. But man, gotta say, don't love being marked like a spot in the line for the bathroom. I also don't like anyone talking to my friends that way. Especially Reagan. She's so sweet and nice.

The Reagan I know is gentle, slow to jump into a conversation, and has never been one to get in the middle of an argument. Dakota is the outspoken one, often speaking for the both of them, but she's across the room and oblivious.

I'm slow to find my words, but I'm about to tell Leah she should find someone else to latch on to for tonight when Reagan morphs into a badass.

"You interrupted him." Her tone is still quiet but firm.

"Yeah, to tell you to get lost. Do you not see me sitting here? He's mine. I called dibs and I'm not going to sit here while you throw yourself at him all night and try to steal him."

Reagan's mouth opens, her cheeks flush. "I wasn't..."

"I think it's time for you to go." I help Leah off my lap.

"Are you serious?"

"Completely. Reagan's my neighbor and friend. I'm not cool with people treating my friends like shit."

She gawks some more as if she can't believe I'm really turning her away.

"Whatever." She adjusts her dress, pulling the hem down to cover more of her bare thighs. "This party sucks anyway." She mutters something about hockey players being stupid, which feels appropriate after I said one word to her most of the night. Leah huffs all the way to the door and slams it shut behind her.

The rest of the room doesn't even bat an eye. Girls running in and out of here, sadly it's not an uncommon occurrence.

"Well, that was interesting." I rub at my thigh with two fingers.

Reagan's large brown eyes go between the door and me, then her shoulders slump forward and she giggles. "Did that just happen?"

"I think so."

"I'm sorry. I didn't mean to scare off your date."

"Eh, it's okay. You wouldn't believe how bony her ass was. I think I'm going to have a bruise on my leg."

"Somehow, I think you'll survive."

"Probably. I definitely need a drink though. Want something?"

Her eyes fall to her lap. "Sure."

In the kitchen, I pour Reagan a glass of wine and grab myself a beer. She's reverted back to looking timid and unsure, quiet. Now I know she has some fight in her, I want to see it again.

"You were scrappy back there."

"Mean girls are the worst. Old wounds, I guess."

I can't imagine why anyone would be mean to Reagan. Aside from generally being one that hangs back out of the center of attention, she's just so sweet and good. She has a way about her that makes people want to be friends with her. I know that's how it was for me. The second I saw her, I wanted to talk to her and find out more about her. Being ridiculously hot probably had something to do with that too, if I'm honest.

Two years later, and I don't know as much about her as I should for the amount of times we've hung out.

Leaning against the counter, I scan the living room. Guys from the team and the group of girls that tend to follow are piled into the tight space watching the Coyotes play Vegas. I've never dated from the jersey chaser pool and now I'm remembering why. They outnumber us and more than one seems to have noticed that Leah left.

"Since you scared off my date, I think you're going to need to stick with me."

Reagan looks to the girls eyeing me up like a prize. "Why's that?" She bats her lashes, playing it all innocent like she doesn't know why. "I think the two next to Ginny are playing rock, paper, scissors to decide which one gets to make a move next."

"That's weird, right?"

"Yeah, that's weird," she confirms.

"If only I had someone else to be my date tonight." I tap my chin. "Keep the crazies away." *Date, friend, bodyguard.*

Her dimples pop out and she gives me a big, wide smile. "Oh, I see. You want me to be your beard."

"You're too beautiful to be anyone's beard. Let's go with date."

Ginny walks into the kitchen and looks between us. "What are you two talking about?"

I grab her a hard seltzer from the fridge and toss it to her. "Reagan's my date for the night."

"He's joking," Reagan says quickly. "He's hiding out."

"I think it's a great idea. You two would be adorable together."

My sister beams.

"All right, easy on the booze," Reagan says to her. "Remember last night?"

"Yes, I do. Do *you*?" Ginny volleys back. They share some sort of look that I can't decipher.

"Baby doll," Heath calls to Ginny from the living room. "You're too far away."

"Gotta go," she says and skips off toward her boyfriend and my roommate. It's easy to see that Heath is crazy about her, but I'm still not loving that my baby sister is dating one of my teammates. Not that she asked. She didn't. My little sister is in a relationship and I'm... I don't know what this is I'm doing yet. If it's playing the field, then I suck at it and I don't enjoy sucking at anything.

"They seem happy." Reagan watches them over the top of her wine glass.

"Yeah. I think they are."

"You don't look as angry as you did a couple of months ago when you're in the same room as them."

"As long as he doesn't hurt her, we're good."

"You should try saying that with a smile."

My jaw loosens. Shit, I do sound like a grump. "What about you? No date tonight, so that must mean last night's blind date was a dud?"

"How did you know?" She nods her head and glances at my sister. "Ginny?"

"Yeah. Before she rushed out of here last night, taking my wine, she mentioned something about your date ordering a salad for you."

"He was a Scorpio. I should have known better. I don't need

a man to order for me, and if he does, it better be something chocolate. Also, the wine was delicious and more than made up for my bad dinner, so thanks for that."

I'm grinning at her. This might be the most I've ever talked to Reagan, just the two of us. And the most she's ever said about herself.

One of the girls that came over with Leah comes into the kitchen and steps closer than necessary. Her friends wait behind her. Our kitchen isn't that big. She could stand on the other side of it and we'd be close enough to whisper.

I wonder if she won rock, paper, scissors, and if so, what she won with. Can I ask that?

"Adam, you have to come outside with us. We're going to play flip cup." She takes my hand and tugs.

"Sorry." I don't budge. "I don't want to ditch my date for the night."

"Date?" Her voice climbs and she searches my face.

I look over her head to Reagan and give her my best pleading eyes.

"Sorry girls." She sweeps in front of them and nuzzles into my side. "Tonight he's all mine. I even had to fight for him," she says that last bit with steel in her voice.

Her hand gently slides up my stomach and rests on my chest. Well, that feels… nice.

"I thought you were just the neighbor," one of the girls says.

It's a good thing one of us is an amazing actress. Reagan doesn't miss a beat. "Is that what you heard?" She laughs sweetly, just a hint of condescension.

"Okay, well since Leah left, we need one more anyway. Both

of you have to join us." The girl motions for us to follow and steps toward the sliding glass door that leads to the deck.

As soon as they're out of sight, Reagan jumps away from me. "Sorry."

Yeah, so am I. Sorry that she's no longer touching me.

"No, that was perfect." I tip my head toward outside. "What do you say?"

"Don't you think they'll figure out we're not really on a date?"

I take her hand in mine. Yep, definitely nice. "No way. Not with Scarlett Johansson by my side."

She grins. "What about you?"

"Well, I'm no Hollywood actor, so I'll just do my best to look like I'm not having too bad of a time with you," I tease. In truth, I don't worry for a second that we'll have a good time.

And for the next two hours, we do. I have to say, being the center of Reagan's attention…I don't hate it. She's outspoken, funny, and she keeps touching me. Just little possessive moves every so often. Physical reminders for our new friends. A squeeze of my bicep, a quick hug around my waist, linking our pinky fingers.

"You are ridiculously good at flip cup," I tell her after she pulls off the win for our team. "Any more hidden talents?"

"Hidden? Where do you think I practiced this talent?"

I nod. Right. Probably in this very spot.

She steps to me so her tits brush against my chest, and she places her hands loosely around my neck. Without hesitation, my hands go around her back.

"You were usually standing on the opposite side of the deck, not paying me any attention," she whispers. There's no malice in her tone, but I still feel like an idiot for not noticing.

I lean down until my lips hover near hers. "I'm paying attention now."

As the sky darkens, we give up on flip cup and sit with our new friends outside on the deck. It's cold out. The heaters are going and I brought blankets outside to help keep us warm. The girls may have been interested in me to start, but it's Reagan they're fawning over now.

She's sitting next to me. A blanket covers our legs and my hand rests on her thigh over the soft material. Winona and Sage—two of our new friends—lean forward and are touching her hair, complimenting her and basically just totally girl-crushing.

"You two should come with us to Theta for the after-hours party."

"Oh, uh…" Reagan looks to me.

"I think we're going to pass tonight," I say and squeeze Reagan's leg.

They prepare to leave, and Winona and Sage take turns hugging Reagan.

"You two are so cute together," Sage says. She's trying to say it so that only Reagan can hear, but her drunk whisper isn't quiet at all.

"The cutest, right?" Reagan says. She waves as they go back through the apartment to leave.

When it's just the two of us left outside, Reagan lets out a long breath and slumps back into her chair, giggling. "Wow."

"Thank you for that. Standing ovation-worthy performance." The few stragglers that haven't left or gone to bed are inside in front of the TV watching Rhett and Heath battle it out on the Xbox.

"You're welcome."

She's stopped acting now and I can feel her growing more distant.

"I had a really good time tonight. I'm sorry if it was weird for you. I really didn't expect that to be an all-night performance."

"No, it's fine. I had a good time too." The wind blows her hair into her face and she brushes the strands back. "Can I ask you something?"

"Anything."

"Why were you avoiding the girls so hard tonight? You and Taryn broke up months ago and as far as I know you haven't dated anyone since."

"Except you now." I tip my beer toward her and then take a drink.

"You know what I mean. A real date and hookups don't count. Those girls were pretty nice. Are you still hung up on Taryn?"

"Are you politely asking me why I haven't jumped into another relationship already? Because the guys have been giving me shit. No need to tiptoe over my feelings. I know I have a reputation for going from one girlfriend to the next."

"It's more than a reputation. You haven't gone more than a few weeks without a girlfriend in all the time I've known you."

I hesitate, nodding. I don't know if that's true, I've never really tracked it, but it's not far off.

"It's okay if you're not over Taryn. She was great. We all liked her a lot."

"She was." My last girlfriend was someone I thought I could picture a future with, but when she transferred schools at semester, we both decided it'd be easier to cut ties instead of trying to make it work long-distance. I'm a romantic, but I'm also realistic. I like spending time with my girlfriends too much to be happy with a weekend here and there. "It isn't Taryn. I'm trying to take some time, be single. Plus, with this being my last year playing hockey, I really want to see it through and focus my energy there."

"Makes sense."

"Also, don't tell the guys I know, but they have a bet going on how long before I'm with someone new."

"Oh, I know," she says. "Heath's out. He had one week."

"I guess between my buddies betting on me and the shit with my parents, it seemed like a good time to break my usual cycle." I still get an ache in my chest when I think about my parents splitting up. They completely blindsided me. I thought they were crazy in love, even after all these years. Ginny thinks I'm taking it too personally, but it is personal. Everything I believe about love and relationships was based on watching them. They were so happy. Or so I thought.

"But what if you found someone you wanted to be with? Would bad timing stop you?"

"No, I doubt I'd let anything stop me." The trouble is I'm not sure if I trust my own instincts. I never get into a relationship expecting it to fail. Yet, they always do. It starts out fantastic and then a month, or six later, and suddenly everything just feels… wrong.

"Adam, I need to tell you something." Reagan angles her body toward me. Her eyes fall to her hands. She looks so serious all of a sudden.

"What is it?"

Seconds pass, my heart rate accelerates in anticipation.

"I…" she starts and then stands quickly. "It's nothing. I should go. See you later."

Reagan beelines inside, says something to Dakota, and then heads out of the apartment. Huh. Well, that was abrupt. What a weird fucking night.

Good news, though. I'm most definitely not broken.

Chapter Three

REAGAN

COMMITTED CANCER, YOU MIGHT BE FEELING BORED WITH A COMPLACENT PARTNER. MIX THINGS UP! SINGLE CANCER, THIS IS THE PERFECT TIME TO JOIN A POLE DANCING CLASS OR READ A BOOK ON SEX POSITIONS. YOU NEVER KNOW WHEN THE RIGHT GUY WILL FALL INTO YOUR LAP.

All the usual suspects show up to open auditions for the spring play. Mostly drama majors, and a few that aren't, but who have done previous performances. We're clearly divided by the level of seriousness we bring. All the drama majors sit together on one side of the stage and the others on the opposite.

As Dr. Rossen starts to explain the audition process to the newbies, a girl I don't recognize steps into the theater.

The door slams behind her, and we all stare. She walks down the center aisle to the stage.

"I'm sorry I'm late," she says, not quite meeting anyone's eyes.

Dr. Rossen looks over her glasses impatiently. "Are you here for auditions?"

She scans the stage, looking at all of us. I can see her gulp. "Yes."

"Very good. Name?"

"Mila."

"Have a seat, Mila." She lifts her clipboard. "As I was saying, Director Hoffman and I will take auditions according to the sign-up. You'll come out, do your prepared monologue or read from the script. If needed, we'll do callbacks at the end of the week. The cast list will be posted this weekend, and we'll start rehearsals next Tuesday. Any questions?" She barely waits a second before ducking her head and walking toward the second row of seats. "Let's get started."

Everyone files off the stage except the unfortunate soul who got stuck with the first time slot. Dr. Rossen and Mr. Hoffman are both notoriously hard to impress. No one ever wants to go first, although, their moods really don't improve much the farther along we get. And this is Mr. Hoffman's first time taking the director role, so I have a feeling he's going to be even harder to win over.

Mila looks apprehensive as people push past her. I remember just what it's like to be the new girl.

"Hey," I say as I approach. "I'm Reagan."

"I know. I mean, I'm kind of a fan of yours. I've seen every student performance for the past two years." Her smile is shy, but she talks fast and animated. "Mila."

"Nice to meet you."

She follows me behind the curtain. There are a few chairs and props that people sit on. I keep going, passing by everyone and dropping my backpack in a corner. "This is my little nook."

"Oh, I'm sorry. I'll go—"

"No, wait. That isn't what I meant. Have a seat, please. I'm more nervous than normal. It would be nice to have some company."

She lets her bag fall to the ground. "*You're* nervous? I've never done this before."

"Really? Never?"

She shakes her head.

"Not in elementary school or summer camp?" I thought everyone had done some theater, however unwillingly.

"That look on your face..." She waves her hand in a circle dramatically. "Is not helping."

"Sorry." I offer her an apologetic smile. "We don't get a lot of new blood around here. Are you doing a monologue or reading from the script?"

Mr. Hoffman is one of the few directors who lets us audition for a specific part. He still casts us however he feels best suits the show, but he at least pretends to take our preferences into consideration.

"I'm not sure." She pulls out a printed script. "You?"

I hesitate to tell her. She'll know in a few minutes anyway. "I'm reading the youngest sister's tantrum at the end of act one."

"Really?" Her eyes widen and her mouth hangs open. "That's so different from anything you've done."

"No kidding." I've been cast as the quiet, the serious, the average girl, but I've never played a comedic or silly role. And I've never been the lead. Both are out of my comfort zone, but I know it's just what I need to take my acting to the next level. I can't play the same role forever—quiet, hot girl. Besides, everyone is hot in Hollywood. I need more than looks and a few college plays under my belt to be taken seriously anywhere outside of Valley University. Assuming that's where I go next. I haven't made plans that far ahead, but I like to be prepared for anything.

And I grew up on a steady diet of *I Love Lucy* reruns and cinnamon-sugar toast. Comedic and silly was sort of my whole jam. My mom was not the most attentive parent. When I got old enough to feed myself, she stopped pretending she wanted to be home altogether. She was gone more than she was at home. I'd stay up late, partly waiting for her and partly too afraid to sleep, and I would watch whatever late-night TV I could get. My cell phone bill rarely got paid, but with a decent antenna, I could manage a few channels even when the cable got shut off.

I got pretty good at taking care of myself. Lucy, and others, kept me company and helped me feel less alone. I probably learned more life lessons from TV parents than my own mother. All but the most important one—not all mothers want to be a mom.

"I was thinking about reading a few lines for the middle sister," Mila says. "She doesn't say a lot, but she's on stage quite a bit."

"Are you worried about memorizing the lines?" I settle in with my script. Another thing I like about Mr. Hoffman; he gives us the script in advance of auditions. I've had it memorized for a week, but it's still comforting holding it in hand.

"Absolutely. It took me three days to learn my audition piece. I have no idea how you do it."

"It's easy. I promise. You'll be able to recite the entire play forward and backward before we're done with rehearsals. Don't be afraid to try for a bigger part."

With that, we go silent, reading over the script and prepping. My audition time is before Mila's so eventually I stand to gather my things.

"Good luck," she says.

"Thanks. Same to you. Looks like I'll be seeing you around."

"Hope so."

When it's my turn, I head out to center stage. The lights are on throughout the theater today giving it a completely different feel than our performances where the audience is darkened, and the spotlight illuminates the action.

"Reagan." Dr. Rossen glances down at her clipboard. "When you're ready."

Nerves I haven't felt in years make my voice shaky as I begin my audition. But no matter how anxious I am, there's a sense of peace standing center stage that I don't feel anywhere else. It's anonymity while still being my most true self.

Mr. Hoffman has a great poker face that never gives away his thoughts, but he has a slight tell in how quickly he writes. If he enjoyed it, he furiously scribbles as if he's trying to get every feeling and thought down before he forgets. If he didn't feel it, he takes his time—the pen moving slowly across the paper.

I close my eyes for just a moment, breathing between words, slipping farther into character until I become someone else. The youngest sister is sassy and crass. She moves with a carefree demeanor. She's free of inhibition and wounds. She holds nothing back because she doesn't know just how cruel the world can be yet. She isn't the official lead, but her character will steal the show if done right.

If only it were as easy to apply some of those carefree characteristics to my real personality. I'm fully confident I can pretend to be anyone, but when I'm me—well, it's not as easy to fake confidence.

When I finish, I pause and hold my breath before I let my

gaze land on Mr. Hoffman. He has his pen up to his mouth, poised between his teeth. Neither he nor Dr. Rossen speaks for several seconds and the theater goes quiet. Too quiet.

He puts the pen down to his paper but doesn't write.

What does it mean when he doesn't write anything? I'm guessing nothing good.

He shifts in his seat. "Okay, thank you, Reagan. Let's take five, everyone, and then we'll resume where we left off."

I step down from the stage, heart racing.

"Can I talk to you for a second?" I ask, approaching them slowly.

Without answering, they give me their attention.

"I know that it was a little rough, but I can do this."

"This being that role?" Mr. Hoffman asks.

I nod.

"I'm surprised you went with that character. I think you'd be a good fit as the older sister or any number of other parts."

The oldest sister. The serious one of the three. A role I could perform without thinking.

"I really want a chance to prove I can do something different. This is the role I'm interested in."

His brow furrows. "Okay."

I back away, not sure if I helped or ruined my chances of being cast. "Thank you for your time."

I MEET DAKOTA AT THE TRACK AFTER BOTH OF OUR CLASSES ARE done for the day. She's already running when I step through the gate. While I wait for her to come around, I stretch off to the side. She's moving at a ridiculously fast clip for as many laps as she's probably already done.

She was a runner. Is a runner, I guess, but she's no longer on the track team. She quit after freshman year.

"Hi. How was the audition?" She stops and checks her watch. She times herself to make sure she hasn't lost her edge. According to Dakota, just because she's not competing doesn't mean she shouldn't be able to on a whim. She's one of those people who could tell me she's decided to try out for the Olympic team, and it wouldn't seem all that crazy.

She lets me set the pace as I fall in beside her, a much slower jog than she's capable of. I'm here solely because I know I need to do something to offset my other unhealthy habits. I dislike exercise only slightly less than giving up junk food.

"He didn't write anything. I think I shocked him."

"Shock can be good." Her red ponytail sways with each bouncy step. Who has bounce in their step when jogging?

My feet shuffle along the ground. "I hope so."

I push down that uneasy feeling reminding me that it's entirely possible I'll be working backstage on this one. "Why were you so late getting in last night?"

"You mean after you were outside getting cozy with Adam and then freaked out and ran home?"

"I already told you, we were *pretending*, and I was tired. Don't turn this around on me."

"Sadly, my whereabouts aren't as exciting as you and Adam flirting. I went with Maverick and Jordan on a taco run that lasted forever. A lot of people want tacos at two in the morning. So… did you finally tell him?" Dakota asks with a smile that takes over her face. My friends are entirely too invested in my crush on Adam. For almost two years I was able to hide it from everyone, and those were much easier times when no one was dissecting every interaction I had with him.

"No, I was his fake date so the group of puck bunnies that came over with Jordan wouldn't harass him."

"O-kay," she says the word slowly. "Since when does Adam shy away from female companionship?"

I feel myself getting defensive of him. "He wants to take some time between relationships before he jumps into something new."

"How is fake dating you for a night different than letting some random girl hang on him?" She huffs a laugh. "Leave it to Adam to figure out a way to not date but still date. Was it awful fake dating a guy you have a massive crush on or amazing? I can't decide if it's tragic or exciting."

"I went into the zone. I barely remember it." Mostly accurate, but I'm never going to forget the feeling of being wrapped up in his strong arms. Tragic. Definitely tragic.

"I'd hoped you'd finally told him. You *have* to tell him, Rea."

"I will. I am. I'm just trying to figure out how." I was so close to telling him last night, but I don't want to ruin everything.

"Easy. Go over there tonight and tell him. Blame it on last night if you have to. We need you to tell him."

"We?"

"Yes. Even Rhett is starting to pick up on it. Oblivious Rhett! Besides, the sooner you tell him, the sooner you'll stop going out on dates with all of these losers."

"They aren't all bad. What about Hunter, the guy from my

psychology class?"

"He brought you dandelions in a Dixie cup."

"I thought that was sweet!"

"If you say so. I think subconsciously you're saying yes to these guys you know you won't like because you don't want to like them. You only want Adam. You're never going to move on until you tell him."

Move on. The way she says it as if the idea of us together is unlikely makes my chest ache. Like I should tell him, let him laugh in my face, and then get over it. Okay, even Dakota isn't that cruel, but is that what she's expecting?

"I will tell him," I reassure her. I just have to find the right time.

When we're done at the track, Dakota heads to work at the Hall of Fame, and I go back to our place.

Adam's coming out of his apartment when I get to the top of the steps of our shared second-floor landing. He's dressed in dark jeans and a T-shirt that hugs his broad shoulders.

He tips his head when he sees me. "Hey there, sexy girlfriend."

"Whaaat?" My heart races and my brain short-circuits.

He waves it off. "Sorry, I was referring to the other night. Thanks again for that. Could have used you earlier today in the cafeteria."

"I think finding a real girlfriend would be easier." I meant me, of course, but the look on his face makes it clear that is not where his head's at. Stupid. Stupid. No, he should not find a real girlfriend if it isn't me. I swear I don't just put my foot in my mouth around this guy; I put the whole leg.

He chuckles softly. "Yeah, I guess I shouldn't complain. Most of them are nice, but I can't tell which ones are in it trying to help the guys win the bet or which ones actually might be interested. Mav is playing dirty to win. Hooking up with someone for a bet..." He shakes his head.

This is my window, maybe? Perhaps I'm overthinking it and I don't need a perfect moment or perfect way to tell him.

"Any girl would be lucky to date you. I'm sure they're all interested. Speaking of, I've been trying to figure out a way to tell you something."

"You have? What?" His hazel eyes soften, but he crosses his arms at his chest. Classic Taurus preparing to hold his ground. He must think it's something bad I want to tell him.

While I organize my thoughts, the door to the guys' apartment swings open and a shirtless Maverick fills the doorway.

"Oh good, you're still here," he says to Adam. He smiles at me and juts his chin. "Yo, Rea."

"Hey, Mav." I wave with one hand.

He looks to Adam. "Can you grab some food while you're out? The pantry and fridge are bare."

"Dude, you don't live here. Go rummage through your own pantry for food." There's no bite to his tone. Adam shakes his head. Maverick lives downstairs in a single apartment, but he spends so much time at their place he's basically the fourth roommate.

Adam's phone pings. He pulls it out and then rolls his eyes as he reads it. "Thanks for the great oral. Seriously?"

Mav cackles and throws his head back. "You're the best, Scott. Get some of those Little Debbie swiss rolls."

"You know my mom has access to my Venmo, right? She's going to see you sent me a hundred dollars for great oral."

"Then she'll be very proud of your oral game. Moms want their sons to give good head, right?"

Adam winces. "Too far."

"Thanks, Scott. You really are the best." With a wink, he disappears back into the apartment.

"I would apologize for Maverick, but I'd spend my entire day doing nothing else." Adam smiles at me. "What were you going to say before?"

"It's nothing." I chickened out somewhere around the mention of good head.

"All right." He's slow to move. "I guess I should go. Good to see you, Reagan."

Inside my apartment, I bang my head against the closed door. I have to tell him, but not today.

Chapter Four

ADAM

"Be back here at seven tonight to watch film. Take a nap between now and then if you need to because if anyone dozes off, you'll all be skating laps." Coach looks at Rhett. My buddy is notorious for falling asleep while we watch game film. "Colorado is going to be tough this weekend." With a nod, he dismisses us.

Maverick ruffles Rhett's unruly blond hair. "Don't worry. I'm sure he wasn't talking about you." He snorts and looks to me. "He totally was."

"It was two times," Rhett says, then adds. "No, three. It's so warm in there, and the lights are dim."

"You must be a firecracker in bed. Carrie is a lucky woman." Maverick slicks back his dark hair with a comb. "Do you guys want to go to The Hideout?"

Rhett rubs his stomach. "If I eat a big meal before coming back here, I'll definitely fall asleep."

"I'm having dinner with Ginny at the dining hall," Heath says. "You're welcome to come."

"I can only take so much of you two in one day. No offense, buddy. Love you, but I'm starting to feel like the third wheel." Mav looks to me. "Scott?"

I shoulder my bag. "Can't. I have a meeting with Dr. Salco. I'm hoping she found a scholarship for me. Later, guys."

After trekking across campus, I stop outside of Dr. Salco's office, then take a deep breath and let it out slowly. She's holding my future in her hands, and she is not known for her bedside, or office-side, manner.

Medical school is expensive. I don't qualify for aid, and if I don't want to end up in debt for the next thirty years, I need the scholarship she funds. One student is chosen each year. She's some sort of multi-millionaire. Her dad, also a doctor, co-founded a pharmaceutical company that took off. Anyway, the only detail that's important is that she has the ability to make my next four years of school a hell of a lot cheaper.

I step into the doorway and then freeze when another student is sitting in the chair in front of her desk. Not just any student. Janine. Also known as the bane of my existence.

"Sorry." I check the clock on the far wall. "I thought we were meeting at five."

"We are." She waves me in. "Have a seat."

The only available chair is crammed into a corner and has a stack of medical journals in the seat.

I hesitate, avoiding Janine's gaze. We've been duking it out for the past three years. Both premed, both at the top of the class, both hate to be outdone.

"You can set those on the bookcase," Dr. Salco instructs.

Once I'm finally squeezed into the small chair, she starts. "Thank you two for coming. I won't mince words. Choosing a recipient for the department scholarship has been difficult this year. You're both straight-A students, hardworking, and each juggling your own extracurriculars on top of school. Your professors have wonderful things to say about you. Both of your recommendations are top-notch. In short, it's been an impossible task deciding between the two of you."

And here I thought I was the clear choice. Sure, Janine is smart and gets good grades, but she relies too much on her book smarts and being ultra-prepared and organized. Not that those things aren't important, but being a doctor requires you to be ready for anything, to think on your feet.

"What does that mean for the scholarship?" I ask.

"You're not going to make us split it, are you? I need that scholarship more than Adam does. Half isn't enough," Janine says.

Dr. Salco raises a hand to silence us. Which is great because I need to keep my cool and that's impossible when Janine spouts off. She has no idea what I need.

"No. The rules are clear that only one student can be selected, but to help the committee choose, we'd like you both to join us for the scholarship banquet. Tell us in your own words why you should be chosen."

"You want us to give a speech?" I sit forward and swallow thickly.

"How long should the speech be? And are there any guidelines for content outside of why I'm a better candidate?" Janine takes notes on her iPad.

I grind my teeth at her eager and prepared attitude, then unzip my backpack for a pen and paper.

"Five minutes is plenty. The focus should be on your accomplishments and plans for the future. The committee is made up of doctors and professors who have been in your shoes. Make your case." Her mouth pulls into a tight-lipped smile. "I will email all the details," she says to me as I continue, elbow-deep in my bag, rummaging for something to write on.

"Thank you," I mutter quietly.

Once she dismisses us, I walk out feeling a lot less optimistic than when I arrived. Janine is a step behind me as we exit. Neither of us speaks until we're outside of the building.

"Don't look so down, Adam. Sweet talking women is your specialty, right?" She rolls her eyes.

"I doubt that's going to work considering the committee is sixty percent male," I fire back. "Also, I don't sweet talk women."

"Sure, whatever you say. At least you don't have to worry about all the old men who still think women should be nurses instead of doctors."

Yeah, that definitely sucks. I've seen it firsthand in a couple of classes too. Extra help, pulling me and a few other guys aside after class to make sure we're doing okay, and probably other instances that I didn't even pick up on.

I level with her. "I need that scholarship."

"So do I. I'm already in debt from undergrad."

I was lucky that I got a full-ride scholarship for hockey, but it's nothing compared to the total we'll need for medical school.

"What do you think they're going to be looking for in our speeches?" she asks.

"I don't know." I glance around the campus greens, mind racing. "Assurances that we won't drop out probably. Or flunk out."

"Do you want to get together to work on our speeches?" she asks, sounding like she'd rather not.

"You know, most people wouldn't share their plans with the enemy so willingly."

She mutters something under her breath that I don't catch, then says, "If I win, I want to know it's because I'm the better candidate."

"Well, when I win, you can extend that same line of thinking and know I'm the better candidate."

"Your ego is obnoxious." She takes a step down the sidewalk. "Tomorrow after biochemistry?"

"I'll be there."

THE FOLLOWING AFTERNOON, I SLIDE INTO A CHAIR OPPOSITE Janine at a table on the second floor of the library. She's already got her laptop open and a printed draft of her speech sitting beside her.

"I worked on it all night. It's rough, but I tried to hit three main points."

I pick it up and scan multiple pages. Jesus. I haven't even started. I drop it to the table. "Okay. Let's hear them."

"Point number one, I'm an exceptional student and dedicated to the medical field. I have an example of my work with the crisis line. Point number two, all the reasons why I want to be a doctor and the justifications for why I think I'll be good at it. I won't bore you with my life story."

"Gonna hear it eventually anyway."

"And point three, my goals and promises for the future as it relates to being a doctor."

"Not bad," I say. Not bad at all.

"Not bad isn't good." She sounds offended that I didn't love it.

"It's just that what you have planned is exactly what they're expecting. We both drone on about our qualifications and hopes and dreams and then they choose based on what? Who they like better?"

"That is the basic setup of this whole thing."

"They already know all this shit about us." I wave toward her papers. "They've seen our transcripts and probably our admission letters, too."

She nods. "Yeah. So, what are you suggesting instead?"

I tap my pencil on the table. "I'm not sure."

"All night and that's what you came up with?" She gives me a look like she expected as much from me. "You know, you won't be able to glide through med school like you have the past four years."

"What does that mean?"

"You show up unprepared. Always. Class, meetings, study group. And it works for you because you're smart and professors like you."

"I'm not unprepared. I thought we were meeting today *to prepare*. Instead, you over-prepared, like you always do."

"I'm sorry if I don't wait until the last minute to do everything."

"As opposed to doing it three weeks before the professor assigns it and then having to redo it because it was wrong."

"That was one time, and I was going out of town. I was trying to work ahead." She throws her arms up.

"Admit it, Janine. We're different and that's fine. Your speech is totally you and I'm sure it's great. I'm just not sure that's the format I want to go with. Maybe going different directions is best. It'll show them who we are at our core."

"Maybe. Just as long as you don't get up there and regale them with tales of your heroic performance on the hockey team."

"Dr. Salco hates hockey so I doubt that would help me." Something about it being responsible for too many injuries, yadda yadda. I mean, that's why we wear pads and helmets.

"All right. Will you at least read over my speech and let me know if it sounds okay?"

"Of course. Email it to me. I'll send you mine when I figure out what I'm going to write."

"I'll be looking for it the day before the banquet then." Janine starts to gather her stuff into her backpack. So much for getting together to prepare. But I have a better idea of what I don't want to do now. "Are you going to the mixer?"

"Haven't decided. You?"

She shrugs. That's a yes.

"What else do you think they'll be judging us on?" she asks as we take the stairs to the first floor.

"Everything, probably. Are you bringing a date to the banquet?"

"My boyfriend, Sean, is coming with me. What about you?"

"Nah. I think I'll fly solo for the event unless my sister wants to tag along or something."

She frowns.

"What?"

"I could be wrong, but I get the feeling Dr. Salco likes that I'm in a serious relationship. She told me once that the only reason she got through school without being evicted from her apartment for forgetting to pay rent or utilities was because her husband took over the bills and everything else so she could concentrate only on studying."

"She told you that? That's so personal. Also, I can't picture her young or married."

"The professors pat you on the back for a good game, and they let personal things slip to me. We each have our secret weapons."

"Well, thanks for the tidbit. I'll take my chances. Maybe they'll think being single is a pro for me—fewer distractions."

Janine looks behind me and smiles. "Heads up," she says without switching her gaze.

I open up my stance to Dr. Salco coming along our path.

"Good to see you both. Did you get my email?"

"Yes, ma'am," Janine says.

"I included the details for the mixer tomorrow night. It isn't mandatory, but it might be nice to get to know the committee before giving your speeches at the banquet next month."

I nod. "We're looking forward to it."

Dr. Salco smiles that pursed-lip upturn that I can never quite read. "Will your boyfriend be joining you? I so enjoyed getting to meet him at the department party. He reminds me a lot of my Michael. Having a support system is so important when you're in medical school. It can be really overwhelming."

"He will be there, and I agree," Janine says, smiling smugly at me.

"And you, Adam? Will you be bringing a date? A partner, friend, or family member are all welcome." Dr. Salco looks to me expectantly.

"I will," I say, keeping it vague. The one time in my life I don't want a date, turns out, I need one.

Chapter Five

REAGAN

TODAY IS THE DAY! SEIZE IT. GRAB IT BY THE BALLS! YOU KNOW ALL THOSE CLICHÉ SAYINGS? OWN THEM. THE WORLD IS YOUR OYSTER! SCARED TO START A NEW JOB? DO IT ANYWAY. LETTING FEAR STOP YOU FROM ASKING OUT YOUR CRUSH? PUH-LEEZE. WHO COULD SAY NO TO YOU? WHATEVER HAS BEEN WEIGHING ON YOUR HEART, GO FOR IT!

Today is the day!!! I tossed and turned all night trying to decide how to tell Adam, or if I should tell him, but this morning's horoscope couldn't be any clearer. There will always be a reason not to tell him. Lots of really good reasons. Like, he might not feel the same and break my heart. They are called crushes for a reason after all.

We're all going out tonight to The Hideout and I'm going to do it. I am! Probably. Hopefully. No, definitely! I pack tissues and wear waterproof mascara in case it goes badly and wear my favorite panties in case it goes very, very well.

"Are you almost ready?" Dakota calls from the living room. She's always ready before me. Fifteen minutes tops. She's so confident in her choices, so unlike me who changed five times before deciding on my favorite jeans and a cropped sweater.

"Two minutes," I yell back. "Is Ginny riding with us?"

"No, she went ahead with the guys."

I shove my lipstick and mascara in my giant purse and take one last look in the mirror. "Seize the day," I mumble under my breath.

The Hideout is a local restaurant and bar. It's the guys' hangout on nights they want to get out without worrying about kicking people out of their place at a decent time.

Get in, have a drink, talk to Adam, and then… we'll see.

It's loud and packed as we push through the bar area. The hockey team is at their usual table. Ginny stands from her seat next to Heath and throws her arms around my neck.

"You made it." She hugs me and then Dakota. "I saved you both a seat."

Maverick moves his legs off the two chairs. "Kota, Rea, looking great as always."

Dakota slides in beside him and then I take the other chair. The pitcher is passed our way and the waitress brings extra glasses. I glance around, looking for Adam.

"What's wrong?" Ginny asks.

I'm still sitting here, the pitcher and an empty glass in front of me.

"Do you want something besides beer? I can grab the server."

I stop her. "No. Beer is fine. I was just wondering where Adam is."

"Sulking," Ginny says at the same time Rhett says, "Hiding from girls."

"That too," Ginny agrees. "He's at the bar."

"Sulking about what?" I pour a drink and try not to sound too interested. Ginny and Dakota know about my crush, obviously, but the rest of the group gives me a pass and at least pretends not to know.

"There's this scholarship. He thought it was a sure thing..." She waves her hand around. "He's fine. I think it's just everything with our parents, plus the breakup, and now this. He's had a lot going on and you know how broody he can get."

I do know. Although I've never known him to sulk and hide at the bar. My stomach sinks. Here I am ready to dump more on his lap when all he seems to need is a friend.

"I think I'll go check on him and buy another pitcher for the table."

I fiddle with my hair and calm my nerves as I weave through tables and groups of people standing around to get to the bar. I follow it around all the way to the far-right corner before I spot Adam. He's positioned behind a pole and the cash register stand where all the servers work. The perfect cover for a guy of his size. Even so, he has two girls standing nearby sneaking glances. They're angled toward him, smiling, completely oblivious to his body language. It's easy for me to tell that he isn't happy to have been found. Elbows on the bar, his eyes are downcast into his beer.

I second-guess adding to his harem, but he glances over and spots me. A slow smile spreads across his face and he sits tall. "Reagan."

I step between him and the girls. "Hiding out over here?"

"Just didn't feel like chatting."

"Right. Of course." *That includes you, dummy.* "I'm just grabbing a pitcher for the table and then I'll leave you be."

"Stay. I don't mind talking to you." He leans forward to speak to the girls on the other side of me. They're standing instead of sitting at the stool in front of them. "Can we grab that seat?" he asks. Then, without waiting for their answer, pulls it closer.

The brush of his shoulder against my arm and the scent of his body wash does funny things to my stomach.

"Thank you." I sit and place my glass on top of the bar. "Is everything okay?"

"Tired, have a lot on my mind. Basically, I'm shit company tonight, but the guys wouldn't let me stay home."

"Anything I can help with?"

"You've already helped." He tips his head toward the girls on my other side. They've turned their attention to another broody-looking guy at the bar.

"Using me to avoid girls again?"

"Not my intent, but also not a terrible idea."

"Is it really so awful having so many girls vying for your attention?"

"No, of course not. I love girls and attention. Falling into something new would be as easy as breathing. It's my cycle. Trying to break it is much harder. Plus, I really do have a lot going on. Seems unfair to bring someone into that. And I suck at hookups."

"Maybe the next girl you date will be the one."

"Maybe." He snorts.

"You don't sound convinced."

"I'm not sure of anything anymore." He takes a long pull from his beer. "Maybe *the one* is a myth."

"I don't think I ever said it, but I'm sorry about your parents splitting. That's tough."

He nods. "Are your parents divorced?"

"Never married, but I'm not close to my parents like you are with yours."

"I didn't know."

"I don't talk about them much." I shrug. "Dakota's more family to me than anyone else."

He smiles. "I get that. You two are close."

"So, what else is going on with you? The thing with your parents happened months ago so that can't be the only reason you're over here brooding."

"It's this scholarship for medical school. They've narrowed it down to me and one other person. We have to go to these two events with the committee before they decide."

"Nerve-wracking."

"Yeah, no kidding. And if I wasn't already worried, I told the head of the committee I was bringing a date. And you know how I feel about those right now."

"Couldn't Ginny go?"

"No, I already tried that. Heath's friend Lincoln is coming into town tomorrow night and they made plans. And I got a tip that the committee might be looking for someone who's settled down."

"Settled down? You're in college. Seems a little old-fashioned."

"Right? I know. It's probably not a big deal, but—"

"You don't want to risk losing because of that."

"I need that scholarship."

"But you also really don't want to go on a date right now."

"Exactly."

"I'm struggling to feel sorry for you on the dating front," I say.

He cuts me a playful glare. "I'm sorry, but just pick someone you trust and try not to make too big of a deal of it. It's just a date."

Slowly, he nods. "Yeah, you're right. Fuck. Thanks for listening to me bitch and moan and then telling me to get over myself."

I smile. "Is that what I did?"

"You did, and I appreciate it. Do you want to order a pitcher and join the group?"

"Sure."

We make small talk while the bartender gets the pitcher. I thank her and stand. I thought he'd meant we'd both go, but Adam doesn't move from his stool. "Aren't you coming?"

"Nah. Go have fun. I'm gonna finish this beer and then grab a ride home. I've got a date to find. Thanks, Rea."

I pause, then finally force my feet to move. So much for seizing the day. Looks like I've seized it for someone else.

I'M STILL UP, SITTING IN THE LIVING ROOM LONG AFTER WE GET back from the bar. Dakota's in bed so I keep the volume low on the TV. I'm only half paying attention anyway. My thoughts of Adam are interrupted only by my worries about the play. Cast announcements are in a few days and I don't have a good gut instinct about it.

A light knock at the door pulls me from the TV. It's so faint I think it might be at the guys' place until it comes again.

I get up and walk to the door quietly, then peek out the peephole to find Adam on the other side. Dressed in sweatpants and a T-shirt, his feet are bare, and his hair looks like he's been running his fingers through it.

I glance down at my outfit, decide there's no time to change, and open the door. "Adam, hey. What are you doing here?"

"I wondered if I could talk to you? I know it's late. Did I wake you?"

"No. I was up. Come in."

He pads in a few steps and stops. Adam Scott is in my apartment. I can count the number of times he's been here on one hand and never when it was just the two of us.

"Can I get you something to drink?" I ask and we stand awkwardly in the space between the living room and kitchen.

"No, I'm good."

"Okay, well then, do you want to sit?"

I get a glass and pour water from the tap, mostly to give myself something to do. Adam sits on the couch next to the spot I just vacated.

"Were you studying?"

"No." I take a seat and fold my legs up underneath me. "I'm a night owl. Late-night TV is like comfort food for me."

"I prefer ice cream." He rests his hands on his knees. "I apologize for barging in, but I couldn't sleep, and I had an idea. What if you were my date to the mixer tomorrow night?"

"What?" I spill the water, curse, then set it on the coffee table. "Are you serious?"

Excitement and disappointment take turns soaring through my body.

"I was. I'm second-guessing myself right now though," he says with a small laugh. He leans forward. "But hear me out. We had fun the other night and you're the best actress I know. Those girls totally bought it. So, we do that except somewhere nicer with all my professors."

"I'm the only actress you know, and that wasn't exactly an Oscar-worthy performance. Playing flip cup and giving you a few flirty looks isn't the same thing as fooling a scholarship committee."

"We don't have to fool them. You *will* be my date."

I hesitate. The water I just drank sits heavy in my stomach. "I don't know."

"Maybe it's a dumb idea. I just thought of all the girls I could take on a fake date, you were the only one I trusted with the job. You get me, get what I'm going through." His eyes are sincere and vulnerable.

I want to say yes, of course I do, but for as excited as I thought I'd be when, and if, Adam ever asked me out, I'm so thrown and torn about how my very real feelings might complicate the situation, that I'm quiet for several moments. Will I be more disappointed if I go on a fake date with him or if he takes someone else? The answer to that is a no-brainer. "What would I say if they asked about us?"

"It won't be like that. No interrogations, just free drinks and mingling. I'll handle any questions that might come up, and as a bonus, I get to be the guy with the hottest date."

"Now you're just buttering me up."

"Is it working?" His grin is boyish and charming. Like I could ever say no to him.

"Yes. Okay. I'm in."

Seize the freaking day.

Chapter Six

REAGAN

CANCER—IT'S BETTER TO LEAVE THE PARTY EARLY THAN TO BE THE LAST ONE STANDING. WALK AWAY AND LEAVE THEM WANTING MORE.

The mixer is held in the back room of Araceli's. The restaurant sits up in the foothills and the scenery from the wall of windows along the room is breathtaking. So is my date.

Adam's wearing a classic black suit, and the combination of the suit with his longer hair is really working for me. It's definitely an added benefit of going on this fake date. He's serious arm candy, and tonight he's mine.

The event itself is amazing too. These doctors know how to do it up right. Small, high-top tables are set up all over the room. There's a bar on one side and a buffet on the other. It's all so classy, so elegant, so rich.

I on the other hand am a mess. Sure, I look good—several hours of primping guaranteed that— but I'm so nervous that my hand shakes as I accept a drink from the bartender.

I have to tell Adam tonight. I should have told him last night before agreeing to come, but I couldn't force the words out of my mouth. And a night out with Adam was too good to turn down. So tonight is the night. For real this time.

"Okay, now what?" I ask as we make our way to the center of the room. "How do you want to play this? Casual date? Serious date?"

He places a hand at my lower back. "Relax."

His touch pretty much guarantees that isn't possible. "I need to know my part."

If I don't turn on Stage Reagan soon, I'll be this bumbling, anxious girl all night and I am not going to spend the evening with the guy I've crushed on for two years being shy and unsure.

He ducks his head and speaks quietly so only I can hear, "Just be you. Beautiful, talented Reagan."

"You went to a lot of trouble to bring a date for this event for me to be myself."

"It's possible that appearing to be in a serious relationship will help my chances, but that's a long shot and I don't expect you to pretend to be in a relationship with me."

"I insist. Otherwise, I might as well duck out of here and leave you to fend for yourself."

"Please don't do that. I need at least one friend in my corner tonight."

"Then let me be both—your kick-ass friend who is also pretending to be in a serious relationship with you." If I can be anything but what I am, a girl on a fake date with her real crush, then this night will be a lot easier to get through.

He looks uneasy, but a man steps to us and says hello to Adam, and then I'm on.

"Professor Picke, this is Reagan." Adam places a hand at my elbow to bring me into the conversation.

"Hi. It's nice to meet you." I shake his hand.

He smiles and nods, but his attention goes back to Adam. "Big game Saturday night."

"Yes, sir. We're ready."

"Good, good." He slaps Adam on the back. "Congratulations on the scholarship."

"It isn't mine yet," Adam says. "But here's hoping."

"You're a bright young man." The way he says it makes the whole thing seem so insignificant, but I know this is important to Adam.

Speaking of, my date seems uncomfortable with all the praise. Adam's hand goes in his pocket and his gaze falls to the floor every so often. Especially when Professor Picke starts talking hockey again. Interesting. I guess his discomfort with attention isn't just with eager girls trying to catch his eye.

I finish my drink and then hold it up. Adam notices. Of course, he does. He's a very good date. "Well, looks like my date needs a refill."

"Yes, yes of course. See you in class tomorrow."

"Thank you for that." Adam dips his head to whisper as we walk away.

"You're welcome, but I think I need to get water if I'm going to have to slam drinks to get us out of any more conversations."

"Let's hope that isn't necessary. I need to convince these people I'm the right person for the scholarship, not chat about the season."

"I've got you," I say. I order a water from the bartender and we hang off to one side. "Who's our next target?"

He chuckles. "Take your pick. I need to talk to pretty much everyone in this room."

Wow. This might be a long night which I don't mind, but I feel a little bad for him. "How about the woman on the far left? Gray updo, gray dress, standing by herself."

"Dr. Hunt."

"Is she a professor?"

"She teaches biology. I've taken a few of her classes."

"She has great taste in shoes. Love the red pumps. Has she ever asked you about hockey?"

He smiles. "No."

"Great. Let's go say hi." I link my arm through his and do my best to ignore the shock of electricity zipping up my side.

Dr. Hunt smiles as Adam and I draw near. "Mr. Scott. Good to see you."

"You too, Dr. Hunt. This is Reagan."

"Hi," I say and extend my hand. "I love your shoes."

"Oh." She looks down after shaking my hand. "Thank you. I didn't realize that students were invited tonight as well."

Adam's throat works as if he's thinking about what to say.

"Only the two scholarship nominees," I say proudly.

"Right, right. Of course." Dr. Hunt smiles. "You've made it very hard for us to choose this year. It isn't often we have two candidates so equally deserving."

"Thank you." He shifts his weight from one leg to the other.

Her gaze flits back to me and narrows. "You look familiar. Are you premed too?"

"Oh gosh, no." I laugh. "I'm a theater major."

Her face lights up. "That's where I know you. The Christmas play was beautiful. You looked like a real angel up there."

"Thank you so much."

Adam grins down at me. "Reagan's ridiculously talented."

My face warms.

"It was wonderful to meet you, Reagan. Adam, good to see you again. I'm afraid I have to make my apologies. My husband is beckoning from across the room." She points and Adam and I swivel to find him. He's staring our direction but otherwise, I can't make out any cry for help. He's standing slightly outside a large group of men, with a drink in hand. By all outward appearances, he seems to be okay. Maybe a little bored.

"Wait for it. He'll tug his right ear every time I make eye contact."

Sure enough, he reaches up and gives his ear a pull when Dr. Hunt looks up.

"We came up with that trick years ago to save each other. He's not much for these types of events. I imagine he's had all he can take." Her smile softens. "Great to see you both."

We watch her cross the room. Adam chuckles when the man lifts his hand to the guys, clearly indicating his departure. "That's awesome. If I tug my ear, can we get the hell out of here?"

"Afraid not."

He scrunches up his face. "No fair."

"Come on, who's next?"

"Dr. Salco just walked in. She's the head of the committee."

"Great. Lead the way."

Dr. Salco is a woman in her mid to late fifties, by my best guess. Her brown hair is stick straight and falls just below her chin. Her features are sort of pinched and not exactly welcoming, but she does smile as Adam and I step in front of her.

"You made it. Very good." Her gaze moves from Adam to me.

I smile big, ready to win this woman over.

"Dr. Salco this is Reagan, my f—" He stops, catching himself before saying friend. There's an awkward beat of silence while he fumbles to correct himself.

"Fiancée." The lie slips from my lips so smoothly. I step closer and rest my head on Adam's shoulder, just like I've thought about doing so many times. In these heels, I'm just the right height to do it.

Adam makes a strangled sound and then turns his body away while he composes himself. He tries to cover his reaction by taking a drink.

I smile sweetly at Dr. Salco.

"Fiancée?" She looks from Adam back to me, eyes widening. "I didn't realize you were engaged, Adam. Congratulations."

He swallows, then starts coughing. Oh dear god, I may have killed him. Miraculously, he clears his throat and then his arm slides around my waist. He opens his mouth like he might want to speak, but then just nods.

My confident fiancé looks like he's about to break a sweat. Maybe I've gone too far, but since I've jumped over the cliff, I do it with flair.

"It's recent, but I've been in love with this man for years. The first time I saw him, I just knew."

Dr. Salco is hanging on my every word, so I keep going, telling her how I crushed on Adam from afar. I do love a captivated audience. Part reality with a dash of drama. The script is juicy, and my costar is the most handsome leading man, if not a bit shy on stage.

We've swapped personalities, it seems. He's stopped coughing though, so that's a plus.

And as Dr. Salco and I talk, more people gather around. That's the thing about a good performance: it tends to draw a crowd.

"That is quite a story," Dr. Salco says. She's not much of a smiler, but her eyes are kind and I think I've sold her.

Taking a sip of my drink, I finally stop talking and lean into Adam. It's easy to look like you're in love when you basically are.

"It really is," someone says.

I search the crowd to find the source. The tone of this new person says she doesn't believe me. When I find my hater, I suck in a breath. "Janine? What are you doing here?"

She smiles and looks like she might want to step forward and hug me, but she doesn't, thank goodness. I might be holding Adam up. He's stunned silent beside me.

Janine's boyfriend, Sean, waves. "Long time no see, Reagan."

"You three know each other?" Adam asks, finally finding his voice. His gaze darts between us.

I'm thrown, grappling for my next line. Maybe I should tug my ear.

"We all went to high school together," Janine says.

I think Adam curses under his breath, but it's so quiet I can't make out the words. Probably, *fuck my life why did I bring this crazy person as my date?*

"I'll leave you all to catch up," Dr. Salco says. "Nice to meet you, Reagan. Sean, glad to see you again. Adam, Janine, enjoy tonight and make sure you do the rounds to meet everyone. They're all very eager to get to know the both of you."

It's just the four of us, and those nerves from earlier are back. Fuck, did I just screw this up for Adam?

"You're his competition?" I ask Janine. "I should have known." She always said she was going to be a doctor. No, not just a doctor—the best there was in whatever field she decided on. The last I knew, she was leaning toward pediatrics, but that was years ago. Another lifetime, it feels like.

"Well, you would have if you'd kept in touch over the years."

Ouch. But also, truth.

"So, you two are together now?" Janine points a finger between me and Adam.

I let him take this one. I have no idea whether or not to keep selling it or back off.

"Uhh, yup." He stares at his feet.

"We're engaged," I say when it's clear Adam's not going to offer more.

"Engaged?" Her brows raise. "Only you could go from single to engaged in a week."

"Not exactly a week. Reagan and I have known each other for years. The relationship moved quickly, yes, but we've always had an…" He clears his throat again, and his voice gets higher. "Attraction."

He wipes his forehead. Is he sweating? Oh my god. My face heats with embarrassment for him. He's so out of his comfort zone and I did this to him. Also, he's a terrible actor. I guess he does have a flaw.

"Well, congrats. I'm happy for you two." She takes a step away and then turns back. "Does Lori know?"

"Who knows what Lori knows." I look away from her scrutinizing gaze.

"You should reach out. She's doing better." She takes Sean's hand. "Come on. I need to make the rounds. Bye, Reagan."

Adam rakes a hand through his hair and lets out a long breath that puffs out his cheeks.

"I'm so sorry. I got a little into the part." I wilt beside him and hang my head in shame. What an abysmal performance.

He chuckles, but the sound is too tight and brittle. He's trying to be a good sport but seriously freaking out. "Don't be. I never should have put you in this situation. This is my fault." He stands a little taller and takes another deep breath. His free hand finds mine and holds it loosely. "Well, we're committed now."

"I'm so sorry," I say again.

"At least we're in it together, I guess. Ready to get this over with?" He drops my hand but then places his arm around my back. I'm sure he's just trying to keep up with my wild story and doesn't really want to be holding me so intimately, but I lean into him, soaking up his touch.

"Ready."

He's definitely never asking me out on a real date after this shit show, might as well enjoy it while it lasts.

Chapter Seven

ADAM

Reagan smiles over at me as she talks to a group of my professors. She leans closer, like she's done a dozen times tonight and I hold my breath waiting for… yep, there it is. Boob alert. Reagan's boob is touching my arm.

My maturity has taken a real nosedive tonight. She's all dolled up in a bright green dress that pushes said boobs up, and from this angle I can see right down into her cleavage. I don't do that though (this time) because that's a crappy way to treat a friend doing you a solid. Instead, I mentally recite all the bones in the hand.

I'm not too busy distracting myself to notice the way people react as soon as she says we're engaged, though. Especially the women, but even the men, get these happy smiles and want to hear more about how we got together. People love engaged couples and they especially love us, it seems. I pause my recital of bones to listen to her retell the story of how we first met. It's at least in part based on truth. I remember that day well.

"I was moving into the apartment next door and he swooped in to help me carry my boxes upstairs."

It was one box, but if she wants to remember it like I carried twenty then who am I to correct her?

I find myself grinning and wrapping my arm around her waist as she rests her head on my shoulder. I know we're not really engaged, but Reagan is a damn good actress which makes it harder than you'd think to play along without forgetting.

Hell, when Dr. Dove, a professor in the physics department, asks to see Reagan's ring, I want to kick myself for not buying her a rock the size of my fist. Then I remember, we're not actually engaged.

Real shame. She's the kind of girl who deserves big diamonds and opportunities to show them off.

As the hours pass and we finish talking to everyone, I start to relax again. I'm usually better under pressure than this, but I've got a lot on the line.

"Wow, I don't know how you do it," I say when we finally get a second by ourselves.

"Do what?"

"Keep up the charade like that. You're incredible. They all bought it. Every single one of them. Even Professor Hammond looked like he was happy for us and I happen to know he just went through a nasty divorce."

"It was nothing." She crosses her arms at her waist, then drops them and stands straighter. "Anyone else we need to talk to?"

"I don't think so." I do a final scan of the room and loosen my tie. "Ready to get out of here?"

She nods.

Once we're in the Jeep, I lean back in the seat and blow out a breath. "That was intense. I'm sorry I put you through that. Holy uncomfortable situation, am I right? I owe you big, and I promise I'll never ask you to do anything like that again."

We lock eyes. I can't read her expression, but I can tell she's dropped the act now. Little disappointing, I gotta say. When someone looks at you like you're everything, it sucks when they stop.

"Do you want to grab dinner or something? It's still early."

"No thanks. I'm pretty tired." She stares out the window as I pull away from the restaurant. She's gotta be exhausted. I am and I was barely doing any of the work.

We're both quiet as we head back. Tonight was a lot to process. I got to see a side of Reagan I've never seen before. She was so... perfect. She said the perfect things at just the right time. She's smart and funny, and obviously observant. She could recall snippets of my life, interests, family, like she was an integral part of my life.

Sure, we've been friends and neighbors for two years but I'm not even sure Rhett could have done better. No one was looking to trip us up on our lie, but if they had been, they wouldn't have been able to. Well, as long as they only spoke to her. She was flawless. And I'm not too proud to admit that I wasn't a lot of help. She carried us to victory for sure.

Reagan walks ahead of me up the stairs toward our apartments.

"I'm sorry for tonight," she says, breaking her silence.

"What? Why? Those professors ate it up. You were great. They loved you." I raise a hand to touch her arm and then shove it in my pocket. *You're not engaged; you're just friends.*

"Yeah, they did, but you looked like you were going to faint for most of the past two hours," she states simply and opens her door.

I chuckle quietly. It was real close there for a bit while my whole future flashed before my eyes.

She steps inside. "I'll see you later. Night, Adam."

I slip into my apartment and practically flop onto the couch. I'm exhausted, but the adrenaline of the night is still pumping.

"How'd it go?" Rhett asks from the kitchen. He's drinking orange juice straight from the container and staring into the fridge.

"Great, I think. I don't know. It was weird."

"Weird? Weird how?"

I'm hesitant to tell him about me and Reagan pretending to be engaged. Rhett's my best friend, I know he's always got my back, but I guess I don't want to admit that I had to stoop to that level. I'm not proud of it. In fact, I've already decided I need to tell Dr. Salco the truth. That's not going to be a fun conversation.

I wave him off. "Want to grab food somewhere or go on a run?"

"A run?" He lifts a brow.

"I need to do something besides sit here. I'm all amped up."

Smiling, he says, "It really must've been a weird night."

"You should have seen Reagan charming my professors. If she were up for the scholarship, they would have given it to her tonight and then probably thrown her a parade. I've never seen anything like it."

Rhett grins at me. "You like her."

"What? No." I dismiss the idea not because it's so crazy that I'd be into her, but the fact that it took Reagan pretending to be my fiancée to get her to open up to me. That tells me how much of a chance I stand at there being anything between us but friendship. "I'm thankful though. I think I have a good shot at the scholarship if I don't blow the speech."

"Maybe you can get Reagan to do that for you too," he jokes.

I stand. I really do have way too much energy to sit around. "Let's go for a run through campus. Remember that old trail behind the dorms we ran freshmen year?"

Rhett grins. "That's a killer night run trail. You think it's still the same?"

"Only one way to find out." I head to my room and change quickly, come back out with my shoes in hand.

"I can't," he says, when I find him still in the kitchen. "I promised Carrie I'd call her again before she goes to bed. It's getting late there."

"Can't you just text her and tell her you'll talk in the morning?"

I can tell by his expression that's not happening. Rhett's girlfriend Carrie lives in Nebraska. They've dated since high school and have been doing long-distance all of college. This isn't the first time he's had to bow out of something to call her.

I get that it's important they communicate, but it's six or seven times a day that he *has* to talk to her. If it seemed like he wanted to, I guess it wouldn't bother me so much, but it feels like it's out of obligation.

And, I've heard their good night conversations. They last all of two minutes. Which means he's blowing off our run for a conversation that could be done through text. I don't get it.

"Sorry, man. I'll catch you in the morning."

I decide to go anyway. I'm smiling when I step outside. My brain keeps circling back to the mixer with Reagan at my side. I swear it was so real. Pausing, I stare over at her apartment wondering if she's in there watching TV like last night. I contemplate knocking and asking if she's up for a run but talk myself out of it with a shake of my head.

You're just friends, man.

Chapter Eight

REAGAN

BEAUTIFUL SUNSETS NEED CLOUDY SKIES. LOOK FOR THE MOMENTS OF BEAUTY TODAY!

"So, how was it?" Dakota asks the next morning as she gets ready. I'm still in bed and she's rummaging through my makeup searching for the eyeliner she lent me.

"It's in my purse, I think," I say and point to where it sits on my desk.

She dumps the contents on the bed and laughs. "How do you find anything in here?"

I sit up and grab the eyeliner. "Like that."

She snatches it and then sits at my vanity to sharpen and use it. Her gaze meets mine in the mirror. "Did something happen? Was he a dick to you because so help me, I'll—"

"No, nothing like that."

"Then what happened? Honestly, I expected you to wake me up when you got home last night to spill every detail."

That's what I'd expected to happen too, but after I got home from the worst date in the history of mankind, I didn't want to talk to anyone. Giving a play-by-play will remind me of the horror. Kind of like now as an image of Adam wide-eyed and swaying flashes through my head.

"It was… awkward," I say finally. "I thought that I could compartmentalize it all, but I like him too much."

And I may have cost him the scholarship if anyone finds out I lied through my teeth. I consider smothering myself with a pillow, but I deserve far worse—like sucking it up and dealing with the awful situation I got us in.

Dakota stands and checks the time. "I have to go, but I want to hear all about it later. I'm doing a tour at the Hall of Fame this morning. Lunch?"

"I can't today. I need to finish the reading for my music theatre history class this afternoon. Dinner?"

She shakes her head. "I'm pulling a double shift today, but why don't you come to my game tonight."

"Game?"

"Spikeball," she says like I should know. "Our first game is tonight."

"You were serious about that?"

"Yes." She picks up a pillow that's fallen on the floor and tosses it at me. "Will you come?"

"Of course," I say because that's what you do when your best friend asks you to go watch her play intramural sports. "It couldn't have been softball or something that I at least understand?"

"Would that really make it better?" She grins as she leaves my room.

No, today I'm not sure anything would make it better.

I don't see Dakota, Ginny, or the guys all day once I leave the apartment. I stay on campus between classes, skip lunch, and throw myself into avoidance. I'm getting an A-plus until Ginny tracks me down.

"How'd you find me?" I ask when she gets to the front of the stage. I'm sitting in the center with my textbooks laid out in front of me but I'm not really studying.

"Please. I know your spots. I tried University Hall first to see if you were drowning in coffee."

"I wish," I mutter.

"What's that?" She smiles.

"Nothing." I sigh. "What did you need?"

"I'll tell you over dinner. Come on."

My stomach growls. "I'm not eating today."

"Umm… why not?"

"Punishment."

"Rea, you cannot punish yourself for indulging sometimes. That's twisted."

"No, it's not like that."

Her brows lift in challenge.

"Fine, I'll go with you to dinner but I'm only eating foods I don't like." That seems like a fair compromise. Healthy foods only—take that self!

After we go through the line at the dining hall and get our food, we take our trays and sit down. I glance around for Adam seeing as how we're sitting at the hockey team's table.

"Their practice is running late," she says as if she can read my thoughts.

I relax and pick around my salad. When I look up, Ginny is

staring at me.

"What's with the all black?" she asks. She looks me over like she's just noticing my outfit.

"I'm in mourning."

"Oh my god, who died?" Her expression is horrified for a moment.

"No one. Just my fake relationship and any chance of ever dating your brother."

She laughs and then coughs and holds up a hand while she takes a drink of her water. "I'm sorry, what?"

I hadn't planned on confessing any details of last night, but once I start, I can't stop. And maybe that really is the punishment I deserve because it's just as awful when I start remembering all the little details that I managed to forget.

Ginny listens intently and even manages not to laugh. Though I can tell how badly she wants to as she smashes her lips together in a flat line.

"It sounds like you did him a solid. I'm sure he was appreciative, and you're just making too big of a deal out of it."

"No, you're wrong. It was the biggest train wreck since Justin Bieber and Selena Gomez."

"Oh, please, it couldn't have been that bad. Also, I loved Jelena."

"I thought he was going to faint. He got sweaty and pale, and no words were coming out of his mouth."

She grimaces. "Yeah, that doesn't sound good. I've only seen him like that one other time when he had to give an impromptu speech at an award banquet."

I groan.

"*But* I'm sure you just took him by surprise."

"Oh, I took him by surprise all right, but not the good kind of surprise. The truly scary kind that should only happen in cheesy horror films."

"Well, let's find out." She nods and her gaze goes above my head.

My entire body lights up and I just know he's here even without looking. Maybe our shared trauma has forever linked us.

"Please don't tell anyone else about the fake engagement," I whisper while we're still alone. "I'll tell Dakota eventually, but I can't do it right now. Retelling it was almost as painful as living it the first time." I'm calling that good as far as punishment goes.

She laughs and smiles. "You're so dramatic, Rea. I love you. I won't tell anyone. But speaking of secrets, t*ell him the truth*."

She stands as the guys join us. "Hey, let's sit somewhere else today."

Heath glances to me and then Ginny trying to figure out what's going on, but she pulls him along.

Mav tries to set his tray down, but Heath pulls him back. "I think she means all of us."

"This is our table. We always sit here," he says.

"Let's switch it up today," Ginny says smoothly, then turns to her brother. "Can you stay and help Rea with a problem she's having?"

She doesn't give him any time to answer before she herds the rest of the group away from us.

Adam places his tray down in front of me. "Is it okay if I sit?"

Instead of answering, I motion for him to have a seat.

He opens a bag of chips as he stares at me. "A problem, huh?"

"Not really. She knows about last night and is trying to give us time to talk."

He nods slowly.

"I'm so sorry. I feel awful about the entire thing."

"I told you, it's fine. Though I probably have to tell Dr. Salco the truth. As much as I want to win, I wouldn't feel right about getting the scholarship based on a lie."

"You're a good guy." Somehow that makes me feel worse. "Blame me. Tell her I had food poisoning, or that I had too much to drink."

"I'm not throwing you under the bus. I could have stopped you and I didn't."

I'm not sure a force of nature could have stopped me, but I appreciate him saying so. I even feel a little better now that I know he doesn't hate me.

"I forgot that you went to high school nearby. What was Janine like?" he asks between bites.

"Smart and dedicated. She's always been really competitive and driven. Her parents were hard on her to do her best and get good grades."

"You two were close?"

A stab of guilt makes me look down at the table. "Yeah. We were."

"What happened?"

"Nothing, really. We're so different. When we got to Valley, we started running with completely different groups of friends and we lost touch. I met Dakota and we became inseparable. Plus, she's been dating Sean forever, so she spent a lot of time with him."

"Makes sense. She's tough. We've been competing for years."

"Yeah, about that. She's my age; how is she already graduating this year?" It's been bugging me since last night. I knew she was premed, but I never imagined she was the person Adam was competing with.

"I think she said she came to Valley with like thirty hours of college credit. Plus, she's always taking big course loads, and she's taken classes every summer. She's intense." He shakes his head. "If we weren't always competing, I might even admire her for it."

"Right. Yeah, I'd forgotten that she took a bunch of college credit courses during our senior year of high school. Meanwhile, I was partying and getting stoned with friends."

"A stoner? Really?" His gaze narrows and he smiles at me. The first real smile I've seen since before I told all his professors we were engaged.

"For a short time. It wasn't really my thing, but I gave it a shot."

He doesn't respond at first but keeps smiling at me to the point I feel a blush creeping up my neck.

"Thank you for last night. Seriously, you were amazing. Everyone loved you. And I'll take care of everything."

Everything being my big, fat lie.

"You're welcome," I say. "So, it's over? Now you just wait to find out who won?"

He gets that panicky look from last night. "I still have to give a speech."

"Right, the speech. What do you have so far?" I am desperate to move this conversation away from last night even if it means making small talk about his speech.

"Nothing."

"Are you going to wing it? Because I feel like I should warn you, Janine is a pretty good speaker. She was valedictorian of our class and had students, parents, even some teachers in tears with her graduation speech. She doesn't come across as someone who could command an audience, but the girl can perform when the pressure is on."

"No, I know. We've done group projects together before. She's great." He blows out a breath. "I don't love talking in front of people."

"You're afraid of speaking in public?" I ask, maybe a little too accusatory. "But you're team captain. I've heard about your amazing pep talks in the locker room and on the bench."

"That's different." He shrugs. "And I prefer my phrasing to yours."

I roll my eyes. "No one loves talking in front of people."

"You do," he points out. "You're unbelievable. Getting up on stage and putting yourself out there. That's so much harder than yelling at the guys to pump them up. You're fearless. I admire that."

"Me? Fearless? You're joking, right?"

"The way you worked the room, talking to people, making them believe we were this bomb couple, and that I was some incredible guy they should all get to know—it was inspiring. You had me believing it you were so good."

"That's because I wasn't acting. Not really. Exaggerating, yes. But make no mistake—I was terrified."

"I don't understand." His hazel eyes hold mine.

Maybe it's more punishment or maybe I've just reached the point where nothing could be scarier than last night, but I decide it's time. Way past time.

"The story about how the first time I saw you and it took my breath away, how I had a crush on you for years..."

He stares blankly. Okay, apparently, I'm going to have to spell it out.

"Adam, I have had a crush on you for years. A really bad crush. So last night, it was scary for me—not because I was in a room full of strangers but because I was telling my story over and over again. Except with a much happier ending than the reality. And, look, I don't want this to make our friendship weird. It's why I haven't told you. Well, that and I've chickened out a dozen times."

He doesn't blink for a long time. He drops the bag of chips to the table and leans back all while looking at me like I've grown two heads.

Yep, more punishment.

A slow smile spreads across his face at last. "You like me?"

Chapter Nine

ADAM

Reagan has a crush on me? A bad crush? What does that even mean? And why does having a crush on me make her look so nauseated?

She nods, shrinks a little in her seat. "Did I make it weird?"

"No, but now I want to kick myself for not figuring it out. Seriously?" I can't help the grin spreading across my face. "You are always so quiet around me…"

"I'm quiet because you make me nervous. I get this total body lock up around you. I can't think or talk. It's sort of humiliating how into you I am." She screws her eyes shut and then peeks out, opening one and then the other.

"Why? I think it's fucking awesome."

"You do?"

I'm not sure why she looks so surprised. "I admit I'm stunned, but hell yeah. Last night was…"

"A disaster," she says.

"I was thrown when you told Dr. Salco we were engaged, but before that… I was having more fun than I've had in months."

"I had fun early in the night too," she says, then mutters, "Before I opened my stupid mouth."

"But honestly," she continues. "It's okay if you don't feel the same. We can go back to being friends. I just thought you should know and that maybe it would help explain my mental breakdown."

I thought I was decent at noticing when girls were into me, but I swear I never had any indication that Reagan saw me any differently than the rest of the guys. No, that's not true. There was one moment, a year ago where I thought maybe there was something between us, but nothing ever came of it.

"Do you want to hang out or something?" I'm fumbling this badly, but my brain is still slow to let this sink in. Reagan likes me.

"Isn't that what we're doing?" She smiles so that one of her dimples shows.

"Right, yeah. I meant outside of the dining hall. Not that this isn't romantic."

"I promised Dakota I'd go watch her play spikeball tonight."

When a pang of disappointment hits at hearing she has plans I realize that I may be more into this than I even realized.

"Then I guess dining hall date it is."

DINNER GOES WAY TOO FAST AND BEFORE I KNOW IT, WE'RE heading back to the apartment complex so she can get ready to meet up with Dakota.

Reagan's somewhere between the talkative and outgoing girl she was last night and the quiet one I've known over the years, and

I'm wondering if this is her – the version I never got to see.

I take her hand and walk her to her door across from mine. "What do you say, can I take you on a real first date another night?"

"I'd like that," she says and then bites her bottom lip. "Are you sure? I don't want to talk you out of it, but you were just telling me a couple of nights ago that you weren't in a good place for dating."

"That was before."

"Before what?"

"Before I knew *you* liked me. This changes everything." I squeeze her hand and force myself to take a step back. "Later, Reagan."

Ginny and Heath are in the living room cuddled up on the couch when I walk into the apartment.

"Dr. Scott!" Heath calls.

"How was it?" Ginny asks. "Did you get Rea's problem solved?"

"Yes," I say and check her expression.

She's wearing this big, uncontained smile. Wait a minute.

"You knew!" I shake my finger at her. Of course, she knew. She and Reagan are close. I can't believe she kept it from me. If your own sister won't tell you when the hottest girl on campus is into you, who will?

"She told you then? Really?" Ginny sits up and her grin gets somehow bigger. "Ahh, I thought she'd chicken out again."

"Yeah." I drop into a chair. "Some sister you are, keeping something like that from me."

"I'm a great sister, but I'm also a great friend. So…?"

"So?" Heath and I ask at the same time.

"Are you into her?" Her face pales. "Oh my gosh, do I need to go over there with ice cream and wine? If you broke her heart–"

"Chill. I admit I was surprised, but yeah, I think she's awesome. We're gonna go out. Good to see whose side you're on though, sis."

"I'd bring you ice cream and wine, too, if someone broke your heart. Back to last night, was it really that bad? She was petrified that she'd ruined everything for you with the fake fiancée thing."

"Wait," Heath says. "What fake fiancée thing?"

"I'll fill you in later," she promises.

I shake my head. "No way. The exact opposite. You should have seen her working the room. Even my hard-ass professors loved her. Oh, and get this, she knows Janine."

"The chick that's always making you look bad?" Heath asks.

"I've only ever heard you refer to her as kiss-ass Janine," Ginny says.

Heath snorts a laugh. "He's always complaining about her note-taking and showing up early then turns around and yells at us at practice for forgetting shit or being late."

"She takes notes and then emails them to the entire class. It's a tad much," I defend myself.

"Sounds nice," Ginny says. "I wish someone took notes for me."

"She's fine. We're different, and that's totally cool, but she's the type of student people want to give scholarships to, and I need them to give it to me instead."

Ginny nods her understanding. "I get it. So, Reagan crushed it. Did you?"

"They're waiting to see our midterm grades, and they want us to give a speech at the scholarship banquet before they decide. Which means I have a month to keep making them all believe I'm the better candidate."

"Okay, now that we're through the boring stuff, tell me more about Reagan. How did she tell you? What did she say?" Ginny squeals at the end of her barrage of questions. "Gah, I wish I'd been there!"

"We could have been if you hadn't made us sit somewhere else," Heath points out.

I stand to head to my room. The excitement I had after spending time with Reagan is wearing off and in its place is that same uneasy feeling about the scholarship and a speech being the deciding factor. It needs to be amazing. Especially if I have to tell Dr. Salco that I'm not engaged. "I think I'll let her tell you the story, if she wants."

"Oh, she wants." She throws the blanket off her and tries to stand, but Heath wraps both arms around her waist.

"You can ask her tomorrow. If you go over there now, I won't get you back until late."

"She's headed out anyway," I say.

Ginny sinks back into Heath. "Fine. If we're going to make out, though, we should get a move on it. I need to go to sleep early."

"Too much information," I say as I go into my room and shut the door. I'm glad my sister is happy, but knowing she's having sex on the other side of the apartment is a definite overshare.

I change into sweats and fall onto my bed with my phone and call Reagan.

She answers on the third ring. Her face fills the screen. "Hi." She's back to sounding and looking timid. "I'm just about to head out."

"This won't take long. I just realized you didn't actually say yes when I asked you out earlier, so I'm calling to ask again. We're flying to Colorado in the morning for the game, but I'll be back sometime in the afternoon the next day. Will you go out with me Sunday night?"

She laughs and the sound hits my chest. "Yes, I will go out with you."

"Good. Also, I wanted to warn you that Ginny knows you told me."

Her eyes widen. "Oh, no. Is she on her way over? I have to meet Dakota in ten minutes."

"No, lucky for you, and unlucky for me, Heath had other plans for them tonight. Did everyone know except me?" I prop my head up with an arm behind my neck.

"I'm not sure. Ginny knew first because I wanted to make sure she was okay with it if I decided to tell you."

"You asked my sister's permission?" Wow, now I know why Ginny hated that so much when guys would tell me they wanted to ask her out beforehand to make sure I was cool.

"We're friends and I didn't want her to feel like I was using her to get to you or anything else. Then Dakota found out, of course."

"And Ginny told Heath," I add. It's easy to see how it got around the group. I'm shocked they all kept it from me.

"Yeah. I don't know if anyone else knows. I wasn't really that subtle, so probably."

"Subtle enough that I never noticed."

"You were wrapped up in your girlfriends and you didn't see me like that. It's okay."

"I promise you; I saw you like that. I just didn't think you were into me. Aside from being so quiet, you never flirted with or dated anyone on the team…" *Fuck.* "Because you didn't want to date one of my teammates. Damn."

Her soft laughter seeps through the phone again. "Yeah, I've spent enough time around you guys to know how you feel about dating a teammate's ex."

Damn.

Neither of us speaks. I'm thinking back to all the times we hung out, searching for more hints, and replaying her actions with this new knowledge. Man, I hate missing things and I definitely missed this.

"You know, I remember the first time we met, too. You were holding a box and scanning the apartments like you couldn't remember where you were going."

"I couldn't," she says.

"I wanted to talk to you, but I didn't know what to say, so I offered to carry the box for you. And if I remember correctly, I did ask you out that day."

"You invited me to a party."

"That's basically the same thing," I argue. "I never felt luckier than when I realized the hottest girl on campus was going to be living next door."

"Flattery will get you everywhere," she says, and I make a vow to do a lot more of it.

SUNDAY AFTERNOON WHEN WE GET BACK, I CALL MY MOM TO check in.

"Hey, I was just thinking about you," she says when she answers. "Congrats on the game last night."

"Thanks. What are you up to?"

"I'm cleaning out the garage. I found a box of trophies from when you were little. Fifth grade spelling bee champion," she says proudly.

"I think you're safe to throw those out."

"No way. Besides, now that your dad got all of his old tools out of here, I have way more room. I'm moving everything that's in boxes into tubs and putting up shelves, so I have space in the garage to park."

Since they announced their separation, they've mostly kept any annoyance or animosity toward the other from me and Ginny, but occasionally it slips out in their tone. Who knew tools in a garage was something they'd ever fight over?

"We have a home game next weekend," I say, changing the subject. "Can you come?"

"Wish I could. Aunt Zoe is having eye surgery Friday, so I promised her I'd drive her to and from the appointment."

Another game where neither parent will be there. I already got a text from dad saying he has a work thing and won't be able to make it.

"Okay, well, there aren't a lot of home games left. You could drive up Saturday."

"Maybe," she says. "I'll check the schedule, but I promise I will drive down soon. I miss you."

"I miss you too, Mom."

"I better go. I think I took on more than I can finish in one day."

Ginny steps into the doorway of my room and I hold up a finger to tell her to wait.

"All right. I'll talk to you later. Ginny says hi."

When we hang up, Ginny walks all the way in and sits on the chair at my desk. "Mom?"

"Yeah, doesn't sound like either of them are coming to the games next weekend."

"They suck lately."

I shrug.

"They said everything would be okay and that we'd still be a family."

"We will," I promise her. Just as soon as our parents stop acting like children, but I keep that part to myself. "Now, help me figure out what to wear on my date with Reagan."

She squeals. I might not know how to fix the shit with our parents, but I know how to get Ginny's mind off it.

Chapter Ten

REAGAN

TUCK YOUR HEART BACK INTO YOUR POCKET, CANCER. NOW IS NOT THE TIME TO BE EMOTIONALLY SLUTTY. WHILE YOU'RE AT IT, KEEP IT IN YOUR PANTS, TOO.

"It's up! It's up! You look. I can't do it." I slide my laptop to Dakota when Dr. Rossen's email comes in with the final cast list.

She scrolls slowly. So dang slowly. I pace and hold my hands up like I'm praying. I want this so badly.

"Well?" I ask when I can't take it any longer.

Her face lifts from the screen, and she smiles. "You got the part of Molly. Is that the one you wanted?"

"I did?!" I jump in front of her so I can see.

"Molly, Mary, and Mara. Those are terrible names for sisters. They sound too much alike," she complains, but I barely hear her.

"I can't believe it. I got it!"

"Congrats!"

I hug her so hard she grunts and gasps for air. "This is going to be amazing!"

"I'm really proud of you," she says when I free her.

And then it really registers. "Oh no."

"What?"

"I might screw up the entire production." Holy crap.

"Wow, that was a quick turn of feelings there, even for you."

"I've never played a part like this. I'm not funny. Why did I think I could pull off a funny character?"

She grins. "Sometimes you're funny. You're making me smile right now."

I groan loudly just as there's a knock at the door.

"Sounds like your date is here. Want me to let him in and sharpen my knives while he waits?"

I laugh, hoping she's joking, as I rush to let Adam in. His hair is still damp, and he steps in with a grin that's so sexy I forget to speak.

"Hey," he says and snaps me out of it.

"Hey. Hi." I wave awkwardly.

Some of my uneasiness around him has diminished now that he knows about my massive crush on him, but I'm still nervous about all the disastrous ways this could go.

My hair and makeup are already done, so I change quickly while he waits on the couch. I send Dakota to her room with a promise that she won't threaten my date.

He stands when I walk into the living room. I clutch my purse against my body. Waterproof mascara and tissues are packed, and I'm wearing my favorite panties. "I'm ready."

"You look great," he says. He looks me over like he can't believe we're really doing this. Like he's seeing me for real. The way I always wanted him to.

With a hand at my lower back, Adam guides me to his Jeep and opens the door for me.

And then we're off. I am on a date with Adam Scott. I pinch myself – which freaking hurts – but at least I know I'm not dreaming.

The thing about all the bad dates I've been on lately is I now know how to spot one early. Little cues like silence on the ride to our destination. It's not foolproof. Sometimes things turn around by the time the appetizers arrive, but more often than not, my initial reaction to the date bleeds through to the end of the night.

And I also know what a good date looks like. Specifically, what Adam looks like on one. I've watched him date so many girls over the years.

So, when Adam and I get to the restaurant and neither of us has said more than two words, I start to panic. All the giddiness about finally going out with my dream guy turns to nerves. And then I start to babble. All through dinner. I barely touch my food I'm so busy regaling him with every detail of my day. It wasn't that exciting to start with and my retelling does not enhance it.

By the time we get back into his Jeep to go home, I'm ready to cry. I fall into silence that would have been helpful an hour ago when I recited my horoscope and his.

He starts the engine but doesn't put the vehicle in gear. I blink back hot tears. I'm so mad at myself and angry at the situation, and just… pissed that I was so wrong. How can I like him so much and then find out we're so bad together?

"Shit, are you okay?" Adam asks.

"Fine." I turn to look out the window and brush away the wetness on my cheeks.

"You're not fine. You're crying." He shifts and leans into my space, takes my chin into his hand and makes me face him. "I'm sorry. That was awful. It was my fault. Since the second you walked out in that tiny, red dress, my heart's been in my throat. My jeans are so tight I'm worried my dick might actually be losing circulation."

"What?" A surprised laugh escapes, and I can't help but stare down at his crotch. "Oh." He's hard. Really hard. "I thought you were counting the seconds until the date was over, and I couldn't stop talking because I didn't want this to be the worst date of all history. Well, second-worst date. Nothing could be worse than me forcing you into a fake engagement in front of all your professors. I'm doing it again," I say. "I can't stop. Before, I couldn't talk around you, and now, I'm blabbering on. Seriously, I can't sto—"

His hand covers my mouth, and I squeak my surprise. He chuckles and removes his hand. "Sorry, that was a dick move. I didn't mean to cut you off. It's just... I really want to kiss you and you're making it hard to find a second to dive in."

I slam my lips together. He's looking at me like he's waiting for me to say something else. "Yeah, never speaking again," I whisper.

Laughing, he leans forward. His breath is minty and soft as he parts his lips. His hand goes to my chin and then slides behind my neck leaving a trail of goosebumps.

The radio's on, but I can still hear the groan he lets out as I press my mouth to his. His kiss is the magic touch that zaps some confidence into me, and I tangle my tongue with his. My hands find his hair, and I thread my fingers through the thick locks and gently tug him closer. He comes so easily you'd think I have super strength. He's basically in the seat with me, which is no small feat considering how big he is.

One arm circles my waist, and he brings us both to his side of the Jeep. All without breaking the kiss. Impressive.

"Ouch," I yelp as my knee hits the gear shift.

I think he mumbles sorry, but that hand at my waist has shifted to palm my ass and – oh, sweet, sweet nirvana. Climbing into his lap, I sink down onto him and it's only then we stop kissing. Our lips are only millimeters apart. His hot breaths mix with mine.

His gaze locks me in place. I don't know how long we stare, neither moving, panting, wanting, reading each other before his dick twitches under me. My eyes flutter closed.

"Tell me to slow down," he pleads as his mouth finds my neck.

I have a choice—slow down, risk that we've salvaged this date enough that he might ask me on another, or go for it. One night is better than none. My horoscope told me to keep it in my pants, but, come on, this has to be the exception. Adam is my every exception.

I roll my hips and claim his mouth. I'm all in. Whether that's just for tonight or more.

After that, there's no more pleading or asking permission. Adam's hands are everywhere, guiding me over the thick bulge and then on my face caressing and tender. When his fingers slide up to cup my boobs, I lean back and the horn blares.

His laughter tickles my throat. "I think we should probably take this back to your place."

Instead, I unzip his jeans and push them down far enough to free his dick. His eyes close and his throat works as I wrap my hand around him and pump slowly.

"Condoms are in the glove box." He grins sheepishly.

Sure enough, a new box waits for me. I'm a little shaky as I rip open a foil packet, but I do it with the excitement that's built for two very long, very frustrating years.

I barely remember covering him with the latex or the short words we share after—him making sure I'm okay and that I'm sure I want to do this, and me asking if he's a crazy person because duh, of course, I'm sure. I don't even bother taking off my panties. With a little maneuvering, I shove them to one side. Crotchless panties seem like a good idea for the first time ever.

When I slowly sink down onto him, it's so much more than I dreamed. I'm breathless and fevered, and there's a frantic energy that courses through me as I hold on to his neck and let him fill me so completely.

He controls the pace. Both hands are at my waist, lifting me and bringing me back down over and over. My dress inches up, and he pulls it even higher so that his palms dig into my hip bones. The expression on his face is bliss and lust, and I put it there.

A thousand times I wondered what this moment might be like, but I never imagined it like this. I left too many things out. Things I know I'll never forget—the nip of his teeth along my jaw, deep groans that vibrate through his body, and the possessive way he grips my skin. And the feeling somewhere deep inside of me that comes alive in a way I can't explain.

My head falls forward, and I bury it into his shoulder as I come. He's only a few pumps behind me, slamming me down onto him and driving his hips up, then stilling as he finds his release.

I stay like that, collapsed onto him, until he brushes my hair away from my neck and kisses me chastely. "That was unexpected."

"Says the guy who had condoms at the ready."

A chuckle shakes his chest. "Come home with me."

We both know going to his place or mine makes this more

complicated. We'll have to answer questions once our friends know we've hooked up. And they'll know. There's no way I'll be able to hide this huge grin on my face and rumpled dress. One look at me and Ginny and Dakota would know everything.

"Okay," I agree. All in.

I TEXT DAKOTA TO LET HER KNOW I'M NOT COMING HOME AND then put my phone away to avoid any reply texts. At the guys' apartment, we get lucky and don't have to speak to anyone.

The TV is on and Maverick's passed out on the couch in front of it. And it looks like by their closed doors, both Rhett and Heath are in their rooms.

Adam hasn't dropped my hand since we got out of the Jeep. He flips on the light of his bedroom and shuts the door. Crowding my space, he stares down at me with a smile. A real one, the kind that make my stomach flip. "We've done things all out of order. I can't decide if I want to get you naked again immediately or ask you all the things I planned to ask over dinner."

"You had questions?"

He shrugs a shoulder. "I realized that I don't know all that much about you. Not like you know me. You've paid attention."

There's no use in denying it. Little has happened in Adam Scott's life these past two years that I haven't noticed.

"Why didn't you ask them at dinner and save me from myself?"

"Couldn't get a word in."

I hide behind my hands.

He laughs and slides my hands away from my face. "It was adorable."

"I'm pretty sure you know all my embarrassing secrets. Including how I blather on when I'm nervous."

"Well, I want to know more."

"Ask me whatever you want." I sit on the edge of the bed and tug him with our joined hands to follow.

"I'm having a hard time remembering what I wanted to ask. Having you here in my room, on my bed, it's pretty distracting."

"The best way to remember something is to focus on something else."

His gaze darkens, and he leans forward to press his lips to mine. Our kisses are lazier this time, and we even manage to go several minutes without letting our hands explore. But soon, he's stroking my legs, slowly moving higher until his fingertips disappear under the hem of my dress.

Listen, I know Adam's dated a lot of girls and therefore slept with a lot of girls, but I've never been more aware of it than the second he finds the hidden zipper of my dress and is pulling the fabric over my head. The man has skill.

"Not fair," I say. "You're still so clothed, and I'm basically naked."

"You can take off whatever you want," he says, voice gruff.

I reach under his T-shirt, but I don't get very far because his mouth covers one nipple, and I suck in a deep breath. He palms the other and then alternates. I've totally forgotten about getting him undressed until he lays me down and covers my body with his.

He helps me pull his shirt over his head and then goes back to worshiping my body as I let my touch roam over his back and chest exploring every muscle. And there are a lot. Adam is tall and broad. His body has been sculpted and defined by years of hockey. I find a raised line and trace the scar on the inside of his bicep with a fingertip.

"What's this from?" I ask.

"Went down on the ice with a defender my first year at Valley and took a skate blade to the arm."

"What about your pads?"

"It got through or around. Not sure. Didn't work."

Well, that's not reassuring. "Have any more?"

He rears back and points to another scar, this one lighter than the last and just below his belly button. "That one is from a stick."

"Good thing it didn't go any lower." I rub the outline of his dick through his jeans.

"You're telling me." He falls back on top of me and that's the last thing either of us says until he's covering himself with a condom.

Adam laid out next to me naked and wanting me—well, there's no horoscope that could have prepared me.

Chapter Eleven

ADAM

There is nothing that could have prepared me for this. Reagan—gloriously naked in my bed. It's like one of those ambiguous images. At first you see a wine glass, but if you squint or flip it upside down, then eventually you see there's two people kissing. Once you see both, you can't unsee them. And I'm never going to be able to unsee this version of Reagan. Lips pink and wet, chest heaving with excitement. So, *so* naked. *Fuuuuck.*

"You're beautiful." I brush her hair back away from her neck and can feel her pulse under my thumb.

As I push inside of her for the second time in an hour, I can't believe this is happening.

With Reagan. Gorgeous, shy, sweet little Reagan's pussy is squeezing me so tight and greedy. Her nails lightly scratch down my shoulders. Her tits bounce every time I pump into her. *Bounce. Bounce. Bounce.*

And I am entranced.

I flip us so she's on top. "Ride me."

She hesitates, but not for long. My hands find their way back to her tits. I sit up so I can lick and bite each one. Featherlight then rougher. She pushes me down onto the bed and takes over, which is absolutely fine with me. Reagan manhandling me… yep, no complaints here. But damn if I'm not going to get off way faster than I want.

We'll just have to go again. I plan to see this date through to the early hours of the morning, making her come so many more times. I'm making plans for all sorts of fun.

This is not how I expected tonight to go. Honestly, my expectations were that we'd have a nice dinner, talk and get to know one another apart from the group. I don't want to say this is better, but she's naked so… yeah, fuck it. It's better. There'll be time later to talk.

When her moans get louder and her movements more frantic, I take over by gripping her hips and thrusting from below. Her skin slaps against mine, her hands at my chest squeeze until her nails prick my skin.

Only by seconds, she gets off first and it is the most amazing performance. Hair wild and face of pure bliss, Reagan having an orgasm is something I want to watch on repeat.

She starts giggling, gulping in air as she collapses on the bed next to me. "Holy crap. That was amazing."

"Understatement of the decade." I stare up at the ceiling, trying to catch my breath. I don't want to move, but I need to do something about this condom.

As I sit up, noise outside of the door catches my attention. The apartment is a constant den of activity, so it isn't surprising, but the fact that the voices are hushed and seem to be centered directly outside of my door is suspicious.

"Uhh, I think we have an audience."

"What?" She snaps upright, and I point toward the door.

The whispers start up again, and I distinctly hear Ginny yelp, "Ouch, Mav, you stepped on my foot."

Then there's a round of shushing from someone or someones. I have no idea how many are out there, but I'm guessing the entire apartment is standing outside my door listening in.

"What do we do?" Reagan asks.

"Nothing. They're the idiots with their ears pressed to the door. They'll get bored eventually." I kiss her and then get up to take care of the condom.

Reagan's got the sheet wrapped around her, staring at the door when I pull out clean clothes. She's more bothered by them than I am. I guess I was expecting it. Nothing happens in this apartment that doesn't open itself up for public scrutiny. I love these guys, but they're nosy as hell.

I pull on sweats, toss Reagan a shirt, and then quietly pad to the door. I wait to be sure they're still there, but when Maverick's deep chuckle gives them away, I swing the door open without warning.

Stepping into the doorway, I stretch out an arm to stop them from getting in and hopefully shielding Reagan from view.

"Can we help you?" I ask. I try for annoyed, but it's been too good of a night for it to ring sincere.

Maverick, Ginny, Heath, Rhett, and even Dakota stand in a huddle with matching guilty expressions.

"Is Reagan in there?" Dakota tries to peek around me. "It's Reagan, right? If it isn't Reagan, then I'm going to kick your ass, Scott."

"It's none of your business. Get away from my door. It's weird.

Especially you," I say to my sister.

"Just tell us if Reagan is in there," Ginny pleads.

I don't feel Reagan approach, but she ducks under my arm wearing the large T-shirt I gave her. It falls past her knees, and I can't tell if she's wearing panties, but I sure plan to find out as soon as these idiots get lost.

"Yay!" My sister squeals the loudest, but even Rhett's got a dopey grin.

"Now, will you please step away from my bedroom door?" I go to shut it, but Maverick slaps a palm onto the open door and holds it there.

"We need details," he says.

"No," Reagan and I fire back at the same time.

"We deserve details."

Mav has absolutely no boundaries, so I'm sure he truly believes that. I wrap an arm around Reagan's waist and pull her against my hip. All our friends track the movement.

"Thanks for your interest in our sex life, but we're not discussing it."

"Their *sex life*." Heath grins. "Implies it's going to continue."

Fuck yeah, it's going to continue.

I don't say that out loud, though. Instead, I say, "Good night. Don't come back."

Reagan waves, and I manage to get the door closed and lock it.

"Well," I start and run a hand through my hair. "They know we are in here together mostly naked, so we might as well make sure it's worth the millions of questions we're both going to get tomorrow."

She wraps her arms around my neck, and the T-shirt rides up, giving me a glimpse of her bare ass. "It already was."

I lift her in my arms and carry her back to bed. "I think we can do better."

THE NEXT NIGHT, REAGAN ASKS ME TO MEET HER AT THE THEATER after hockey practice. I'll admit I was hoping she was going to do some sort of sexy performance for me. Maybe put on one of those costumes she's worn and strut across the stage. Okay, that makes her sound like a stripper, but they're my dreams and I refuse to apologize for them. I can still vividly recall her dress from the last play. It was a deep green and had a V-neck that made her boobs look huge.

I've seen just about every performance she's done since she and Dakota moved in across the breezeway from us. A private show—yeah, that sounds like a great follow-up to last night.

She sits with her books laid out in front of her, a notebook on her lap. Her hair is pulled into a low side ponytail with a black scrunchie. Black with gold stars.

"You found it." I hop onto the stage.

"What?" She glances side to side.

"The lucky scrunchie?"

"Oh." She reaches up and touches it and then glides her hand down to the end of her ponytail. "Yeah, I did. It was in my purse."

I gaze out into the empty theater. "Man, I don't know how you do it. I feel nervous just being up here thinking about what you do."

"I love it. This is my favorite place." There's a reverence to her tone.

"It's kind of creepy being in here by yourself." The more I think about it, the less I like the idea of her alone in this dark place with no one around. It might be my dislike of public speaking and standing on a stage facing rows and rows of seats, but this feels like a scene straight out of a horror movie.

"Mr. Hoffman's office is right outside, and I'm pretty sure he'd hear me scream."

"That is not reassuring."

"I'm fine. Besides, you're here now."

I pull her to her feet and kiss her. Crazy. I still can't believe we're kissing now. This is a thing. We kiss. A lot. And it's fire.

"Besides making out, what did you have in mind when you invited me here?" I'm about five seconds from distracting her from whatever plans she has if they don't include my lips on her body.

"No plan, I just went with the one place I thought we couldn't be hammered with questions. Do you know how many texts Ginny sent me today?"

"If it's half as many as she sent me, then I have a pretty good idea. What did you tell her?" I ask.

"Who?"

"Ginny. When she texted and asked *what happened?* and *what does it all mean?*" I change my voice to mock Ginny's bubbly and excited tone.

"I sent a series of GIFS indicating my silence on the topic, and I've been hiding out here. And you?"

"I didn't respond, which will drive her crazy. She's probably waiting at the apartment to pounce on me when I get home."

"That's as good of a reason to stay as any." Reagan presses her lips to mine and kisses me hard. Glad we're on the same page with our plans for tonight. Kissing. Because kissing is awesome.

There's too much adrenaline pumping through me to stay still. Attacking her mouth, I back her up, moving to one side of the stage. It's dark, but I find a wall and pin her against it.

"I can't seem to get close enough." I'm flattening her against the hard concrete, and still, it isn't enough.

I boost her up, and she wraps her legs around me.

"Any closer and we'll be one person." She tugs on my hair and sucks on my bottom lip.

"I forgot to ask about your day."

"My day?" Her laughter is the best damn sound. "My day was good. How was yours?"

"Better now."

"We're not going to be able to hide from them forever."

"I'm not hiding. I just want you to myself." I bite down on her neck, and she squeals and laughs.

There's so much I don't know about Reagan, and I want to get to know her. I honestly do, despite the way I keep mauling her. It just seems like in order to get to know each other, we have to get some of our physical feelings out of the way. And stay the hell away from our friends.

"Hello?" a male voice calls out from the back of the audience.

"Shit," Reagan whispers and jumps out of my arms. She smooths a hand down her hair frantically and steps out toward the middle of the stage. "It's just me, Mr. Hoffman."

"Reagan?"

I stay hidden, but I can see Reagan wringing her hands. Then she starts talking fast.

"Yeah, sorry, I was studying and then decided to run some lines. I guess I got a little carried away."

"All right. I thought I heard screaming."

I peek out from my hiding spot. Hoffman is a balding, middle-aged man. His hands are on his hips as he interrogates Reagan.

"I'm sorry. I was really getting into it."

Yeah, she was.

"I'm about finished," she assures him.

"Okay. I'm heading home soon. You should too."

"I will. I promise." Reagan glances over at me quickly. She doesn't move until the theater door closes.

"Oh my gosh." She walks toward me in a fit of giggles.

"Good to know you're safe in here."

"From everyone but you." She hugs my waist. "Come on, let's get out of here."

Chapter Twelve

REAGAN

EAT YOUR VEGGIES, WEAR SUNSCREEN, DAYDREAM, AND SPEND MORE TIME WITH PEOPLE WHO MAKE YOU SMILE.

My heart rate climbs with every step toward the theater Tuesday afternoon. Mila is the first person I see. She stands off to the side as if she's unsure of where she should be.

When she spots me, her face lights up. "Congratulations!"

"Thank you. You too. Understudy for not one, but *two* parts." Molly and Mary, the middle sister played by a sophomore named Harriet.

Mila tightens her grip on her backpack. "I'm so nervous. Now I have double the lines to memorize."

"Don't be." I nudge her with my elbow. "This is going to be fun."

I hold on to that hopeful attitude until after my first scene. Director Hoffman's face is pinched as he calls for us to take a break.

"Reagan." He beckons me with a wave of his hand.

I hop down from the stage and meet him in the second row.

"Are you sure you want this role?"

"Yes, I'm sure."

His mouth pulls down into a frown. "You look uncomfortable. Your lines and movements are right, but it isn't believable."

"It's the first day," I argue, feeling a prick of annoyance.

"This isn't the casting I wanted for you, but you seemed so determined I went against my instinct. If we need to make a change, I'd rather do it now than halfway through rehearsals."

"We don't need to make a change. Tell me what I need to do."

"It isn't one thing, Reagan. It's everything." He sits and crosses one leg over the other. "I think we can alter the character a little in some of the big comedic scenes, make her less over the top."

"No."

He stares at me, unspeaking.

"I can do this."

With a tilt of his head, he says, "Okay then. Let's try it again."

The first weeks of rehearsals are always grueling and frustrating, but I've never felt more picked on and discouraged than when we finish for the day.

My body hurts, which doesn't even seem like it should be possible. I was holding myself so tightly, my muscles scream from overuse.

"Good job today," Mila says as we're grabbing our bags from backstage.

"Thanks." I groan quietly. Who knew playing the silly character would be the most exhausting? I have a whole new appreciation for how hard this is going to be.

OVER THE NEXT TWO DAYS, CLASSES, REHEARSAL, AND ADAM take up every waking second. After Sunday night, we stopped making plans, and he just texts to tell me to come over as soon as I'm done for the day. We avoid our friends with muttered apologies and lock ourselves in his room, so it's just the two of us.

On Thursday, I have to throw a wrench in our routine to work on a paper I've neglected.

"There you are." Ginny opens my bedroom door and pokes her head in.

"Hey. Yeah, I have a paper due tomorrow. I've been in here since noon trying to finish." I glance out the window to see the sun is setting and then rub my eyes. "What's up?"

"What's up? Really?" Ginny walks in and makes herself comfortable, kicking off her shoes and sitting on the end of the bed. "You've been avoiding me all week."

"I'm not avoiding you." *Just spending every free second getting naked with your brother.*

"I don't know what to make of the silence from you two. Neither one of you has said a peep."

"It's only been a few days."

"I know, but usually when you come home from a first date, I get the whole scoop."

"Well, technically, I didn't come home from our first date."

Ginny smiles, but then her lips fall into a pout. "Is this going to be weird? Are you going to stop sharing things with me?"

"He is your brother. Wouldn't it be weird to hear details?"

"No," she says too quickly. "Okay, maybe. But you're like a sister to me, and I don't want to lose you to my smelly brother."

"You won't lose me. Promise." I take her hand and squeeze.

"So?" She perks right up.

"Did you just play me?"

"Give me something. I'm dying to know if you guys are like a thing now. Are you his new girlfriend? Is the bet off?"

"We haven't talked about it or labeled anything. We went on a date and hung out a few times. That's it."

"You've been banging nonstop. You're telling me you haven't had any conversations between sex rounds?"

I feel my face warming. "Sure, we've talked, but nothing heavy. I don't want to jinx it. Everything is great. We're having fun, and I think we both wanted to keep everything away from our friends until we figure it out. The last thing I want is to screw up the group dynamic."

"Well, you better figure it out quickly because we're all hanging out tonight."

My expression must give away my hesitation.

"No excuses. I'm totally cool with my brother hooking up with my best friend, but I am not cool with it driving a wedge between us. Plus, Rhett and his girlfriend broke up, and we need to be there for him and help take his mind off it."

"Rhett and Carrie broke up?"

Ginny nods.

"Wow." Rhett's had the same girlfriend as long as I've known him. Since high school, or maybe even longer. They've been doing long-distance since she's at a college in Nebraska, but I thought they were solid.

"Okay." I give in. "But I have to finish this paper first."

Ginny leans forward and hugs my neck. "No matter what, Adam doesn't come between us, okay?"

"Okay," I reply automatically. Of course, that's the last thing I want, but hearing Ginny voice the concern makes me wonder exactly what she thinks is going to happen that she'd need to choose sides.

***

When I get to the guys' apartment an hour later, everyone is outside on the deck. They've got the fire pit going and music playing.

Adam smiles when he spots me, and the guys all say hey.

Dakota's holding two glasses of wine and lifts one toward me. "Celebratory wine for finishing your paper or *fuck it, I'm dropping the class* booze. I figured it was appropriate to drink either way."

"Celebratory," I say as I take the wine. "I finished. It might be crap, but it's done."

I sit next to Adam. Not on him or any closer than I'd sit to any of the guys, but Mav grins. "You two are gonna hook up again tonight, aren't you?"

Adam throws an arm around my shoulders and pulls me closer. "Get it all out of your system. We can take it."

"We can?" I whisper to him.

"I got you."

And he does. He holds onto me as the guys tease us. Mostly, Mav. It breaks the ice, and it isn't as weird after that. I relax. I don't think I realized how nervous I was about this screwing up the group's vibe. They're important to me. They're more than friends and the only type of family I really know anymore.

Rhett's always quiet, so it's hard to get a read on his mood until Maverick turns his questions on him.

"How are you doing, buddy?"

"Fine." Rhett continues to stare off into space as he answers.

Maverick hands him the bottle of Mad Dog. "Every time you give a one-word answer, you have to do a shot."

Rhett doesn't even bother arguing, just takes the bottle and a healthy pull.

"Now, how are you doing, buddy?" Mav asks again.

"Doing fine." He holds up a hand with two fingers. "That was two words."

"Is he okay? I can't tell," I ask Adam quietly.

"He'll be fine."

"Let's play sardines tonight," Rhett says. "I don't want to sit here. I need to move around."

Everyone mumbles their willingness. We head inside to get warmer clothes. I go with Adam into his room where he pulls a sweatshirt on over my head and then a beanie.

"You're on my team tonight," he says as he adds his own warm layers.

"What about Rhett? We have an uneven number, and he shouldn't be on his own."

"He can be on a team with Dakota and Maverick."

"Do you think Dakota and Maverick are the most supportive decision?"

"Fuck," Adam curses. "I was really looking forward to having some time alone with you. I missed you today." He fists my sweatshirt and tugs me toward him. "You're staying over tonight, right?"

"Yes, but we have to sleep some tonight. I fell asleep eating lunch today."

He chuckles. "Well, come on then. Let's get this over with."

We hold hands on the walk over to campus. It's cold out, and I huddle into the sweatshirt Adam lent me. It's one of his many Valley Hockey sweatshirts, but he's worn it recently because it smells like him.

Once we arrive, Dakota and Maverick head off to hide, and the rest of us wait. This wasn't a game I'd ever played before meeting the guys. I didn't grow up with siblings or cousins, and I rarely had sleepovers where games like this might have been played.

Dakota's told me that traditionally it's played indoors, but given the limited space of our apartments, we use the main area of campus. One person or group hides, and the rest of us try to find them. Though instead of regular hide and seek, you have to join and wait for everyone else when you find them. And sometimes, we throw in crazy rules like making the seekers chug a beer or swap shirts with their partner. Pretty much anything goes so long as you don't go inside of or on top of buildings. That opens up too many possible hiding spots.

Ginny and Heath are standing off by themselves hugging and talking which leaves me with Adam and Rhett.

I'm still holding on to Adam's hand, but I keep some distance between us so that Rhett doesn't feel weird. He isn't much of a talker, so I really can't get a read on his emotional status.

"How'd I get stuck with you two?" he asks as he pulls a beer from his coat pocket and pops the top.

"What do you mean?" Adam sounds downright offended.

"I got stuck with the happy new couple."

I drop Adam's hand and cross my arms over my chest.

Rhett chuckles. "It's fine. You can touch around me, whatever. I'm fine. Totally fine."

Yeah, that's convincing. "What happened?"

"We were fighting all the time. Every day she was pissed about something else. I just couldn't take it anymore."

"You broke up with her?" I ask. For some reason, that surprises me.

He nods, takes another long drink.

"Wow."

"You did the right thing," Adam says. "You'll find someone who treats you better, who you click with, and things will be easier."

"Or maybe you two will get back together," I offer. "You were together a long time. Maybe you just need some time apart."

Adam shoots me a confused look.

"Nah, I don't think so." Rhett runs a hand through his hair, making the long top fall to one side. "It's weird, though. I haven't been single since I was fifteen."

"You were together for six years?" Now I feel even worse about them breaking up. That's such a long time to have history with someone.

"Yeah. Fucking forever, right?"

"That's way longer than I've ever dated anyone. I can't imagine."

"What about you two?" Rhett asks us. Then he looks at me. "Is this a thing? Are you his girlfriend?"

"Oh, uh…" Nothing like being put on the spot.

"You haven't talked about it, huh?" Rhett grins. "You know what might cheer me up?"

"What?" Adam asks. He steps closer to me, almost as if he's

trying to reassure me with his presence.

"If you wait another three weeks to make it official. I'll be fifty bucks richer and, really, what's another month?"

The bet. Of course. Rhett is the most competitive guy of the group. It probably would make him feel better. Boys are strange.

"We're not jumping into anything," I say. Adam and I haven't talked about it, but I think that's true. It's true for me. While being Adam Scott's girlfriend sounds amazing, he was just telling me how he needed to switch things up and get out of old patterns.

"Except each other's beds?"

Adam's phone alarm goes off. "It's time," he calls loud enough that Heath and Ginny can hear.

"Let's go." He shoves Rhett. "You keep talking, and I'm going to forget about your broken heart and get pissed at you for saying shit like that to my—"

"Your girl?" Rhett grins. "You were going to say your girl, weren't you?"

Adam's mouth pulls into a straight line. I link my arm through his. "Come on, you two. I think I know where they are. Dakota mentioned something about finding a good hiding spot near the library."

"I gotta take a piss."

"Now?" Adam complains.

"I'll be quick," Rhett promises and jogs toward the nearest building.

When he disappears inside, Adam turns to me. "Sorry about that."

"Don't be. I expected it. Though not from Rhett."

"I guess we should have talked about what to say. It's my

fault. Any time I've hung out with a girl this much, she's been my girlfriend."

"It's okay. Really. You don't owe me any explanations. I'm perfectly content not labeling this and hanging out. You want to break your routine, and I just want to spend more time together."

"That's the thing, though. I'm not sure I'm okay not labeling it." His lips come down to meet mine, and his hands circle my waist. His face is cold, but his mouth and body are warm, and I snuggle in closer to both.

"I'm back." Rhett falls in beside us.

He's opening another beer when I pull myself away from Adam.

"How many have you had tonight?" Adam juts his chin toward the can.

"Don't know. Not enough. Maverick promised there was a point in which I'd forget everything, including my name, but I still know it. Rhett. R-H-E-T-T."

"Are you drunk?" I ask through a laugh. I don't think I've ever seen Rhett drunk. Sure, he drinks when we all hang out, but it's never altered him in any way I could tell.

He winks at me and keeps on spelling his middle name and then his last name. Well, this is new. I don't even think he's looking for Maverick and Dakota. I've been his partner more than anyone else, and I can say without a doubt he takes it far more seriously than the rest of us. He gets off on the competition.

Speaking of the competition, we're the last group to find Mav and Dakota. It's been over thirty minutes of us searching when we hear whispers and find Ginny, Dakota, Heath, and Maverick crammed together underneath a table outside of University Hall.

"Finally." Maverick stretches out his legs. "Cramp. Fuuuck. I have a cramp." He holds his calf and cries out.

Everyone else is laughing as he dramatically curses and rolls to his side. Adam crouches down beside him.

"Massage it," he instructs. "Try to stretch out your leg again."

"Fucking hurts when I do that," Mav complains.

"All right. Stand up. Maybe that'll help." Adam helps him to his feet, and Maverick slowly puts pressure on the leg with the cramp.

"Damn, that was a bad one," Mav says once he's hobbling around a little.

"You need to make sure you're stretching out really well every day."

"Sure thing, Dr. Scott."

On the way back, Adam sticks near Maverick. He's walking on his own, but slowly and stopping every twenty feet or so to rub the muscle.

Ginny and Heath make their excuses as soon as we're back and head to bed. Rhett starts up the Xbox. I sit next to Maverick on the couch. He's screwing off the top of his Mad Dog when Adam comes from the kitchen with a Gatorade. "Perhaps you should try this instead?"

"I'll use it as a chaser."

Adam laughs quietly and sinks into the cushion beside me.

"I think I'm off, too," Dakota says with a yawn. She stops at the door. "Are you sleeping here?" she asks me.

"Yeah. Running after classes tomorrow?" I've seen less of Dakota this week, and I think that's harder on me than her. I need her, and I need us to be close like we've always been.

"I'll meet you there." She says good night, and then it's just the guys and me.

Adam places a hand on my thigh, and I nuzzle into his side. He's talking to Rhett and Mav about practices and then the game they're playing on the Xbox. The long week of late nights has caught up to me, and at some point, I fall asleep only to wake when he lowers me onto his bed.

It's dark with just a small amount of light from the sliding glass door that leads out to the deck from his room.

"Sorry," I say, my voice is deep from sleep. "I guess I was tired."

He strips down to his boxers and gets into bed next to me. "It's okay. Been a long week."

He draws me against him and kisses me. He tastes like toothpaste.

"I need to brush my teeth and wash my face," I say as I pull back.

I also really need to take off this bra. It's pretty and lacy with some awesome padding that makes my boobs look A-plus, but the comfort is more C-minus.

"Hurry back." His tongue sweeps into my mouth, and he kisses me deeply before letting me go.

I do hurry, but by the time I get back, his eyes are closed, arm thrown over his face. I grab one of his T-shirts and change into that. Carefully, I get into bed, trying not to wake him. One arm reaches around my waist and pulls me tight against his chest. His nose nuzzles into my hair, and he places a kiss on my neck. "Night, beautiful."

Chapter Thirteen

ADAM

I'm stretching out as the rest of the team arrives for our morning skate. They take the ice slow and quiet.

"What do you say, boys?" I force a pep into my voice that I definitely don't feel.

Last night was the first time I got more than a few hours of sleep all week. I'm not complaining. Far from it. I'd do it all over again, but it makes being a leader and setting the tone for this weekend's games a little tougher when I'm fighting back a yawn.

We've got the team playlist going—a mix-up of songs submitted by each guy that Maverick puts together. We skate for thirty minutes on game days—no more and no less. It's a light skate. We go through a few drills just to get the nerves out, and, in the case of some of the guys, work out the alcohol from the night before. Food and a nap and they'll be good to go tonight.

Rhett's dragging today. Not surprising considering the breakup and the amount he drank last night. I'm glad he finally ended things with Carrie. Not liking your best friend's girlfriend is a real bummer. I tried to warm up to her, really, I did.

He gave so much, and it was never enough for her. If he called her twice a day, then why wasn't he calling three times? She hated that he played hockey because it meant he couldn't travel to see her on the weekends, but did she visit? Rarely. Maybe once a semester. It was hard to watch him with her these past four years we've been teammates and roommates.

Not that my relationships have been the picture of excellence. Hopefully, that's changing, though. Things with Reagan are going so well I have to remind myself that I'm trying to break my cycle of jumping in and getting too serious too fast. From night one, I planned to take it slow, but there's just no doing that with Reagan.

We're spending every night together, I think about her during the day, and it still doesn't feel like enough. I want to be with her all the time. I don't want to date anyone else, and I sure as hell don't want her to date anyone else. I should probably mention that. You can have a casual but exclusive thing, right?

I shake my head. This is what I do. Give myself completely, jump in headfirst, and live in that new relationship until the little things I overlooked in the beginning start to pile up, and I realize it'll never work. I want this time to be different. I need it to be.

Reagan isn't like the girls I've dated in the past. She's my friend and neighbor; she's tight with Ginny. No matter what happens, she's going to be part of my life. It's almost like it automatically became serious when we crossed over that line. Or hurdled over it in our case. I care about what happens between us, of course, but also just about her.

I should probably do the opposite of whatever I think is right—put some space between us, slam the damn brakes on. She's got a full day of classes, and I've got the game tonight and another tomorrow, so that shouldn't be too hard. Though, I'm already itching to text her, kiss her…

"How are you feeling?" I ask Rhett as I fall in beside him.

"Like I put my liver through a shredder last night." He smells like the sweet liquor he drank, and I put a little more distance between us to breathe some nonalcoholic air.

"I'm sorry about Carrie. I don't think I said that last night."

"You definitely didn't, and no, you aren't." He cuts me a knowing look.

"Fine. I'm not sorry you broke up, but I am sorry that you're bummed."

"Bummed?" He scoffs. "We've been together since high school. I've known her since I was four years old. I'm not bummed. That makes it sound like I'm a child disappointed that there's no more ice cream. My world is rocked."

I search his face for understanding. "But you broke up with her."

"And I feel awful about it. Sick to my stomach."

"Then why did you do it?" Honestly, I never thought he would. He's grumbled about her before, mentioned in passing that things seemed harder between them this past year, that they had less and less in common, but then he'd be on the phone with her twenty minutes later, and everything would be great again.

"Because I don't want to hate her or dread talking to her. She might not be the person for me, but I care about her. She saw something in me when no one else did. I was nothing before I met her. Miserable and lonely. I owe her a lot."

Rhett's made no attempt to hide that he was a skinny, unpopular kid until he started dating Carrie, but I think he gives her too much credit. He's a great guy. I have no doubt he was also a great kid, and I know he was a great boyfriend. I saw it day after day. She liked him for who he is instead of what he looked like. That doesn't make her a saint. Besides, he grew into his giant frame and big nose. He's a good-looking guy now, according to the girls that often hang around trying to get his attention. He'll have no problem finding someone new.

"I'm here for you. Whatever you need. You want to have people over tonight and get stupid?" I secretly hope that isn't the answer because we need to be sharp for our games this weekend. One night of heavy drinking he might be able to push through, but two?

"No, man. I'm good. It's just going to take time."

"The offer's good anytime. Whatever you need."

"Thanks." He nods his appreciation. "What about you and Reagan? Did you lock that down yet?"

We get in the back of the line for passing drills. "We're taking it slow. You heard her last night. We're not jumping into anything."

"Why not? Reagan's great."

"Because I want this to work, and in the past when I've been too quick to label things, it's blown up in my face."

"But you're still doing it." Rhett gives his head a shake. "You can call it, or not call it, whatever you want, but you're treating her like you do all your new girlfriends."

"I'm not," I say, though I can't offer any evidence of that. I grind down on my molars. He's right. Of course, he is, but I'm in unchartered waters. I want to make her my girlfriend, but it's only been a week, and that's exactly what the old me would have done. Acknowledging that is like admitting that I'm setting us up for failure.

"All I'm saying is, I've seen you date a lot of girls. So has Reagan. If you're not being clear about whatever it is you're doing, then you're both assuming something. Make sure that something is the same thing."

"Your advice is that I should clarify that we're not together?"

He chuckles. "Or that you are."

GINNY'S AT MY APARTMENT WHEN I GET BACK. SITTING ON THE couch braiding her hair, she nods in greeting.

"What are you still doing here?" I ask, tossing my bag in the general direction of my room and sitting next to her on the couch. Heath had to go straight to class after our skate, so she's not waiting for him.

"Eww. You're sweaty, and you stink."

I wrap an arm around her and pull her into my armpit. She squeals and punches my chest until I free her.

"Gross. I'm going to stink for class. Thanks a lot." Her mouth pulls down in disgust, but her eyes are twinkling with laughter.

"You are welcome." I get a whiff of myself as I bring my arm back down, and yeah, a shower is definitely in my future.

"Did you move in, and I missed it?" I elbow her. She's here most nights now.

"I really miss when you slept at your girlfriends' places instead of here," she teases me back.

"I'm glad things are good with you and Heath," I say honestly.

"Me too. And now you and Reagan..." She trails off like she's waiting for me to give her more information.

"Yep, things are good."

"That's all I get?"

I lean closer and whisper like I'm going to share some deep, dark secret. "That's all there is to tell."

She rolls her eyes and shoves at my shoulder. "Mom texted me earlier. She said to tell you good luck and sorry again that she's not coming to your games this weekend."

I shrug. They haven't made it to any games since they announced their separation. Considering they barely missed a game before that, it's just one more reminder that our family is broken. "It's fine."

"No, it isn't. This is your last year."

There's a familiar ache in my chest at the mention of hockey ending with an added gut-deep annoyance that my parents are missing it. There's only a month left of the regular season.

"Dad assured me he was coming for family night." I might be frustrated with our parents, but I try not to let Ginny see just how much it bothers me. She doesn't need to add my issues to her own.

Ginny nods. "So weird. I went from sad to pissed at them. I want to shake them both. They're being ridiculous."

"They're figuring it out. We're all figuring it out. It's going to be all right."

Ginny smiles and rests her head on my bicep. "At least we have each other. I'm glad you're going to be here for med school."

"Me too."

She sits up and pins her gaze on me. "Things are good between you and Reagan? Really? Your favorite sister doesn't get any more details than that? You know, I bet if I told Mom and dad that you were engaged…" She trails off, smiling innocently as she looks down at her lap.

"You little shit," I say and tickle her sides.

She elbows me hard, and I back off.

"Don't you dare." If I weren't already sweaty, I would be thinking about their reaction. Especially mid-divorce. "I gotta shower."

"Booooo!" she huffs when I stand and head toward my room. "Can I at least get a ride to campus?"

"Leaving in five," I say over my shoulder.

I GET TO CLASS A FEW MINUTES AHEAD OF SCHEDULE. JANINE'S already here. I think she must arrive at every class at least five minutes early.

I drop my backpack onto the floor and slide into the chair next to her. "How's it going?"

She has her iPad out and continues to stare at it for a few seconds before putting it down to answer me. "Fine. I was just finishing the chapter on immunology."

"Isn't he covering that today in class?" I snicker.

"Yes. I read ahead. It helps me retain the information in class better." She rolls her eyes. "I'm sure your big head has no problem soaking it all in at once, but I have to work hard for this." What she doesn't say is she thinks I don't have to work hard period, and that's just not true.

"I like to read it again after class. I prefer getting the professor's take first and then going over it a second or third time on my own.

I work hard too."

"Sorry. I didn't mean to imply you don't. I'm stressed about the scholarship and grades this semester."

"Your grades are fine." I know this because we're in almost all the same classes. I've rarely seen anything other than a shining A on her returned work.

She rests her elbows on the desk and leans forward. "So, you and Reagan?"

Right. I almost forgot that Janine was there for the whole fake fiancée thing. The thought of coming clean to her and Dr. Salco makes me shudder. How do you bring that up? "We're together, yes."

I could tell Janine the truth right now, but if she mentions it to Dr. Salco before I do, that'd be shitty.

"Not just together, *engaged*. When did that happen?"

A little of that panic from the other night returns. I'm no good at acting the part without my leading woman. "We've known each other a long time."

"Please. *I've* known Reagan a long time. You've known her what, three years?"

Two, actually. Since she and Dakota moved in next door. I nod. "Something like that."

"Well, I'm surprised to see my childhood best friend engaged to my college rival, but I can see you two together." I struggle to form an appropriate response before she adds, "It was good to see her. I've worried about her over the years."

"You've been worried about Reagan?" My brows lift. "Why?"

"We lost touch when we got to college. That's probably my fault. I've been so focused on grades and making sure I got into med school. But she's doing well?"

I'm missing something, but I don't know what. And I can't really ask since I'm supposed to be her all-knowing fiancé. "She is."

"Good. I really am glad. Lori was a mess for most of her life. She does seem to be doing better now, not that I blame Reagan for not forgiving her. Will you tell Reagan that for me? I tried to tell her the other night, but she didn't seem like she wanted to hear it."

Other people are starting to arrive to class, including the professor, so I nod, and then close the conversation by turning in my desk to face the front. "Of course."

THE MUSIC IS LOUD, THE CROWD EVEN LOUDER, AS WE TAKE THE ice for warmups. I stand at the gate and give each of the guys a word or two of encouragement. I'm always the last one out. I see to them first. We're only effective if each one of us is at our best, and that's my job. I give them whatever they need to be their best.

Some guys like Jordan get pumped with a tap of the helmet, where other guys like Liam require "atta boys" periodically throughout the game. Mav likes me to check him into the boards during warmup. I know how to motivate each of my guys. It's why Coach made me captain.

It's never been my dream to play hockey after college, so it's easier for me to look out for the team than guys like Heath or Mav who have already been signed. I love it, but it never felt like enough to base my entire life around. Here, with these guys though, it's an experience that I know I'll hold on to forever.

When I finally step onto the ice, I stretch and scan the crowd. I already know my parents aren't here, but I can't help but look for them anyway out of habit. They've had season tickets since my freshman year, same spot halfway up the lower level next to the bench.

I wonder if they'll sit together when they come now or maybe the seats will be a bargaining chip in their divorce. Season tickets for the china set or some other sentimental piece they acquired in the twenty-three years they were together. Since they split, I'm continually getting tripped up on things like that.

As far as I know, there haven't been any real fights over furniture, but watching them divide the items that make up every memory of my childhood has been awful.

But tonight, since they're not coming, Ginny, Dakota, and Reagan are in their place. Reagan's wearing my hockey sweatshirt. It's huge on her, but she is working it. My clothes have never looked so good. I tip my head at her, and a shy smile pulls at her lips.

Even sharing a smile in a stadium packed with people feels intimate. It's been a great week and it feels good to have her here. I like her. I want things to keep being great with her. Do I resist every natural instinct I have? Do everything different than I have in the past?

I don't know what the secret trick is to lead our relationship as well as I lead the team, but I'm determined to figure it out.

Chapter Fourteen

REAGAN

THE PLANETARY CONFIGURATION MAKES IT LIKELY THAT YOU'LL REAP THE BENEFITS OF YOUR HARD WORK. YOU'LL BE TEMPTED TO RELAX. DON'T! LEAN IN! YOU CAN SLEEP WHEN YOU'RE DEAD. KIDDING! YOU'LL ALSO NEED LOTS OF REST TO PUSH THROUGH, SO GETTING PLENTY OF SLEEP AND EATING HEALTHY IS MORE IMPORTANT THAN EVER.

Valley is winning by two at the start of the third period. Adam stands at the edge of the ice near the bench as the guys file in. He's a giant—broad shoulders accentuated by all the padding and the added inches to his already massive height from the skates. I like how tall and big he is. I feel safe with him.

I didn't have many male role models in my life (or role models of any gender, actually), so maybe it's daddy issues that make something like safety seem sexy to me. I don't care. Knowing Adam could physically maim someone but is choosing to go into a career where he'll help people makes him incredibly attractive.

Ginny leans over me to speak. "Heath says they're going to The

Hideout after the game."

"Don't they always?" Dakota asks.

The answer to that is yes. Or almost always yes.

"I can't tonight. I promised Matt I would go with him to their frat formal tomorrow. It's at a resort a couple of hours away, so we're leaving early in the morning."

I huff a laugh. "I love how you say, 'I promised' like it's this casual, friend thing."

"It's an overnight date?" Ginny asks.

"No." Dakota shakes her head, then says, "Yes, it's overnight, but it's not a date."

"She's wearing her high school prom dress. It's absolutely a date." I nudge Dakota and smirk at Ginny.

"Whatever. He's a guy I know from when I ran track, nothing more. I'm wearing sneakers with the dress. Not a date. We're just friends, and I'm doing him a solid."

"When have you ever worn anything but sneakers on a date?" I ask. Dakota rocks a pair of sneakers, but if I ever saw her in heels, I might die of shock.

"Once upon a time, I'm sure. Seriously, just friends. I've seen him in running shorts—not interested."

"Well, I'm in for The Hideout," I say and link my arm through Ginny's. I'm in for wherever Adam's going. I haven't seen him since very early this morning when he left me in his bed to go to their team skate. And I've missed him.

My feelings are moving fast despite us taking things slow. Everything about him makes me happy. It's hard to ease into something you've wanted for eternity.

After a Valley win, Dakota drops Ginny and me at The Hideout.

The guys are only a few minutes behind.

Adam wraps me in his arms.

"Congratulations." I inhale as I rest my head against his chest. He smells like soap, and my mind wanders to the shower we took together two nights ago. My nipples tighten, and my face flushes.

"Thank you." He pulls back, obviously not lost in dirty fantasies. "I'm going to grab another pitcher."

Someone claps him on the shoulder to offer their congratulations. He turns to say thanks, and I stand just behind him. Ginny's already planted herself on Heath's lap, and people are filling up the table we secured. Adam doesn't look like he's going to be able to escape conversation anytime soon, so I leave him to claim a chair.

Rhett drops into the one next to me with a sigh. He places his phone on the table.

"Nice game tonight."

"Thanks." He pours a beer and then offers the pitcher to me. "You want a beer?"

"Sure." I move my glass closer, and he fills it.

I scan for Adam, but don't see him anymore. The seats around us are almost gone.

"Should we save Adam a place to sit?"

"Nah." He shakes his head. "When he's ready to sit, he'll make someone move."

"Right." I angle toward Rhett. Without Dakota or Ginny, I feel a little out of place. Which I know is silly, these guys are my friends too, but I rarely interact with them one on one. "How are you doing?"

"Okay." He shrugs and then runs a hand through his unruly

blond hair.

"Have you talked to Carrie?"

"She texted, but I haven't responded. Adam told me to leave it alone."

"Can I see?"

He unlocks his phone and slides it to me. My heart breaks for him when I see his contact name for her: *Care-Bear* with a heart emoji.

That will suck to change.

The last text from her is a freaking novel but basically says she wants to see him in person and talk.

"You don't want to see her?"

"I'm not going to change my mind. Is extending this out and telling her that in person really going to help anything?"

"I don't know. She seems to think so." I hand the phone back. "Can you even take time off to go see her?"

"No. She'd have to come here."

"I don't see the problem if she wants to make an effort; let her."

"You think?"

I second-guess myself. "I'm probably not the one that should be giving advice on this. I've had exactly zero serious boyfriends."

"Really?" His head cocks to the side, and his hair flops over one eye. He pushes it back. "That surprises me. And now you're dating the guy that only knows serious. Weird how things work out."

Speaking of Adam, he's back in view. Standing at the opposite end of the table talking to some guys on the team.

"Why doesn't Adam think you should see her? Did he say?"

"He never liked Carrie. They got off on the wrong foot freshmen year."

"Why?" I laugh.

"Oh, it was a mutual dislike. She hated that I was rooming with the campus playboy—obviously that was her word, not mine. He was bringing chicks back to the dorm and—" He stops. "Shit, I'm sorry."

"I'm well aware that Adam's dated a lot of girls. It's fine."

"Anyway, I guess she was worried he was going to corrupt me or some shit. Adam and I are different. I love him, but…" He doesn't have to finish that sentence for me to understand.

That's not who I am either.

"He's a good guy," Rhett reassures me.

"I know. I'm a little worried he's going to get sick of me in a few months, and I'll lose him and the rest of you." I laugh it off like I don't believe it, but it's a real concern.

"Never gonna happen." He lifts his glass and waits for me to do the same, then clinks them together. "You're stuck with us, Rea."

As the night goes on, I chat with Rhett and Maverick, and a bunch of other hockey guys. Ginny pries herself away from Heath to hang for a while, too. The only person I don't spend any time with is Adam.

He bounces all around the bar. He catches my eye once or twice and smiles, but otherwise we don't interact.

I'm having a great time, but something feels off with him. Maybe he's already sick of me. I don't generally worry about coming off as clingy, but we do share all the same friends, so maybe this is him trying to make space? The later it gets the more I worry that might be true.

"Where's Adam?" Ginny asks as she and Heath get ready to leave the bar.

I nod in his direction.

"Is everything okay? I haven't seen you two together all night." Ginny's brows pull together. "Do I need to get Heath to kick Adam's ass?"

"Hey, now. Let's not get your boyfriend into any fights tonight," Heath says from behind her.

"No need for violence. We're fine." At least I think we are.

"Do you want us to stick around for a little while longer?" Ginny asks. Heath does not look stoked about that, but he nods his head in agreement. He'd jump through fire if Ginny asked.

"No, you don't need to stay," I say with a small laugh. I catch Adam's eye, and he smiles. I'm making too big a deal of this. "You two go home. I'm fine. We're good. Seriously," I add with a little pep to my tone.

Ginny puts her arms around my neck and hugs me. "Love you. I'll talk to you tomorrow."

When they're gone, I weave through the still-packed bar to reach Adam.

"Hi." I step up beside him.

"Hey." His arm goes around my waist and then quickly drops. He stands tall. "Having fun?"

"Yeah, but I think I'm just about funned out. Heath and Ginny left, and I think I'm going to go too."

"Oh, really? Already?"

I can't read the expression on his face. Disappointment? But he's made no effort to talk to me tonight, so that can't be right.

"Yeah. I'm tired. It's been quite the week."

"Okay, well, there's still a few guys out, so I'm going to stay and make sure everyone gets home before curfew."

"Right. Of course. Do you want me to wait?"

"No, go home and get some sleep." He pulls me to him for a quick embrace. I pause expecting him to say he'll call or see me later, but he doesn't.

"O-kay."

Briefly, his lips brush against mine, and then someone calls his name.

With an annoyed groan, he says, "Later, beautiful."

I take a step toward the door on wobbly legs. "Later, Adam."

But he's already dismissed me and is talking to someone else. I'm more embarrassed than angry. Embarrassed that I showed up and made myself so available. Embarrassed I assumed he wanted me there.

I hurry out to the parking lot in time to catch up with Ginny and Heath. He's got her pinned against the passenger side door, kissing her so hard *I* have tingles.

I stare at the ground. "Uhh, hey, is it still okay if I catch a ride back to the apartment with you guys?"

Heath pulls away so reluctantly I want to laugh. Ginny's head comes into view. She's flushed, and her hair is a little messy. "Of course. We were waiting to see if you'd change your mind."

"We were?" Heath asks.

Ginny shakes her head at him and moves to open the car door, forcing Heath back. He tips his head toward the car in invitation, and I hop in.

When we get back to the apartment complex, Ginny looks at me with sad eyes as Heath opens his apartment door. "Call or text if you need anything."

"I'm fine. Everything is great. I'm just tired."

I change clothes but don't go to sleep. Sitting in front of the TV, I hold my phone in my hand. I consider texting Adam, but I have no idea what to say.

Being disappointed because we didn't hang out, after an entire week of hanging out almost nonstop, seems a little pathetic. It's really my expectations that need adjusting. We spent so much time together this week, and I thought it'd be the same tonight. No big deal.

But my stomach cramps, and I feel gross all over because I know Adam. I've seen him with so many different girls that I know his playbook by heart. Hanging out after a game at The Hideout is definitely part of that playbook. So is leaving with said girl.

I'm still awake when they get back. Our apartments aren't exactly great at blocking outside noise, plus let's be honest, I'm listening for him. I give it five minutes, and then I text him, *Can I come over?*

While I wait for his response, I think back on the night. I can't shake this uneasy feeling that something isn't right even though he hasn't really done anything wrong.

His response chases away some of my doubts, *Absolutely.*

The living room is dark as I enter. Adam's bedroom door is open. He's changed into sweatpants and is pulling a T-shirt over his head.

"Hey." He smiles when he sees me.

I linger in the doorway as he gets ready for bed. It isn't until he's pulling back the sheets that he realizes I haven't moved.

"Everything okay?" he asks.

"I'm not sure. I have this weird feeling like I did something wrong?"

"What?" His expression tells me I clearly caught him off guard. "Why would you think that?"

"It's just that I barely saw you all night. I was hoping we'd be able to hang out. I realize how ridiculous that sounds, but I know you. I know how you are when you're dating someone you really like."

"Reagan," he starts.

I wave a hand in front of my face, embarrassment making me flustered. "No, I think I'm going to go. This was a bad idea. It's been a long week, and you have a game tomorrow. We can talk about this later. Everything is great. 'Night, Adam."

He's in front of me, blocking my exit before I get to the front door.

"I don't think so," he says, and picks me up and carries me back to his bedroom. "We'll talk about this now."

Chapter Fifteen

ADAM

Well, clearly, I'm an idiot, and Rhett was right. Not that I'll ever admit that to him.

As I set Reagan down on my bed, she looks like she's either going to burst into tears or claw my eyes out. I'm hoping for the latter. I do not think I can survive a crying Reagan.

"I don't want this to be like every other time," I say.

"Does that mean you want to date other people?" Her tone is fragile but hard as nails. I don't know how she manages to be vulnerable and badass at the same time, but it's hot.

And wait, what? Date other people? The fuck?

"No, it sure as shit doesn't mean that."

"Oh." Her lips form the sound and stay that way while she processes my words. She's probably thinking I'm a moron. Welcome to the club.

"I was working with a theory tonight that if I did the opposite of what I wanted, maybe I wouldn't screw this up. I need to take this slow. We've been hanging out every second, and it's been amazing, but I want to do things right this time. I should have just told you what was going on, but this is new territory for me."

What I don't say is I really like her. A lot. This week has been awesome. When this started, I didn't give my past much thought. I was so excited to spend more time with her and explore this thing between us. But now that I'm starting to develop real feelings for her, I have to wonder if I'm leading us down a path that ends like all my other relationships.

"You ignored me because you like me?"

"Yeah, next I'll be kicking your shins and pulling your hair." I hang my head for a second, trying to get my shit together. Doubting myself is new. I don't like it.

"That last one doesn't sound so bad."

I look up as she swallows, and her gaze drops to my chest.

That look—the one of desire as she checks me out, I can work with that. In here, we make sense. This is uncomplicated. It's everywhere else that I haven't quite figured out. How do I date her without falling into the same old cycle?

I climb onto the bed, forcing her on her back. "It doesn't, huh?"

Instead of answering, she pulls my face down to hers. It's a lot easier to shut down my brain when she's touching me.

Her kisses are as hungry as mine. You'd think it would be easy to slow it down. I'm good at following rules, especially my own. But where Reagan is concerned, I'm turning into a loose cannon. I let go of my worry about going too fast. Slow is dumb… and, well, slow.

I undress her fast and drop my pants even faster. Damn, she's beautiful. Blonde hair tumbling past her shoulders, brown eyes the color of cinnamon. And those dimples. They knock the air out of me when she flashes a big smile that makes them appear. And somehow, below the neck, it just gets better.

Why would anyone want to deny themselves this? They wouldn't. I really am an idiot.

I turn her onto all fours and latch on to her pussy from this angle until she writhes and moans. While I rip open the condom packet and then cover myself, she hums impatiently. "I need you."

"Yeah?" I ask, nudging the head of my cock at her entrance.

I get an unintelligible response as she pushes into me, driving me farther inside of her slick heat.

Sliding my hand up her back to the nape of her neck, I bury myself as far as I can go then still. "Does it feel like I want to date other people?"

She shakes her head.

I tangle my fingers in her hair and gently tug. Her graceful neck twists until she's looking me in the eye.

"No one else, baby. This pussy." I pull out, slowly, letting her squeeze me all the way to the tip before driving back in. "It's mine."

Words aren't necessary, or possible, after that. I take her hard and fast, showing her the only way I know how that I want her. There's nothing I can say to make her believe doing things differently with her isn't purely selfish. She knows me and my patterns. I keep forgetting that. I settle for leaving us both panting and limp against the mattress. Actions speak louder than words, baby.

I discard the condom and fall beside her.

"I hope you don't mind if I sleep over because I don't think I can move."

I wrap an arm around her waist and bring her closer. "Nah, I don't mind at all."

I'M IN THE KITCHEN THE FOLLOWING MORNING, COOKING OATMEAL and downing a Gatorade. Reagan's sitting on the countertop next to the stove, sipping coffee and watching me. Looking damn good doing it too. She pulled on one of my T-shirts earlier, and it hangs off one shoulder and leaves her legs bare. My closet has become her new wardrobe, and I'm not mad about it.

I drop a kiss on her lips. "You want some?"

"Uhh, no. I'm good."

Rhett stumbles out of his room in sweatpants with his phone in hand.

"Morning, sunshine," I quip. His hair sticks up all over his head, and his eyes are barely open. "Are you expecting a call from Carrie, or are you just used to carrying that thing with you at all times?"

He stares down at his hand as if he's just realized he's holding it. "Habit, I guess." He places it on the counter and takes a seat at one of the barstools. "What's for breakfast?"

"Oatmeal," Reagan says and makes a face over her mug.

"I was hoping your presence had inspired something more flavorful." He grimaces.

I'm used to the guys ribbing me and then eating it despite their complaints. I look to Reagan. "You don't like oatmeal?"

I add blueberries and turn the heat down.

"It's so boring and healthy," she says.

"Right?" Rhett chuckles.

I didn't even think to ask her. Before Reagan, I always stayed at my girlfriends' places instead of having them stay here. I'd get up, usually before them, and be gone before breakfast. I eat the same thing almost every day, but my boring oatmeal never came up.

"Do you want me to make you something else?" I ask her.

"No." She shakes her head. "Breakfast before ten isn't really my thing. Healthy or not."

"I'll take pancakes," Rhett calls.

"Someone say pancakes?" Mav busts through the front door, Charli at his heels. He's still in his boxers, no shirt, like it's perfectly normal to walk up a flight of stairs from his apartment to ours half-dressed searching for food. And with his dog, no less.

"Oatmeal's done." I grab a bowl for myself and then let them have at it.

I step between Reagan's legs. "Are you sure you don't want a bite?"

"I'm sure. I'll wait until an appropriate hour and grab a muffin and coffee somewhere."

"But I've got this perfectly cooked oatmeal." I spoon some up and wave it in front of her face.

Her lips draw into a flat line, and her head shakes side to side.

"Come on. Open up. You'll like it. It's good for you."

She smiles but doesn't open.

"Fine." I eat it and then press my mouth to hers.

"No fair." She opens, and I sweep my tongue inside. What was meant to be a quick, teasing kiss turns into a mini make-out session.

"Maybe I do like oatmeal."

When I step back, I realize the guys are watching us. And at some point, Ginny and Heath joined.

"Good morning," I say to the room.

"It certainly is." Mav smirks. "Breakfast and a show."

Reagan hops down from the counter. "I've gotta get going. We have rehearsal this afternoon."

I abandon my oatmeal and follow her into my room. She strips out of my shirt and starts to pull on her own clothes. To which I greatly detract progress by running my hands along her bare skin and kissing her stomach and then her neck.

"Are you coming to the game this afternoon?" I ask as I sit on the bed and use her hips to pull her closer to me.

"Do you want me to?"

"Yeah, of course, but you said you had rehearsal."

"I'll be done in time, but you're sure? You want to take thing slow, and—"

"I suck at slow. No more trying to go against the grain. Everything is different because it's us. Come to the game."

"Okay." Her lips pull into a smile. "And us, we're what? Dating? Sleeping together?"

"We're.... whatever," I say. "Exclusively."

"Exclusively whatever. Got it."

"Let's not label it. That part seems to get me in trouble. I like you."

Her light laughter does funny things to my chest.

"Some might say I'm your girlfriend," she quips.

"Totally different thing," I assure her with a grin.

"Good, I've got money on you being single until summer."

My mouth falls open.

"Gotcha!"

"Let me walk you home," I say as she heads to leave.

"I live fifteen feet away. I'll manage. Besides, that sounds like something a *boyfriend* would do."

So it does.

She brushes her mouth against mine so quickly I almost miss it, and then she's gone.

When I go back out to the living room, it's just Rhett and Mav. I drop into a chair.

Maverick's grinning at me like a fool.

"Something to say?" I ask.

"So many things. I'm trying to decide where to start."

"Get it all out." I raise my arms to my side. I can take whatever these guys can dish.

"What are your intentions?"

"Excuse me?" A chuckle escapes.

"I like Reagan. Always have. And let's face it, buddy, your track record is shit." Mav crosses his arms over his chest. Charli whines.

"Thanks for the vote of confidence." I flip him off.

"What *are* your intentions?" Rhett asks.

"You too? Seriously?"

He shrugs. "I was hanging with her last night. She likes you a lot. I can tell."

"I like her too."

"Have you made it official?" Mav asks. His gaze darts to Rhett and then back to me.

"He knows about the bet," Rhett tells him. "You don't need to dance around it."

"How?" Mav wails.

"You idiots weren't exactly quiet about it," I say.

"The bet's off then. You've got a new girlfriend." Mav claps his hands and looks to Rhett. "Who won?"

Rhett pulls out his phone. It's of no surprise to me that my best buddy is the one who's running the betting circle around my relationship status. He's the most competitive guy I know.

"Looks like you're the closest, Mav."

He shoots up off the couch and starts dancing around the living room. He's bumping into shit and knocking things off the coffee table.

"Sit down. No one won. She's not my girlfriend."

"But..." Mav looks so crestfallen.

"What is going on?" Ginny comes out of Heath's room. He's right behind her.

"Your dipshit brother is still single." Mav sits back down on the couch with a frown.

"That's it?" Ginny places her hands on her hips. "I thought something awesome happened."

I just smile as the guys grumble about the bet. Maybe she's not my girlfriend, but something awesome has definitely happened.

Chapter Sixteen

REAGAN

YOU CAN'T ALWAYS TRUST THAT PEOPLE ARE WHO THEY SAY THEY ARE. WAIT AND LET THEM SHOW YOU THEIR TRUE COLORS.

Monday morning, I ride to campus with Adam. He's got classes an hour earlier than I do, but the extra fifteen minutes riding over and holding his hand as we walk toward his building make it totally worth it.

"Thanks for walking with me," he says, swinging our joined hands.

"Any time."

"What are you going to do for the next hour?"

"I'm not sure. Maybe go to the library and study."

He stares at me with narrowed eyes. "Really?"

"Okay, fine. I'm going straight to University Hall for coffee, and then I'll probably watch videos and look at TikTok until class time."

I love his deep laughter and love it even more when I'm the

one to bring it out of him.

"Hang later tonight?" he asks.

"Yeah." I nod, and he pulls me into him and wraps his arms around me. "I'll text you after your rehearsal."

He keeps holding on to me, leaning side to side. "This was a good plan up until I realized I have to leave you for class."

I squeeze his middle to show him I don't want to go either.

"Okay. On three," he says. "One, two—"

Before he says three, I push at his chest. "Get out of here, Dr. Scott."

He scoops me up and heads toward the building. "Maybe I'll just take you with me."

"Oh no. Put me down. I need coffee."

Inside, he finally sets me on the ground, but he doesn't make any more progress on getting to class. His mouth slants over mine. I could kiss him like this for hours, but one of us needs to make sure he makes it to class. I really didn't expect that person to be me.

"You need to go learn things, and I need caffeine. Later, stud."

I'm grinning like a fool as he reluctantly heads off to class. I watch him until he starts into the room. He waves and winks, then disappears.

I'm lost in my own little Adam bubble when I hear someone call my name.

She says it twice before my brain snaps out of it. I peel my gaze from the doorway Adam went through to Janine walking my direction.

Her gait slows the closer she gets.

"Hey, Janine."

"Haven't seen you in years and now twice in a month."

I ignore the subtle jab. "I was just walking with Adam to class."

She adjusts her backpack on her shoulder. "Do you have class now?"

"No."

"So you're free?"

Well, crap. I walked right into that.

"Oh. I'm actually on my way to University Hall."

"I'll walk with you."

"O-kay."

We're quiet as we exit the building and start down the sidewalk. A memory of the two of us walking along campus our junior year of high school flashes through my mind. Janine looks just the same. She's someone who knew early on exactly who she was. It takes a lot of confidence to be who you are, unwavering and steadfast. I always admired that about her. It's probably why I was drawn to her as a kid. I had no idea who I was or what I wanted to be. Some days I'm still not sure I have it figured out.

She heads straight for the café when we enter University Hall. "I assume you still live on coffee?"

It's unnerving being around Janine again. Someone who knows me so well. Every part.

We place our orders at the coffee counter. Awkward silence hangs between us. When the barista rings us up, I hand my card over quickly.

"I've got it," I say. I owe her too much as it is.

"Thanks."

With our drinks, we meander to a small table in the center of the hall.

"You look good. Happy," she says after we're seated. "I can't believe you're with Adam. Makes sense though. He's totally your type."

"I am happy." I fidget with the lid of my coffee. "How are you?"

"I'm good."

"And Sean?"

"Really good. He switched his major, just as you predicted."

"Yeah?" I ask. "What did he settle on?"

"Law school."

"I knew it!" I smile big, forgetting myself.

She laughs softly. "Yeah, you did. The day he told me, I thought of you."

I nod and take a sip of my coffee. Her somber tone smacks me back to reality. We are not two friends catching up. Not anymore.

"I've thought about you often," she continues. Honest, open Janine. My heart thumps too fast in my chest.

"Me too," I admit, then plaster a smile on my face. "But it sounds like things have been great for you. Graduating early, med school, this big scholarship. I'm really happy for you."

I'm working on an excuse to get me out of here when she goes for the kill.

"I saw Lori last weekend when I went to my parents for Sunday dinner."

"Oh, yeah?" I look anywhere but at her.

"She's doing really great, Reagan. The old house is cleaned up, and she's working at the elementary school as an aide."

"They let her work with children?! Someone should be fired for that hire."

Janine doesn't react like someone else might to my outburst. She smiles sadly. "My mom got her the job, but she's working hard."

"Whatever. Good for her. Is that what you want me to say?"

"I just thought you should know. She's still your mom, Rea."

"Yeah, well, she didn't act much like one for the first eighteen years of my life, so I'm sorry if I'm not eager to hear how great she's doing now. Those kids at the school probably see more of her in a week than I did for months at a time when I was their age." The more I talk, the angrier I get. She's doing great now, really? Now that I'm capable of taking care of myself. Now that I don't need her.

"I'm sorry. I can't imagine how you feel."

"You're right. You can't." Janine with her perfect family. A mom who dotes on her and a dad who would go to the ends of the earth for her.

"She asked how to get in touch with you. Said the number she has for you doesn't work, and she wasn't sure your email was still the same."

"Are you kidding me?" I roll my eyes.

Janine's lips flatten.

"If I wanted to talk to her, I would have responded to one of the many emails she's sent over the years."

"So you are getting them?"

"What is this, an interrogation?"

"No, of course not." Janine rests her palms on the table. "This isn't going like I imagined. You have every right to your feelings, but if there was even a chance you wanted to know how she was, I thought I should tell you."

"Well, you've told me." I push back in my chair. "See you around."

I rush out of University Hall, holding back angry tears. Outside, I hang a right, then slump against the brick building and take deep pulls of the cold air.

Janine finds me. I should have expected her to follow me. She left me alone for three years, and that's longer than I expected. She has a good heart, wants everyone to be happy. She still believes that everyone can have what she does, even after watching me grow up with a mom who didn't give a shit.

"Go away, Janine. There's nothing you can say to fix this."

She shakes her head slowly. "There's something else." She pauses and wets her lips, tugs her hat down over her ears. "I told her that you were engaged."

"What?!" A shiver of dread runs up my spine.

"I wanted her to know how well you're doing."

"She doesn't deserve to know anything about me. You had no right."

"I know. I'm sorry."

"Does Adam know about any of this?"

"No." Her brows pull together in confusion. "Why?"

"It's none of his business or yours."

"I'm so sorry, Reagan. I know that it's not the same, but I was mad at her all these years too. I saw what she did to you, and I guess I wanted her to know that despite all of that, you had still found a way to make a great life. You didn't need her."

I may not have needed her, but how much easier might my life have been? I may not have needed her, but I wanted her. Janine's family always made me feel welcome, but they weren't mine.

"What can I do?" Janine asks. She reaches out and squeezes my arm.

"You can tell Lori to stay out of my life." I swallow hard and step away from her. "And you can do the same."

She doesn't follow me this time. I skip my next class and wait for Adam in the same spot I left him. When he sees me, he grins, and those long legs erase the space between us.

"Have you been waiting here the whole time?" He takes me in his arms, and my heart rate finally starts to even out.

I breathe him in and relax against his chest. "No, I grabbed coffee first. I was thinking maybe we could play hooky."

"I'm free until one. I can't miss my lab. What'd you have in mind?"

"I've never been to this place," Adam says as we walk into the arcade.

"A blind date brought me here once," I admit.

He cocks a brow. "A date?"

"Yeah. The location was the best part of the date. I always wanted to come back with someone I actually liked."

I feed dollar bills into the machine. As the coins clatter into the dispenser, Adam kisses me. The place is quiet. I'm surprised they were even open this early, but a few groups of young kids and families are already milling about.

"Gotta keep it G-rated in here. There are small, innocent eyes."

He laughs against my mouth. "What about PG?"

I smack him playfully on the chest.

"What? Their parents are here."

I grab our coins and duck under his arm. "Come on, stud."

Adam and I hit Skee-Ball first, then table hockey. He takes

it easy on me, but still wins. I edge out victorious at a basketball shooting game and Dance Dance Revolution. It's been great, but I still can't completely shake the awful interaction with Janine. I'm frustrated with her, but I hate that I was so mean to her. We were friends for a long time. Good friends.

"Let's go in the photo booth," he suggests as we're making a second round looking for games to spend our last coins on.

"It's a total scam. Five dollars for a strip of tiny, blurry photos."

He inserts money in the slot and pulls me inside. The bench is cold and barely big enough for the two of us. We watch the screen for the countdown.

"Are we going serious or funny?" I ask.

"Serious on the first one. Funny on the second."

"What about the others?" I ask as the countdown ends.

We press our faces together and smile. After the flash, I stick my tongue out at the camera, and Adam gives me bunny ears. On the next one, he kisses me.

And then I lose track of the flashes. His tongue invades my mouth, and I cling to him desperately, filling the ache, erasing the worry. I don't need Lori or Janine. I have Dakota, Ginny, Adam, and our friends. They're enough.

Chapter Seventeen

ADAM

Reagan and I get doughy pizza from the snack bar and take it to one of the kid-sized tables. My legs do not fit underneath, so I'm sitting sideways.

"This was fun," I say.

"It was. Thank you."

"Any time." I've been waiting for her to tell me what spurred her sudden desire to skip class and come to the arcade, but it looks like I'm going to have to pry for information. "Want to tell me what happened while I was at class this morning?"

She wipes her hands on a napkin and takes a drink before answering. "Caught on to that, huh?"

"Hey, I'm not complaining. Pumped to spend more time with you."

"I ran into Janine."

"Oh." I still don't know exactly what the story is there. When I passed on Janine's message last week that Lori was doing well, Reagan shut down and changed the subject. Whoever Lori is, she isn't a popular topic.

"She still thinks we're engaged."

"Yeah, I've been meaning to tell Dr. Salco myself. Janine will find out eventually."

"I am sorry again for getting so carried away and pulling you into the mess to start with."

"Nah, it's fine."

I think that's the end of the conversation, and I'm prepared to let it go for now, but Reagan starts talking. "Janine and I have known each other our entire lives. Our moms were friends as kids and stayed close until I was two or three. It's hard for me to picture. They're so different." She says different like it's a bad word, which has me swallowing and worrying about what that means. "When I was in high school, I actually lived with Janine's family for almost two years."

"You did? Why? Where was your family?"

Reagan shrugs. "My mom was in Vegas, mostly. She traveled there for work almost every week. Usually, day trips so she'd be home by bedtime, but then day trips turned to overnight trips because she'd stay at the casinos too long and miss her flight. That turned to her booking extra days so she could sightsee." Reagan rolls her eyes. "I doubt she ever left the casino floor. After a while, she didn't even make excuses. I stopped asking when she was coming home, and I guess that gave her the freedom not to care."

"She just left you to fend for yourself? How old were you?"

Reagan nods. Her face is red, and I can't tell if she's on the verge of tears or ready to throw something. "Nine or ten, I guess, the first time she didn't come home for an entire weekend. It wasn't just that she was absent. I was pretty self-sufficient even at an early age. But every year, things seemed to get worse. She gambled away all of her savings, then sold everything we had, which I guess was good because we eventually lost everything else. She got in so deep. I only had a roof over my head because my great aunt left the house in my name."

"That's fucked up."

"Sometimes things were great. If she won, we'd splurge and celebrate—make plans for awesome vacations. But of course, before we ever took any, she'd lose it again." Reagan shrugs. "Eventually, I realized it was going to be on me, and I found creative ways to pay the utilities and basic needs. Recycling cans, doing odd jobs, babysitting, I even did some modeling."

I get to my feet and move to her side of the table.

"I'm so sorry." I cradle her against my chest.

"I wanted to tell you the other night when you mentioned her, but it's so embarrassing. Even now."

"You didn't do anything wrong. It isn't your fault."

"I know."

"Do you?" I brush her hair away from her face and stroke her cheek.

"Yeah, but I'm still ashamed. It was so humiliating."

"What about your dad? Other family?"

"I never knew him. He was gone long before I was born, and I was always too scared to press her for details. She got pissed when I asked about him, and she was home so little that I didn't want to give her any reason to leave. And as for other family, what was I going to say? I didn't want to tattle on my own mom. I missed her. I just wanted her to be home. I didn't want anyone else to take me."

"Fuck." My chest splits wide open. "I'm so sorry, baby."

"Janine says she's doing better now. She even has a job at my old elementary school." Reagan snorts. "Ironic, huh?"

"When's the last time you talked to her?"

"She showed up to my high school graduation asking for money. I guess she knew that I'd have extra cash coming in from relatives."

Damn, that's cold. I stroke her arm as she continues, "Janine and I moved to Valley the next week and I haven't been back. I can't forgive her."

"You don't have to," I assure her. I don't know if that's the right thing to say, but it seems to calm her.

"Thank you for letting me steal you away for a few hours. I needed this."

"It doesn't have to end. Come on, let's go back to my place."

"What about your lab?"

"I'll make it up."

"No, I can't let you do that." Reagan straightens. "My shitty childhood isn't taking any more from me, and it definitely isn't touching you. I want to be good for you. Your dedication to school is something I've always found really attractive."

"It wasn't my stellar personality or flowing locks?" I ask and shake my head to make my hair fall in my face.

"I like those things, too," she says and slips her fingers through my hair. Feels good.

"Are you okay? Really?"

"Yeah. I'm fine. Seeing Janine brought it all up again."

"Is that why you've avoided her?"

A small smile graces her lips. First genuine one I've seen since this morning. "How do you know I've avoided her?"

"You said you haven't seen her in years. Valley campus isn't that big, baby."

OVER THE NEXT TWO WEEKS, REAGAN AND I SPEND MORE TIME together than apart. I'm humming to myself in the locker room, looking forward to seeing her again just as soon as I get out of here. She should be finishing with rehearsal, and I'll have her to myself all night.

Heath corners me before I can leave.

"We need to talk," he says, looking nervous. Nervous can only mean one thing.

My heart skips several beats, and I see red. "What did you do to my sister?"

He flips me off. "Fuck you. This isn't about Ginny."

"Oh." My shoulders relax. "What's up?"

Heath laughs at me. "You're ridiculous."

"Noted." I wave my hand for him to continue.

"It's Rhett. I'm worried about him."

I glance over to where he's sitting on the bench, leaning forward and running a towel over his sweaty hair. "Seems fine to me."

"Yeah, well, no offense, man, but you're in a love bubble right now, so your judgment is shit."

"Love bubble?"

"You're completely engrossed in Reagan and this thing between you two, and you can't see anything else."

"I see you right now wasting my time." Time I could be with Reagan. I leave that part out so I don't add fuel to this love bubble theory.

"Let's go out tonight."

"Fine," I relent, mostly to shut him up so I can be on my way. "Text me the details, and Reagan and I will meet you guys there."

He grabs my elbow to keep me from leaving. "No girls. Just the guys."

"For serious?"

Chuckling, he nods. "For serious. Shouldn't be hard to get away since you're not in a love bubble."

"What about your *love bubble*?"

"Oh, I'm still in one, but after a while, you start to remember that other people exist."

"Whatever. Text me the details." I shrug out of his grasp and head for the door.

"Be in the living room ready to go in an hour," he calls after me.

Reagan is cool about it when I stop by and tell her my plans for the night. It might help that I eat her sweet pussy until she screams my name and then drop the news that I have to go out with the guys. She's picking up her discarded clothes around the room while I resist moving from the bed.

"I was hoping you were going to throw a fit and demand I stay here," I say and pull her down onto the bed with me. Her oh so glorious, naked body.

"No, it's good. I've been neglecting my school stuff and Dakota." She lies on top of me, her tits pressed against my chest and my dick smashed between us.

"Love bubble," I mutter.

"What did you say? Love bubble?"

"Heath told me I was in a love bubble."

Her mouth drops to mine, and she sucks on my bottom lip. "More like a sex bubble."

I flip us so I'm on top. It's so much more than sex with Reagan. She's a hunger I can't abate. I tease her, rubbing my cock against her clit.

"You're going to be late," she taunts as her eyes flutter closed and her hands come up to tweak her nipples.

"I can be fast," I say like I'm not about to explode all over her stomach just watching her touch herself.

She grabs a condom from her dresser. While she rips the foil open, she takes my dick into her mouth and sucks.

"Not going to need the condom if you keep doing that." A tingle runs up my spine as her sweet mouth slides down to the base one more time. Fuck me.

"Baby," I groan.

She keeps going. Obviously, she thinks I'm joking about how close I am.

"Reagan, baby, I'm not kidding."

She stops long enough to look me dead in the eyes and says, "I know."

Those two words alone are almost my undoing. I run a hand through her hair, guiding her gently down the length of my cock at a faster pace.

I give her one last warning, but she keeps right on swallowing my dick as I come down her throat.

"Holy..." I can't even finish the sentence. There are no words.

Reagan smiles proudly as she wipes her mouth. "I've never done that before."

"Well, I sure as fuck hope you want to do it again sometime."

I'm a little lightheaded as I sit back, trying to catch my breath.

She hums. "Definitely, but now you have to get out of my bed."

"Kicking me out?"

"Only for a few hours." She gets up and pulls on a shirt and panties. "Will I see you later?"

"I don't know. It'll probably be late when we get home." Rarely does a guys' night end early, and if Rhett really is having a hard time, we'll go harder to try to cheer him up. Booze is the cure for heartbreak.

"I hope he's okay."

"He'll be fine. He's better off."

She starts gathering her school stuff up to study, so I guess it's time for me to leave. Maybe I am in a love bubble because I don't want to go anywhere.

I get dressed and send a text to Heath to let him know I'm running five minutes late. That gives me four more minutes to kiss Reagan.

"Have fun." She squirms out of my hold when Heath and Mav get tired of waiting and bust into the apartment. They're calling my name and threatening to come in and get me. They would too.

Reagan stands on her toes to kiss me once more and then opens her bedroom door. "Try to stay out of trouble."

"I'll be good." I wink. At least until I see her later.

INSTEAD OF GOING TO OUR USUAL SPOT, THE HIDEOUT, WE venture to the Prickly Pear. It's a quieter bar a little farther away from campus.

We get a pitcher of beer and Rhett orders a round of shots. Captain Morgan—his favorite.

"Are the girls coming?" Rhett asks.

"Nope," Heath says. "Just us tonight."

"Ginny and Reagan aren't coming?" Rhett stares at me with a confused expression as the server brings our liquor. "What's the occasion?"

"No occasion. Just having a guys' night for a change."

We each grab a shot glass.

"Is this because of Carrie?" He holds his shot near his lips. "Am I on a fucking pity hang?"

"Take your damn shot. No, it's not a pity hang." I give him my most convincing face. Fuck, he figured that out way too fast.

He tosses his drink back, and the rest of us do the same.

"I'm gonna cue up some good tunes." Maverick pushes back his chair. "Any requests?"

Rhett and I shake our heads.

"I better supervise so he doesn't pick thirty songs by Christina Aguilera and get us kicked out like that time last year." Heath stands to follow him.

"Good call." I chuckle and tip my beer to him in appreciation.

It's just Rhett and me, and I study him a little closer. Aside from those first few days where he drank too much, I haven't really noticed any major differences in him since he broke up with Carrie, but I have been a little preoccupied.

"Have you talked to her?" I ask. No reason to beat around the bush.

"Nope." He takes a long swig of beer, draining his glass.

He pours another as I stare down into my full drink.

"Do you want to talk to her?"

"You don't have to do this," he says as he leans back in his chair.

"Do what?"

"Pretend to care about Carrie. I know you're not her biggest fan."

"Doesn't matter what I think. So, do you?"

"Of course, I do. I want to know that she's okay."

I take a drink, choosing my words carefully. "Then you should call her."

"Seriously?"

I shrug. "What the fuck do I know about lasting relationships? I don't think she's the right girl for you, but if she is, then I'll gladly shut up and be happy for you."

"Wow. Reagan's good," he says as Heath and Maverick return.

"Sex talk. Finally!" Maverick looks between us. "Reagan's good in bed, huh?" He nods. "That doesn't surprise me. Her body is killer. And that mouth."

Heath and Rhett are trying hard not to laugh.

"If you want to keep breathing, I suggest you stop talking." I glower at Maverick.

Heath finally stops fighting it and chuckles quietly. "Kind of possessive. Almost like a boyfriend."

"She's not my–"

"Girlfriend," they say in unison. "We know. You mention it daily."

"I do not." I bite back a grin.

"Are you two just hooking up, or is it leading somewhere?" Heath asks. I swear he's the last person I would have imagined asking me that before he started dating my sister. He was the king of casual hookups.

I can't come up with an answer easily, so I shrug.

"Is this your first fuck buddy?" Maverick asks. "Because I don't think you're doing it right."

"He's right," Heath adds. "The whole point of not making a girl your girlfriend is to avoid sleepovers and spending time together that's not naked. You and Reagan are together all the time. You even let her sleep at our place."

"So?"

"She's your girlfriend, man." Heath waves his arms around. He's a pretty chill dude, so I know he's frustrated with me when he starts getting loud and talking with his hands.

"What does it matter?" I lean forward. "Bet aside. We're having fun. I like her. She likes me. I'm trying really hard not to fuck this up."

"You're trying so hard not to screw up that you can't even see how badly you're screwing this up," Heath says.

"What?" I look around the table for help. Reagan and I are solid, which is exactly what I tell them.

They snicker and hang their heads.

"What am I missing?"

Heath doesn't look like he wants to share, so I look to Rhett. "Well?"

"Hold that thought. We need another round of shots." Maverick scoots his chair back, the wood screeching along the floor. He hustles back a minute later with four shots of what looks like Jägermeister. Fuck, it's going to be a long night at this pace. "What'd I miss?" he asks as he hands them out.

"I was about to drop some enlightenment." Rhett grins.

"Cheers to that," Heath says and raises his glass.

After we take the shot, Rhett starts in. "It's like pulling the goalie late in the game so you can have an extra skater on the ice."

I think. Hard. I've got nothing. "How does this relate to me?"

"Yeah, I'm lost too," Mav says. "And I know the punchline."

Rhett fidgets with his glass. "Forget it. The point is you're doing everything you can to make this time different, but in doing so, you're denying Reagan exactly what she wants."

"No," I refute it. "She's happy. We're good."

"Dude," Mav starts. "Reagan has been into you for a long time. She's seen you with girlfriends, and she's wished that girl was her." He places his hands over his heart and bats his lashes at me. "Wait, I think I finally figured out where you were going with that. Reagan's the goalie in that scenario, right?"

"No," Rhett says, sounding annoyed.

"Scott's the goalie?" Mav tries again.

Rhett groans. "No. No one is the goalie. I was trying to make a point that he switched things up late in the game."

"I so didn't get that," Heath says.

They're bickering back and forth over metaphors, but my stomach suddenly feels like I swallowed a bowling ball.

Rhett pins his gaze on me. "If you'd been secretly pining after someone for years and finally got your chance, would you want that person to switch things up? Or be relegated to some weird non-relationship thing different from everything you knew about how they acted in the past?"

"No, I guess not." I think back to all of our conversations about it. "She hasn't said anything. In fact, she's been great about all of this. She's cool with us not labeling it."

"Yeah, but what could she say? I'm sure you gave her the same speech you gave me," Rhett says and waits for my answer. I don't though because the answer sucks.

"You told her that you wanted to do things different, that she was different, or some combination or variation of that?" He nods his head. "That right?"

"Yeah," I manage to admit and shift in my chair.

"All she wants is to be your girlfriend. The kind of girlfriend she's seen you have in the past. She doesn't give a fuck about all your perfectly logical reasons why she shouldn't be."

A quick glance around the table tells me they're all in agreement.

"I'm gonna use the bathroom." I stand. "Rhett, grab us another round of Captain."

"Me? Why? I got the first round."

"Because you're about to be fifty bucks richer."

All three of them study me for a few seconds before they realize what I mean.

"What?! But? You..." Mav flounders for words looking like I kicked his dog. "No way," he whines. "That's it? But what about all of your really good reasons for not jumping into a new relationship?" He curses under his breath. "If I'd known you were going to listen to us, I would have suggested guys' night last week."

"Aww, cheer up, Mav," I tell him. "You can help me figure out how I'm going to ask her to be my girlfriend tomorrow."

"Something big and bold?" He grins.

"The bolder, the better."

"Wait, why tomorrow?" Heath asks.

"She's with the girls. I'm hanging with you guys." I leave out the part about tonight's purpose being cheering up Rhett and making sure he's doing okay. I still don't know if he's all right, so leaving feels wrong.

"Nah, let's do this thing tonight." Rhett finishes his beer and nods.

"Really?"

"Yeah. Look, I know this was some sort of intervention to help me get over Carrie."

"No, we—" Heath starts, but Rhett holds up a hand.

"I've been moping around and sucking at practice. I get it. But I made a decision tonight. I'm going to call her, get closure, and then move on."

"You decided that in the thirty minutes we've been out? Damn, we're good," Maverick says.

"I decided the second I realized you three were trying to help me. Like you fools have your shit together. So, yeah, please, let's do this thing tonight. I think seeing you ask Reagan to be your girlfriend might be the cure to my shitty month."

"All right then. Make those shots doubles."

Chapter Eighteen

REAGAN

THE ELEMENT OF SURPRISE IS A GREAT WAY TO MAKE AN IMPRESSION. TODAY, YOU'LL HAVE THE OPPORTUNITY TO SURPRISE SOMEONE. LEAVE THEM WONDERING WHAT YOU'LL DO NEXT! ALSO, PACK CLEAN UNDIES—YOU NEVER KNOW.

My face is tingling." Dakota brings her hands up to her face but doesn't touch it.

"That means it's working," I say, wiggling my nose. It does tingle, but it also itches.

"These are hilarious." Ginny hands me her phone. "Take a picture so I can send it to Heath."

"Yeah, I'm sure a creepy-looking tiger face mask will really turn him on." Dakota snorts as I snap a picture of Ginny and hand her phone back.

"You'd be surprised what turns Heath on."

Dakota and I both burst into laughter.

"No, honey, we wouldn't be surprised at all," Dakota tells her.

"He says, '*Rawr*,'" Ginny tells us, staring down at her phone.

"Reagan, you should send Adam a picture."

"You think he's into llamas?" I ask and pose with my hands under my face. She snaps a picture.

"Absolutely do not send that to him. We are not at that stage." The tingling gets worse as my face flames with embarrassment at just the idea of him seeing me like this. "Promise me?"

"Okay, okay." She puts her phone down. "But you look adorable."

"What stage *are* you at?" Dakota asks.

"It's hard to take you serious with that on your face," I deflect. Her mask is a narwhal and makes her face almost entirely blue.

My friends, or the tiger and narwhal they've become, stare back at me. They don't look like they're going to let this go.

"We're at the 'everything is great and everyone else should mind their own business stage,'" I say.

"She has no idea," Dakota says to Ginny.

"My brother is an idiot." Ginny's shoulders sag, and she sticks out her bottom lip. "I'm sorry."

"There is nothing to apologize for. Everything is great." I smile, though I'm not sure how effective it is through this mask.

I get up and go to the kitchen to grab another bottle of wine. The truth is, everything is great. Do I have an uneasy feeling wondering if Adam is as into me as I am him? Yes. Do I think I'd have this same uneasy feeling regardless of what label we slapped on this thing between Adam and me? Also, yes. I've been crazy about him for years. It makes sense that I'd fall harder, faster.

There's a knock at the door, and all three of us look at it but don't move.

"Go away. We're too poor to buy anything, and we've already

found Jesus," Dakota yells.

Ginny giggles. "What if it's Girl Scouts selling cookies or hot firefighters checking smoke alarms?"

"If you have cookies, knock three times," Dakota yells again.

"What about the firefighters?" Ginny asks.

"My stepdad is a firefighter. Kind of ruins the fantasy for me."

The knock comes again.

"Only once must not be Girl Scouts." Dakota shrugs, and I sit back on the floor where we've got a whole home spa thing going on. Wine, nail polish, face masks, and magazines.

Ginny gets to her feet. "The suspense is killing me."

"Can you hand me the white polish?" I ask Dakota while Ginny goes to see who it is. We see our fair share of solicitors here, and the only person I really want to be on the other side of that door is out with the guys tonight.

"Uhh, Reagan," Ginny calls from the door. "I think you want to see this."

"Who is it?" I ask. "Firefighters?"

She doesn't answer, just smiles, and opens the door wide.

Adam steps through.

I gape at him. He's so handsome. He still takes my breath away sometimes. "What are you doing back so early?"

I can barely pull my eyes away from him, but I do note that Heath, Rhett, and Maverick file in behind him.

"Go away. You're supposed to be at guys' night," Dakota says from behind me. "I never get these two to myself anymore."

"What exactly are you supposed to be, Kota?" Maverick asks her.

My hands go to my face.

"I'm a narwhal, Ginny's a tiger, and Reagan's a llama. Duh," my roommate tells him.

Oh shit. I'm a llama. I'm a llama standing in front of my incredibly sexy crush. A freaking llama.

I duck my head and use my hand as a shield. "We're having a spa night. You guys aren't supposed to be here."

"I know, but I needed to see you." Adam steps forward and leans down to see my face.

"Uh-huh." Can llamas blush? I motion toward the bathroom. "I just need a few minutes."

"Don't go." He grabs my hand. "This can't wait."

Slowly, this llama faces her dream man. "Okay."

"Reagan, I…" Adam's brow furrows. "I've been thinking…" He stops again and looks around. "I'm no good at speeches, so I wrote it down."

Maverick steps forward and hands him a stack of poster boards. The first one says my name. Maverick plays a song from his phone. He even holds it over his head and sways in time with the music.

Adam smiles shyly as he drops the first poster board, the next one reads, **The past few weeks have been amazing.**

I smile. They really have. The guys must know what the poster boards say, which makes sense since they came over together, but they're watching me instead of Adam, and I'm blushing hard.

The next board falls.

You are the coolest girl I've ever known.

My stomach flutters as he keeps going.

You're smart, talented, kind, and gorgeous.

Somewhere behind me, Ginny says, "Awww."

Your butt's nice too.

Mav chuckles and whispers, "That one was my idea."

"Thanks, Mav," I say.

I don't know how I got so lucky.

Adam drops the board, and the last one reads, **"Will you be my girlfriend, Reagan?"**

I step closer and whisper, "But, what about... everything?"

"Maybe we should give them some privacy," Rhett says.

"But," Mav starts. "It's just about to get good."

"Come on." Rhett puts an arm around Mav's neck and guides him back out the door. Christina Aguilera's voice gets quieter as they cross the breezeway into their apartment. Ginny squeezes my arm as she and Heath follow.

"Pretend I'm not here," Dakota says. "Just grabbing more wine and going to my room. Where I have knives, just FYI."

Adam leaves the posters on the floor and shoves both hands in his pockets. "So, what do you say? Want to be my girlfriend?"

"Me or the llama?" I joke. I need a minute to process this. "Come with me. I need to take this thing off," I say as I pull him toward the bathroom.

While I peel off the mask, Adam leans against the doorframe. I feel his gaze on me, but I wait until I've rinsed my face and dabbed it dry before I speak.

"That was probably the nicest thing anyone's ever done for me."

"But?"

"How come you changed your mind?"

"Talking to the guys tonight, I realized that I'd only taken what I wanted and needed into consideration. I never once asked how you felt about it."

"I want you. The rest isn't all that important."

"Then maybe it is all about me. I want you to be mine in every way. I want to do boyfriend things for you. Take you on dates, walk you home, make you oatmeal in the mornings."

I laugh at his oatmeal remark. I might even eat it. That's how crazy I am about him.

"And all your worries?"

"Maybe I am in a love bubble, but I don't have those worries when I'm with you. It's only when I'm by myself and second-guessing everything."

"What you just described is a lust bubble, and your dick is doing all the thinking for you when I'm around."

"Maybe." He chuckles and places his hands on my hips. "Me and my dick like you a lot."

"I like you too." I settle between his legs, leaning against his chest.

"But you won't be my girlfriend?"

"Remember how I said I wanted to be good for you?"

I glance up, and his hazel eyes narrow playfully. "Not being my girlfriend is good for me?"

"According to the guy I talked to before he fell into the love bubble, yeah."

I want more than anything to be his girlfriend, but maybe he's right. And even if he isn't, I don't need him to make it official. I feel it when I'm with him. This is enough for now.

"Using my own words against me." Adam rests his forehead against mine. "Your face feels really soft."

"It's from the mask."

"You were a cute llama."

"Can we never speak of that again?"

A slow smile spreads across his face. "Got any other animals? Maybe something badass like a grizzly bear or a lion?"

"I have a unicorn or a shark."

He rubs his palms together. "Let's go with shark."

"You're going to wear a face mask?"

"Will it help me convince you to be my girlfriend?"

My heart squeezes. "No, probably not, but it'll be funny."

"WHAT EXACTLY AM I LOOKING AT HERE?" DAKOTA ASKS THE next morning as I hand her my phone to show off the pictures of Adam wearing the shark face mask. I conveniently left out that the mask was all pink before he let me put it on him.

He chased me around the apartment demanding payback, which he took in the form of sex against the wall. I can't even pretend to be mad about it. However, sex with a guy in a pink shark mask is a little disorienting.

"He was a shark."

"I love how you can see his facial hair through it. Creepy." She gives my phone back and takes a drink of her smoothie. "So, it's official, then? You're Adam Scott's new girlfriend."

"Not exactly."

She tilts her head and stares at me.

"I'll explain later. Anyway, I'm sorry our girls' night got crashed."

One brow quirks up with disbelief.

"Okay, it was an awesome night, but I really do what to hang out—just the girls. The guys have away games this weekend, and I was thinking we should have a do-over."

"Ginny had the same idea."

"She did?"

"Yeah, she was by early this morning. Pack your bags, little lady, we're taking a road trip this weekend."

Chapter Nineteen

ADAM

"Are you ready to go?" I ask, stretching my legs out in front of me. My right foot is asleep from this weird angle I've been sitting in for the past hour. Reagan's study spot on the stage in the theater is about the most uncomfortable I can imagine. But she's here, so I keep coming back.

I should be home packing for our away games, but I couldn't resist spending a little more time with her.

"Just about. First, I have an idea." She stands, then takes both my hands and helps me to my feet.

"Oh yeah?" It's amazing how fast my mind can conjure a dozen dirty images.

"Not that kind of idea." She shoves at my chest. "Stay here."

She leaves me on the stage and hops down, and walks toward the last row of seats. There is a podium that I never really noticed before, but within a couple of seconds of stepping to it, Reagan has the lights dimmed and a spotlight on the center of the stage.

I squint to see her. "I can't see shit now."

"That's the idea. But we can see you."

"We?" I scan the darkened theater.

"Royal we. It's just me but use your imagination. It's the night of your big scholarship banquet, and a room full of doctors are eager to hear your speech."

Sweat beads on my forehead. "You want me to give my speech here?"

"Why not?"

"I have about a thousand really awesome reasons why not."

"You said you need to practice." Her voice sounds closer, but I still can't see her.

"I know." And I really do. The banquet is coming up fast, and I'm not prepared. I jump from the stage and instantly feel calmer. Reagan stands in the aisle halfway between me and the podium.

"How about I give you the speech back at my place?"

"You tend to get distracted with all this when we're at your place." She makes a circle with one hand, motioning to her boobs.

"It isn't my room. I'm distracted by them right now."

She crosses her arms over her chest like that's gonna help. I still know they're there, and I can recall them in oh so vivid detail from memory.

"Okay," I give in.

She grins, lets her arms fall, and my eyes go straight to her rack. I can recall them, but it's always better to get a good look in person.

"Get back up there, stud."

I groan, but I walk back to the stage and hop onto it. I shield my eyes again as the spot blinds me. "Can you at least turn off the homing beacon?"

"Oh, fine, but for the record, you look damn good in the

spotlight."

In the dark, I can make out her silhouette, but I can't read her expression.

"I don't know how you do this. I'm sweating bullets, and I know there's no one out there but you."

"I find it much harder to speak to one person versus a crowd of people."

"I so don't get that." I blow out a long breath. My pulse ticks faster.

"You're stalling, Dr. Scott."

"Okay, okay." I pace a few steps getting my thoughts together.

I don't hear her walk onto the stage, but the next thing I know, she's standing in front of me. "Breathe."

She inhales through her nose and then holds it and lets it out slowly. I feel ridiculous, but I mimic her.

"Why do you want to be a doctor?" she asks and then continues breathing with me.

"When Ginny was little, she got trapped in a pantry closet at our grandparents' house. She was fine, physically, but she was so upset by the time we found her she was having a hard time breathing."

"She told me about that," Reagan says.

"I was young, but not so young that I didn't realize I couldn't help her. It was an awful feeling."

"So, you decided to be a doctor because you couldn't help Ginny?"

"Well, that's where it started anyway. Who doesn't want to play Superman?"

"I don't, but I'm glad there are people like you who do."

"I can't tell them that story, though. Ginny would be horrified. Also, I don't want to be the guy who gives the downer speech."

She laughs. "You could focus on the positive. Ginny was found, and she got the help she needed, thanks to a doctor."

"Still kind of sappy."

With an eye roll, she says, "Okay, then what do you have planned?"

"I was going to tell them about the time I broke my arm playing hockey. The bone was sticking out, and—"

Reagan squeezes her eyes closed and shakes her head. "Okay, never mind. Maybe I don't want to hear the speech."

I pull her against me and drop my mouth to hers. "Thank you for this."

"For what?"

"Helping me."

"I didn't do anything, and you still didn't practice your speech."

"Do you know that when someone has a panic attack, the best thing you can do for them is stay by their side, talk calmly, and remind them to breathe?"

"You were having a panic attack just now?"

"No, but my point is sometimes helping someone isn't flashy. Just being here with me, supporting me, pushing me to practice when all I want to do is kiss you until the bus leaves tomorrow afternoon, it helps."

"You're welcome."

"Be my girlfriend."

She doesn't answer, but I get an amused smirk.

"I'm serious. I'm better with you. I really like you. This time is.... Fuck, I hate to say it's different, but it is. And, yeah, it's because you're different, which I know you're going to roll your eyes about, but you make me different, too. I have a good feeling about this."

I'm sure she's going to say no. I haven't exactly made a compelling argument, but instead she says, "Yes."

"Really?" I scoop her up.

She nods. "Yeah, really. You're kind of hard to say no to. Kiss me, stud."

"That's boyfriend to you."

"YOU SEEM TO BE IN A BETTER MOOD," I SAY THE NEXT AFTERNOON on the bus to State. Rhett's phone is nowhere in sight, and he's playing on his Nintendo Switch.

"That's because I talked to Carrie," he says without taking his eyes off the game.

"You did?" I brace myself for the news they're back together.

Instead, he says, "She's coming to the game."

"She is? But that's, I don't know—a fuck long way for her to drive."

"She's flying, and it's as close to neutral ground as we could get considering we have games or practice almost every weekend."

Rhett and I have been friends for a long time, so I'm quiet for a moment as I collect my words. As the captain, I want his focus to be solely on hockey. As his friend, I want him to get the closure he needs. But I'm also afraid it's the opposite of closure he's going to get. "Is this the best idea?"

"It won't affect my game if that's what you're worried about."

"No. Okay, yes, that is a concern. The games this weekend are important. We're getting down to the final month of the regular season and we need to be our best every single time we step onto the ice, but I'm more worried that talking is going to lead to you two getting back together when that isn't what you want."

His gaze pops up from the video game in his hands to me. He studies my face and then huffs a laugh. "I can't decide if I should be insulted for myself or Carrie."

"I'm sorry. I think you can do better. I want better for you."

We're quiet for the rest of the ride.

When we get to Arizona State, the team files off the bus, and the Sun Devil's team manager greets us at the door to take us to our locker room.

As is his pregame routine, Rhett's dressing and listening to music with Maverick. They have this thing where the two of them share one pair of headphones—each of them getting a single earbud. I don't get it, but it's their thing, and I don't mess with guys' routines.

"What d'ya say, boys?" I ask as we walk down the tunnel to take the ice for warmups. "What d'ya say?"

They file past me, stepping into the rink.

When I finally take the ice, I breathe in the cool air and relax. I've always loved hockey and skating. Especially this moment just before the game starts when everyone is optimistic and ready to do whatever it takes to win. Nothing else matters in this moment. We all have a single focus.

After I've stretched, I skate over to Rhett. "I'm sorry about earlier. Whatever you need, man, I'm here."

He grins. "I was hoping you'd say that. I'm gonna need the

room later."

With a pat on the shoulder, he skates past me, and all I can do is laugh.

"IF THEY'RE IN YOUR ROOM, WHERE ARE YOU?" REAGAN ASKS LATER when I call her.

"I'm hanging out in Heath and Maverick's room. Can't you hear them?"

"I thought you were at a bar or something. They're loud."

"Yeah, no kidding."

"Well, you'll never guess where I am." I can hear the smile in her voice.

"I hope you're about to tell me you're here."

"Sadly, no, but I am in your room."

"You're at the apartment? I thought you were doing some sort of road trip with the girls."

"We did. We drove up to your mom's house for the weekend."

My mom's house. The phrase forms a pit in my stomach. I'm not sure I'll ever get used to them living apart.

"Ah. Ginny's been saying she wanted to go back." I know it's as weird for Ginny as it is for me to be there now that our dad's moved out, so I'm glad she has her friends with her. "What are you girls going to get up to there?"

"Wine, sappy movies, junk food—the usual."

"Sexting your boyfriend?" I ask hopefully.

She hums. "Maybe. First, I'm going to snoop around your

childhood room and look for dirt."

"Good luck. Hasn't been a girl in that room in a long time."

"It's pretty boring in here. Not a single picture of an ex in sight."

I picture her walking around my old room, which leads to picturing her in my bed.

"Probably shoved in a drawer somewhere."

"I haven't gotten to the drawers yet," she says. "Ginny's yelling for me. I better go. How long will you be up? Can I drunk text you later?"

"You can always drunk text. I'm hoping Carrie will be gone soon, and I can go back to my room, but I'll be up for a few hours."

"You don't think she'll stay the night?"

"I don't know. I hope not. How long does it take to tell her it's over?"

"You really dislike her, huh?"

"I just don't think she's good for him, and I think he's kidding himself that talking to her in person is going to give him closure. She wants him back, and she knows that in person, she's far more persuasive. He never should have agreed to it."

"Actually, that might be my fault," Reagan says.

"Yours. How?"

"A while back, we were talking about the breakup. He sounded really upset, and I told him I thought seeing her could help."

"It won't help." The words come out harsher than I intend. "He's only ever dated her. He needs to move on, date other people. That will give him closure."

"He was with her for a really long time, Adam."

"Yeah, exactly. He has no idea what a good relationship is."

"And you do?" She gasps as if she can't believe she said it out loud. The line goes quiet. "I'm so sorry." Reagan's voice is small when she finally speaks again. "I didn't mean that."

"No, you're probably right. What do I know about a successful relationship? I haven't dated anyone more than a few months at a time. And all of those failed spectacularly."

"Adam, I'm so sorry," she says again.

I believe her, but I don't think it's an accident she said it. She's obviously been thinking about how I've blown up all my previous relationships. I can't blame her, but it still stings.

"Have fun with the girls. I gotta go." I press end and stare straight ahead.

"Yo, Scott," Mav calls from across the room. "You want in this game?"

I put my phone in my pocket and join them.

Chapter Twenty

REAGAN

YOU MAY FIND YOURSELF ACTING AS A MEDIATOR FOR TWO PEOPLE YOU CARE ABOUT. DON'T FEEL OBLIGATED TO TAKE SIDES, AND DO REMEMBER THAT WORDS SAID IN THE HEAT OF THE MOMENT CAN HAVE AN IMPACT FAR BEYOND THE IMMEDIATE DISAGREEMENT. IN SHORT, WATCH YOUR DAMN MOUTH!

Numbly, I walk downstairs to find the girls in the kitchen. We went a little overboard at the grocery store on the way to Ginny's mom's house, and the counter is littered with bags of chips and candy, booze, and other things that we randomly threw into the cart.

"Red or white?" Ginny asks as she holds up two bottles of wine.

"I don't care."

"What's wrong with you?" Dakota asks as she opens a bag of chips.

"I think Adam and I just had our first fight."

"Oh, honey, what happened?" Ginny asks. She sets the wine on the counter and then proceeds to open both. She must read on my face that it's going to be a two-bottle night.

I slump onto a barstool. "We were talking about Rhett and Carrie. Carrie went to their game tonight so she and Rhett could talk."

"She did?" Dakota's eyes widen.

I nod. "Yeah. Adam is totally against them talking or reconciling in any way. I don't get it. It's like he thinks everyone should be able to break up with someone they love and move right on to the next. He said Rhett didn't know what a good relationship looked like, and I kind of threw that statement back in his face." I bury my face in my hands. "It just slipped out. I didn't even realize I was thinking it until the words left my mouth."

"That is sort of his thing." Ginny gives me a small smile.

"How did Adam react?" Dakota asks.

"I apologized immediately, and he acted like it was fine, but then he said he needed to get off the phone." Me and my big mouth. "I feel like such an ass."

"You two will work it out," Ginny says, sounding so sure, but she didn't hear the hurt in his voice.

"Words said in the heat of the moment have an impact far beyond the immediate disagreement," I grumble.

"What?" Dakota asks with a laugh. "You sound like a fortune cookie."

I wave her off. "It was in my horoscope this morning." I look between them. "What do I do? Do I call him back now? Wait, and hope he forgets?" If only I could be so lucky.

"Give him the night," Ginny says. "They'll be back tomorrow night. I'm sure by then all will be forgotten, and if not, you make it up to him."

"You realize you're talking about your brother, right?" Dakota grins.

"Gross. That isn't what I meant." Her face scrunches up, and she tosses a chip at Dakota.

I know that waiting is the right call, but tomorrow sounds so far away. I don't know how I'm going to make it through the night worrying about it. "Okay. Yeah, that sounds practical."

"Unless..." Dakota starts.

"Yeah?" I ask, hopeful she has a genius idea. Screw practical.

"We could go to the game."

Ginny and I share a confused look, and Dakota shrugs.

"You want to go to the hockey game?" Ginny narrows her gaze at our friend.

"I thought you wanted to spend time just us girls." I study her closely. This feels very unlike Dakota.

"And I do, but we can do that in Tempe. I love a good road trip." She avoids eye contact completely. Her phone buzzes on the counter, and she jumps for it, and then she smiles.

"Who's that?" I ask.

"No one." Her thumbs tap on the screen.

"Are you texting one of the guys? Is it Mav?" Ginny asks.

"What?" Dakota looks up. "No, I told you, it's no one, okay? So, are we going or what?"

"Your mom won't mind?" I ask Ginny. "We just got here."

"She has to work, and it isn't like I'm here to hang out with her anyway." She grins. "I'm up for it. Heath will lose his mind."

"I'm not so sure Adam will be as happy to see me."

"He will," Ginny reassures me. "Now, let's go watch the movie and drink all the wine."

THE FOLLOWING AFTERNOON WE ARRIVE AT THE GAME AND FIND seats behind the Valley bench. I sent Adam a text this morning wishing him luck on the game, but his response was a one-word, *Thanks*.

Needless to say, I don't feel great about how he's going to react to me coming to the game. Heath spots Ginny right away. He gets this goofy grin on his face anytime she's around. I love them together.

Adam's slower to spot us. Maverick nudges him, and he looks up and scans the crowd until he finds me. One side of his mouth pulls up, and he lifts a hand. I wave back and try to communicate how sorry I am and how much I don't want this thing between us to end before it's even really started.

I doubt he gets that from my meek wave, but I send it out into the universe anyway, hoping he feels it.

Valley won the game last night, but today the guys look sluggish. Or that's what Ginny says after the first period when Valley is down by two. I'm watching, but really only seeing Adam.

"They can't lose," I say. That would feel like a seriously bad omen for the night ahead.

When the guys take the ice to start the next period, Adam looks up at me. His smile is bigger this time, and I feel just a little bit hopeful that we're going to be okay.

Adam wins the face-off, and Heath chases a long pass. Ginny's on her feet, yelling and clapping. Heath and a guy from State are up against the boards fighting for the puck. He manages to kick it out, and Maverick is close enough to take possession and send it to Adam, who is waiting on the right side. The puck sails toward the goal, and the lamppost lights up.

Dakota and I join Ginny, and the three of us scream so loudly you'd think he just won them the game. Adam skates toward the Valley bench and points. At first, I think he's pointing to the guys—it's kind of hard to tell with the big gloves he wears, but when he winks, I know it's for me.

Valley ekes out a victory, and as soon as the game's over, we head to the parking lot behind the arena where the Valley bus sits, waiting for the guys.

"Is that Carrie?" Ginny asks, looking toward a girl standing next to a shiny red car.

"I think so," Dakota says. "Things must have gone well."

"Should we go talk to her?" I ask. I've only met her once, and it was brief, but she's important to Rhett and therefore indirectly important to us.

Before we can decide, the guys start filing out of the arena. Adam's one of the last, like usual. I've noticed it's a thing with him. He doesn't just lead by example; he knows when he needs to follow. I don't run to him, but it's only because I have on heeled boots, and tripping seems likely. Neither of us speaks at first. He hugs me and lifts me off the ground, squeezing me so tightly I can practically feel his forgiveness.

"I'm sorry," we say at the same time.

"You were right. I don't know shit about their relationship."

"You just want what's best for him. For everyone."

He nods. "But he's a grown-ass man. He'll figure it out."

"Did he say that to you?"

"Yeah." Adam chuckles. "Verbatim."

"You want to protect the people around you. It's one of the things I like most about you. And I didn't mean what I said about you. I think I just got freaked out being in your room and realizing if this doesn't work out..." My voice trails off. "I don't want it to end."

"I get it. I don't want it to end either."

All around us, the guys are heading onto the bus and the managers are loading up the equipment.

"Can we hang out later?" I ask.

"Definitely. I want to take you somewhere. Dress warm. I'll come by to pick you up as soon as we get back."

"Okay," I say with a smile.

"I'VE HEARD ABOUT THIS PLACE."

Adam pulls into the drive-in movie theater. It sits on top of Mount Loken. I'm giddy with excitement. We haven't been on a real date since the night I babbled through dinner. And this is official playbook date material.

"You have?" He looks guilty. Probably because it's a known fact this is Adam Scott's favorite date location. Someone once told me there's an Adam Scott special on the menu – two drinks, one large popcorn, and a bag of candy. I'm pretty sure they were making that up, but it's also not entirely out of the question considering how many girls he's brought up here.

"Yes. It isn't exactly a secret you bring all your girlfriends here."

"Okay, yes, that's true. But it's because it's my favorite place. Wanna see why?"

"Oh, I know why." I glance to the back hatch of his Jeep.

He laughs a deep-throated chuckle that makes my stomach flip.

"You think I bring chicks up here to get laid?" he asks as we get out of the vehicle.

"Yeah. That's the whole point of drive-in movie theaters, right?" I don't actually know since I've never been to one, but I always assumed.

"I'm not saying I've never felt a girl up in public or slid my hand up her skirt," he says as his hand slips under the hem of my dress. I'm wearing leggings, but his fingers trail all the way up to my ass, and then he palms one cheek. "But no, I'm not banging my dates at the drive-in." He looks at me like I'm a crazy person for even thinking it. And now I really want to have sex in the back of his Jeep to see why it's such a bad idea.

"Okay, well then, why?"

He leads me past the concession stand. It's dusk, and the temperature is much cooler up here. It feels like winter instead of the warm February weather in Valley.

I'm forced to walk behind him as he heads down a narrow path. I'm looking at the ground, watching my step when he stops, and I finally glance up.

"Oh, wow," I say. All of Valley opens up below us. Dots of light litter the dusk sky.

He holds my hand as we stare down. Everything looks so

small. Something about being on top of the mountain reminds me of how insignificant we are. We're just two people in a world of billions. It's reassuring and scary all at the same time.

"This is amazing." I pull my gaze from the view and drape my arms around his neck. "You're good at being a boyfriend. And this is a good date. I'm glad you brought me."

"Yeah, maybe," he says. "I feel like an ass now that you mentioned I bring all my dates here. It's a cool spot. Everyone should see it. Especially you."

"You're always thinking about other people. Do you like coming here because you enjoy seeing it so often or because you think your date will like it?"

He hesitates. "I'm not sure. Both, maybe."

"Do you come here alone?"

"No."

"Hmm."

"What?" he asks.

"What's your idea of a perfect date? Something you would want to do."

"I don't really care. I like being with you, any old where."

"That's not an answer."

"I don't know. Me, you, the rest doesn't matter."

"Well, come on then. I want the full Adam Scott drive-in experience with the Reagan twist."

"Do I even want to ask?"

"I'll give you a hint, stud," I say as I cup him through his jeans.

Chapter Twenty-One

ADAM

That's all," Dr. Salco says, staring up at the big, ancient clock that hangs on the wall of the lecture hall. She never lets us out early. Not even by a second. "Don't forget we'll be having a quiz on Monday."

There's a collective groan as students file out.

"Mr. Scott," she says, catching me before I leave. She motions me to the front.

I take my time, letting the room empty.

She's shoving papers into her tote when I approach. "The banquet is next week. Are you ready?"

"I think so, yeah."

She lifts a brow, calling my bluff without saying a word.

"I do have my speech written," I assure her. "I just don't love it yet. Speech writing is not my calling."

"Write from your heart and edit with a heavy dose of logic." She waves a hand. "That's what my advisor told me once. You'll be okay."

It isn't the words I'm worried about, though. I'd just rather not say them to a crowd of people. "Thank you, Dr. Salco."

"And will your fiancée be joining us?"

"Right, about that." I've somehow managed not to come clean on the subject of my fake fiancée. On the one hand, it hasn't come up. On the other, I haven't brought it up.

"She seems like a lovely girl." Dr. Salco's mouth tips up. I'm pretty sure she's smiling. Wow. Reagan's good.

"She is." I nod my agreement. "Reagan is the best."

"So, she'll be there?"

Slowly, I nod. "She will."

What's the harm, really? Reagan and I are together. We're just not quite as serious as Dr. Salco believes. We can tell her together at the banquet if it comes up again.

"Wonderful. Have a good day, Adam."

I PICK UP GINNY FROM OUTSIDE OF HER DORM.

"Yo," she says as she gets into the passenger side of my Jeep.

"You've been around Heath too much. You're starting to sound like him."

"I am, aren't I?" She settles in and buckles up.

I pull away from the curb and head off-campus. "The usual?"

"Sure," Ginny says and then starts messing with my phone to change the music.

Our usual is grabbing burgers and fries and driving around. It was something we started when she first got to Valley so I could show her around the campus and town, but now it's just nice to spend some time with her away from everyone else.

Today, I head for the outskirts of town. Valley is a decent-size city, but there's still plenty of desert land when you get outside the city limits.

"I heard you and Reagan went up Mount Loken to the drive-in last weekend." Ginny scrunches up her nose. "You took her to your usual spot?"

"Yeah, yeah, I know. She called me out on it too. I like it up there. It's a great date location."

"You need to get more creative."

Oh, we did. I smile as I think about our night on top of the mountain. That's the thing about Reagan. Even doing the same old things with her is fresh and exciting. I see things from a new perspective when I'm with her. But Ginny isn't wrong.

"Any ideas or are you just gonna bust my balls?"

"Hmmm…" She chews and stares out the windshield. "Something uniquely Reagan, but that only you could give her."

I wait for her to come up with something. She's quiet for too long.

"Well?" I ask when I can't take it anymore.

"I have no idea." She laughs. "Sorry."

My hands tighten on the steering wheel.

"Why are you so stressed about this? I've never seen you so spun up over where to take a girl on a date."

"You were just telling me I need to be more creative."

"Yeah, but I've told you that before, and you just brushed it off." Ginny grins. "You really like Reagan."

"Yeah, of course. She's great."

Ginny squeals—a high-pitched sound that makes me wince.

"I'm not sure why you find this so surprising. She's your friend. You know how great she is."

"I know, but honestly I've been afraid you were going to break her heart."

"No one's worried about her breaking my heart?" I ask, shooting her an annoyed look.

Ginny rolls her eyes. "Please. You're a pro at moving on to the next girl. Reagan's been crushing on you for a long time. When you two got into it over the phone, she was a wreck."

"Yeah, that was rough," I admit. "But that wasn't even about us. I was annoyed about Carrie weaseling her way back into Rhett's life, and I got short with her."

"Maybe it wasn't a fight about the two of you, but it absolutely had everything to do with her concerns about you. She's worried that what happened with Carrie will happen to her."

"What? No."

"Yes," Ginny insists. "Carrie and Rhett broke up, and you've been very vocal in not wanting them to get back together. And I get it. I didn't like them together either, but it's very much your MO. You end things, and you move on, never speaking to them again. Reagan doesn't want that girl to be her."

"I don't think I could ever move on from Reagan like that. If things didn't work out with us…" My jaw tightens.

"Maybe you should tell her that, and I have the perfect plan." Even with food in her hands, she manages to flail them around while she talks. She's clearly excited about whatever she has cooked up, and I find myself hopeful that it will give me clarity on how to move forward with Reagan.

"Can't I just text her and repeat what I said?" I'm kidding, but the outrage on Ginny's face is totally worth it.

"I'm going to pretend I didn't hear that." She finishes her food and turns toward me. "Maverick's birthday is on Sunday. Let's throw him a party."

"I'm failing to see how a party for Mav is the perfect plan to tell Reagan how I feel about her."

"Do I have to figure it all out for you? The place doesn't matter."

"Then why do I need a party?"

"You don't. I just really want to throw a party at your place."

I chuckle. "Does Maverick even want a party? This is the first I've heard about his birthday." And when it comes to Johnny Maverick, he shares everything, so it's suspicious if he's not mentioned it yet. Then again, I have been preoccupied lately.

"Who doesn't want a party thrown in their honor?"

"Whatever. As long as the rest of the guys are cool with it."

"I already asked." She claps. "Let's go by the store."

"Wait, the party is tonight?"

"Didn't I mention that?" She smiles sweetly.

I shake my head. Such a pain in my ass.

GINNY DOES MOST OF THE WORK, AND BY THE TIME WE GET BACK to the apartment with party food and alcohol, the entire team is already here.

Someone's made Maverick a crown out of beer tabs, and he wears that shit proudly.

"Happy Birthday," I say, handing him a bottle of Mad Dog

20/20.

"Aww, thanks, Scott," he says and pulls me into a hug. He's already missing his shirt. It's not a party until Mav's half-naked. I don't understand the guy, but he's definitely a good time.

I pat his back and pull away. "Seen Reagan?"

"Outside," he says. He twists the top of the bottle and takes a drink, then passes it to me.

I manage to swallow the grossly sweet liquor and hand it back. "Enjoy."

I grab a beer and head out to the deck. My gaze goes right to her. Sometimes I wonder how I went two years without looking at her—I mean really seeing her.

She's standing in a group with Dakota, Rhett, and Liam. Reagan looks up as I approach and smiles. Stepping toward me, she wastes no time kissing me. I fucking love that.

I wrap an arm around her waist and lift her so I can kiss her harder.

"I missed you," she says, tearing her mouth away. The girl I once described as shy and reserved never misses an opportunity to shower me with affection or tell me how she's feeling. And I eat that shit up.

I suck on her lower lip. "Missed you too. Wanna get out of here?"

She laughs, and I place her on the ground.

Holding my hand, she pulls me into the circle. Guess that's a no.

"How did everyone get here so quickly?" I ask Rhett.

"What do you mean?" He and Liam share a confused look.

"It's barely been an hour since Ginny texted Heath to let

everyone know."

Dakota starts laughing. Then Rhett joins her. Reagan looks at me with a placating smile.

"What am I missing?"

"Uhh…" Liam starts. He's a freshman and probably the nicest guy on the team, so I wait for him to tell me what's going on because he'll be straight with me.

Reagan squeezes my hand. "Ginny sent out a group text this morning."

"But…"

"She knew you'd say yes. Besides, it's Maverick's birthday."

I shake my head. It wasn't about Reagan and me at all. Though maybe that's the point.

For the next few hours, the party grows. More people arrive, and the music gets louder. I'm leaning against the railing, and Reagan stands in front of me, her back to my chest. The wind blows her hair away from her neck, and I dip my head to kiss her.

"This is kind of perfect. Me, you, our friends," I say against her soft skin.

"It is, isn't it?"

"How long until I can steal you away?"

She laughs like I'm kidding. My kisses on her neck become harder. It's real easy to get carried away where Reagan is concerned.

"Mav requested that we play sardines later."

"I don't think that's happening." I point toward him across the deck. He's kissing one girl, and another is plastered to his side, sucking on his neck.

"Oh," Reagan says. "That's kind of hot." She turns in my arms. "Have you ever had a threesome?"

"Ummm…"

"Tell me. I don't care," she insists.

"Just once. It was… tricky."

"I think I'd lose my mind if some other girl put her hands on you." She slides her hands up my chest.

"Good because I'm not big on the idea of sharing you either. I like this. Us. Just the two of us. Though I can think of some ways to get… tricky if you want later."

Her smile is so big I want to keep talking to let her know how much I'm digging this, but my dick is growing harder against her. Talk of sex, threesomes, or Reagan tends to have that effect. Combined, and I'm ready to fuck her right here. I guess she has the same idea because she pushes her hips into me and inhales sharply.

"Maybe we could sneak away just for a few minutes?"

I tug her, already halfway across the deck before she's finished the last word. "I'm never going to say no to that."

Chapter Twenty-Two

REAGAN

EXPECT GOOD THINGS—FLOWERS, JEWELS, AMAZING SEX. LOTS OF IT. MANIFEST YOUR OWN DAMN LUCK.

I'm sitting on Adam's lap, one arm around his neck, fingers absently playing with his hair as our friends argue over whether butter and margarine are the same thing. I have no idea how we got on this topic. It's late, and most people have gone home.

We're all outside because Mav is celebrating his birthday in the living room. And by celebrating, I mean there's a good chance he's having a threesome on the couch. Happy freaking birthday to him.

I kind of miss him, though. Our group never feels quite right without his shenanigans.

"Margarine is processed bullshit," Liam says. It's maybe the meanest thing I've ever heard him say. He's got this wholesome goodness about him, from his perfectly kept blond hair and preppy clothes to the polite way he talks and acts. I'm surprised he's out this late, to be honest. He's the kind of guy I assume follows a strict curfew, and also takes vitamins.

I scan our friends. Heath and Ginny, Rhett, and Dakota. All of us sitting here just enjoying the night and each other's company. My heart squeezes. This group is so much more than just my friends. Before when I was pining away for Adam, it was hard for me to really feel this at peace when we were all together, but now I can't imagine a group of people that could feel more like family.

"You good?" Adam whispers next to my ear. His arms slide around my waist holding me protectively.

I turn to look into his hazel eyes. "So good."

His gaze drops to my mouth, and he kisses me softly. "I'm crazy about you. Can't seem to get enough, but right now—somehow it feels like enough. Tonight's been perfect."

My heart flutters, and I'm putty in his hands. I can't think of a response. All of my emotions feel too big and overwhelming to put into words. Instead, I nuzzle into him, enjoying the warmth it brings me inside and out.

Dakota's next to us. She smiles and winks when we make eye contact. She's been hesitant to trust Adam, afraid he'd break my heart, but I know how happy she is for me.

"I think I'm out," she says. "I can't miss my eight o'clock class tomorrow."

"Good luck getting through the house without going blind," Heath says as she stands to go inside.

She leans down to hug me. "I'll survive."

"I'm out too." Liam stretches his long legs and then gets to his feet.

"You need a ride?" Adam asks him. I grin up at my considerate boyfriend. Always looking out for his guys.

"Nah, I didn't drink tonight."

"You were arguing over butter and margarine stone-cold sober?" Heath shakes his head and takes a drink from his beer, emptying it. Ginny's on his lap, and he leans forward. "Ready for bed, baby doll?"

Ginny nods, and Heath stands, carrying her with him. I hear him tell her to cover her eyes before they walk in.

"I don't want to go in yet," I say. "It's so nice out."

"We can stay out here as long as you want." Adam brushes my hair away from my neck and kisses me. I want to soak up this night, this feeling, as long as possible.

Rhett kicks his feet up on an empty chair. "I'm giving it another thirty minutes before I go in. I do not need to see Mav's O-face."

"It's all clear," Heath calls from inside.

Rhett doesn't move. "I'm still not ready to go in yet. Sorry, you two are stuck with me for a little while longer."

"We're good," I say. Adam pulls me closer, wrapping me up in his arms, and I lean my head on his shoulder. "You can stay as long as you want."

Rhett's gaze narrows, a slow smile spreads on his face. "You two snuck away and boned earlier, didn't you?"

Adam chuckles. My face heats.

Rhett sighs. "Man, that must be nice to have your girl here every night. My hand-to-girl ratio is pathetic."

"Hand-to-girl?" I ask.

"Amount of times I've fucked my hand instead of my girl."

"Oh." My face flames even hotter. Poor guy. "So, you and Carrie are back together?"

"No," he says immediately, then. "Yes? Fuck, I don't know. We're talking."

Adam's quiet, but I can read his silence well.

"Nothing to say?" Rhett grins over his beer. Obviously, he can read Adam well too.

"Nah, man. I just want you to be happy."

"Thanks. I am." Rhett looks at us and points one finger from around his bottle. "Maybe not that happy, but happy enough."

The thing about being this happy? I don't think I'll ever be able to settle for happy enough again.

SATURDAY MORNING, I WAKE UP TO STRONG HANDS SQUEEZING MY ass and pulling me against a very hard male body.

"Good morning." Adam's deep morning voice is straight sex. Or maybe that's just what's on my mind.

I mutter my greeting and wriggle closer. Sex before coffee is fine but talking is not.

Someone knocks on the door, and Adam tells them to go away as he climbs on top of me.

There's a lot of noise in the apartment for a Saturday morning. I pry my eyes open enough to look out the sliding glass door. "It's still dark out."

"You can go back to sleep in ten minutes," he says as he peppers kisses down my neck and over my collarbone.

His skin is warm under my hands as I slide them down his back.

"Yo, Scott," Mav calls and knocks on the door. "Buddy, 9-1-1. Time to get up."

"Fuck." Adam groans. "Let me just make sure they haven't set the place on fire. Don't move."

When he opens the door, Mav's standing there in a Hawaiian shirt, backward hat, smiling like it's a perfectly acceptable time to be awake. I pull up the sheet around me.

"This better be important," Adam grumbles.

"I'm sorry for the early morning wake-up call." Mav steps into the room carrying a tray of coffees as Adam pulls on a T-shirt and sweats. "'Morning, Reagan."

"Hey, Mav. I'll give you a thousand dollars for one of those coffees."

He walks to the edge of the bed and extends it to me. "No money necessary, but I do need you to get up and pack a bag."

I'm too tired to ask what the heck he's talking about, but he grins and adds, "I'll explain everything, but we have to hurry. It'll be worth it. Promise!"

He leaves, and Adam and I exchange a confused look.

"This should be interesting," he says.

We get dressed and head out to the living room, where Mav tells us his plan for a weekend getaway to Palm Springs to celebrate his twenty-first birthday.

"Didn't we celebrate your birthday last night?" Dakota asks. She waves off the coffee he tries to offer her.

"Yes, and it was amazing. Thank you guys for that, but my parents already booked the house. It's a five-hour trip, so if we hurry, we can be drunk in our own private pool by lunchtime."

"Well, that doesn't sound safe," Ginny says.

"Come on," Mav begs.

"Are your parents going to be there?" Rhett asks.

"Nah." He shakes his head and makes a face like the idea is ludicrous. "The Maverick family doesn't do birthday celebrations, but we do enjoy showering people in gifts instead of affection."

"They got you a house in Palm Springs for one night?" Heath asks.

"Technically two, but we already missed the first night."

"Maaav," Ginny whines. "Why didn't you say anything?"

"Because you guys went to all that effort to invite people over." He waves her off. "I loved it. Really."

Adam is the last one I expect to jump in and offer his support of the idea, but that's exactly who speaks up first. "Yeah, okay. It's the last weekend we're going to have off until the end of the season. Sounds baller. I'm in."

"You had me at private pool," I say.

"You had me at drunk," Heath adds, and Ginny elbows him.

"Kota?" Mav asks.

My roommate nods. "Yeah, fine, but I call shotgun, and I need to be back early Sunday afternoon to study for a test."

We all look to Rhett.

"I don't know," he says when he realizes it's down to him. "I need to check with Carrie."

"Are you serious?" Adam asks.

"How would you feel if Reagan went on a road trip with three dudes?"

The vein that notoriously pops out on his forehead when Adam's agitated starts to appear, but he nods.

"I already thought of this," Maverick interjects. "And there's enough rooms for us to all have our own when we get there." He looks to Rhett. "I'm sorry our friends are hot, and they're going to be in bikinis, but to be fair, that could happen here too."

Rhett's quiet. His leg bounces as he stares at the phone in his hand. "Okay. Fuck it. I'm in, but no giving me shit for calling her to check in every few hours."

"No promises," Heath says as he coughs into his hand.

Chapter Twenty-Three

ADAM

We get to the rental house just after lunchtime. The place is nuts. The grounds are palatial! A phrase I never thought I'd use, but I saw it on the brochure when we walked in, and they really are. There are six bedrooms, a massive living room with a fireplace that takes up most of one wall, a huge kitchen inside, a bar outside by the pool, and covered patios—yes plural. Everything in this place is ridiculously over the top.

Maverick is behind the outdoor bar playing bartender. Rhett and I sit in front of it, and the three of us watch Dakota and Reagan chicken fight with Heath and Ginny in the pool. Mav brought Charli, and she's running around the yard investigating every inch.

"Five bucks says Reagan falls first," Rhett says, tipping his drink toward them.

I jump to my girl's defense. "No way. Reagan's scrappy."

"Guess we're on." He holds his beer out, and I clink mine against the side.

Mav hops onto the bar and sits, his legs dangling over the side. "Dakota won't let her fall. Guarantee."

Reagan's blonde hair is slicked back, and she's concentrating hard as she and Ginny both try to push the other over. They're pretty evenly matched as far as size goes, but Heath's height advantage over Dakota gives Ginny the upper hand.

Reagan's looking unsteady as Ginny pushes hard. Dakota moves backward, and they readjust. This time when they come together, Reagan grabs Ginny's hands and intertwines their fingers. Then, Dakota walks backward, and that pulls Ginny forward. She teeters and almost falls over Heath's head, but he catches her in time.

Rhett chuckles. "This is quality entertainment."

"Let's go Kota," Mav yells.

Heath looks over to him. "What the hell, man? I thought we were friends."

"He's so sensitive," Mav says quietly, then yells, "Sorry buddy, love you."

Heath flips him off, and with one hand not protecting his partner, Reagan pushes my sister backward and off his shoulders.

Reagan raises her hands overhead and cheers as Ginny goes under. She shoots a grin over at me, and damn, she's stunning. I'm totally gone for her.

"Well, fuck," Rhett says. "Double or nothing?"

"I'm going in." Mav puts his sunglasses on and runs toward the pool. He jumps in and holds his beer up to keep it from going under.

They get set for another chicken fight, but this time Dakota gets on Mav's shoulders, and Reagan sits on the side of the pool cheering them on.

I glance over at Rhett. I haven't seen him on the phone all day. "How's everything with Carrie?"

"Eh."

"Do you want to talk about it?"

His brows lift toward the hat covering his head.

"I'm a good listener," I insist.

He hesitates as if he's considering it, but then shakes it off. "Nah, thanks though. I'm cool. Things with you and Reagan seem good."

"Deflecting. Nice."

A grin tugs at his lips.

"They are good. She's great, man. I didn't realize what it could be like. It's…" I struggle to put it in words.

A real smile spreads across his face. "Congratulations, my man. Sounds like you're in love."

AFTER A LONG DAY OUTSIDE IN THE POOL, WE GRILL AND THEN head inside. The fireplace is going, and we're all in the living room drinking and talking.

Half-empty bottles of liquor litter the coffee table. Maverick went all out, buying everyone's favorites, including his own.

"Happy twenty-first," Heath says and lifts his cup.

We all mimic him, and Mav grins shyly as he raises his bottle of MD 20/20. "Thank you guys for being here. This is the first birthday in a long time that hasn't royally sucked."

Reagan's sitting between my legs. She reaches over and squeezes Mav's arm, and I wonder if she feels that way too. Reagan's parents aren't around, and Maverick's think they can buy him off instead of spending any time with him. I'm irritated with my own parents for how they've acted recently, but not one birthday has gone by, my entire life, where they haven't made it feel special.

I dip my head lower to kiss her shoulder. "We should play sardines or something."

"I bet this house has some killer hiding spots," Rhett says.

Dakota groans. "No, let's play something different. We're on vacation!"

"Truth or dare?" Ginny suggests. "Or I've never?"

"I love I've never," Mav says. He puts his beer down on the floor and rubs his hands together. "I'll go first. I've never kissed a girl."

"We all drink except Reagan and Ginny."

Mav cackles at Dakota as she drinks.

She glares. "I told you that in confidence."

"Yes, I know. I'm sorry, babe, but it's such a great visual."

She rolls her eyes. "I've never had a threesome."

We go around the room, taking turns. I've played with the guys before, so I know most of their secrets, but it's fun finding out a little more about Reagan. Like, she's kissed more than one guy in a single day, and she's had a one-night stand. Stupid things that don't change how I feel about her, but just peel back more layers and remind me what an idiot I was not to notice her before.

"Maverick, why do you like this game so much exactly? You've had to drink every single time," Rhett asks. His experiences are a lot more limited than the rest of us since he's dated Carrie for so long.

"Precisely. Plus, I'm an open book, but the shit you can find out about your friends with a little I've never is gold. Like who would have thought you and Carrie have tried anal?"

Rhett's face turns red.

"I have one," Ginny says and lowers her gaze to the floor as she continues, "I've never been engaged."

Maverick, Rhett, and Dakota look around the circle to see who is going to drink.

"Who is it? And how do I not know about this?" Dakota asks. She looks at Mav.

He raises his hands. "No way, sweetheart. Not me."

"Not me," Ginny and Heath say at the same time.

Mav and Dakota look to Rhett. "No. Definitely not."

Slowly, Reagan lifts her drink to her lips, and I do the same.

"What?!" Dakota screeches. Her voice bounces off the walls. "You two are engaged?"

"Fake engaged," we say at the same time. Then we have to tell the entire story. Honestly, I figured they all knew. Especially Dakota.

"Wait, only Ginny knew?" Dakota asks.

"And Heath," Ginny says.

Mav looks hurt. "Bro?"

"I'm sorry. I didn't realize this was such hot gossip, and I figured the rest of you already knew if I did. I'm never the one in the know first." He shrugs.

Dakota excuses herself and heads toward the kitchen.

"I should go talk to her." Reagan places a chaste kiss on my lips and stands.

I grab her hand and tug her back down. Her cheeks and legs are red from the sun, and her hair falls in waves over her shoulder. She's all sun-kissed and glowing, and it's been a long day with our friends where I haven't been able to kiss or talk to her like I want. I have this uncontrollable urge to tell her how I feel. That this thing between us is so much more than I could have imagined.

That I'm falling for her.

She smiles. "I'll be right back, stud."

"I'm going to bed. Meet you there. Hurry."

Chapter Twenty-Four

REAGAN

YOU CAN'T ALWAYS PUSH FORWARD. GIVE YOURSELF SPACE AND TIME. WAIT FOR THE RIGHT MOMENT.

Ginny follows me into the kitchen. "I'm sorry. I thought you'd told her by now."

"It's okay," I say. Dakota's cleaning up, tossing empty beer cans in the trash, and basically just avoiding my gaze. "I'm so sorry you found out this way."

"How could you not tell me about this?" When she finally looks up, I see just how hurt she is by her expression, and I feel twice as awful.

"I was going to tell you, but I was so humiliated over the entire thing. I didn't even plan to tell Ginny, but she coerced it out of me."

"It's my sweet and innocent face," she says. "People always want to tell me their secrets."

"I don't understand why you were so humiliated?" Dakota tosses a bottle into the trash with a clang.

"Because I went too far. Adam wanted a date for the night, and instead, I made him pretend to be engaged to me. He was horrified, and I was humiliated that he was so horrified at the idea."

"But now look at you two," she says and smiles.

I nod. "Yeah, it worked out, but I really thought that I ruined everything. Even thinking about it now, I feel so stupid. I mean, really, who does that? I'm a mess."

"Hey, that's my best friend you're talking about."

"I'm really sorry."

"I've always got your back, you know? There is nothing you can tell me that would change that."

"Same. You're my family."

"Awww," Ginny says.

Heath walks in and glances around the room. His gaze stops on Ginny. "Ready for bed, baby doll?"

She goes with him, and then Mav appears. "I'm hitting the sheets. Thanks for today, guys."

"I should go to bed, too." Dakota hugs me. "Love you. See you in the morning."

I squeeze her extra hard.

It's a maze finding my way back to Adam's and my room. I crack the door open and peek inside to make sure it's the right one. He's lying on the bed, totally naked. His dick is hard and pointing up, making his intentions very clear. He smirks at me. "Lost again?"

I walk all the way in and shut the door. "I was afraid I was going to walk in on your sister and Heath."

He makes a face. "Almost lost my hard-on."

My gaze goes back to it. Yeah, I don't think so.

"Everything okay?" He sits up as I approach.

"I think so."

His arms circle around my waist and he pulls me on top of him. Calloused hands slide under my shirt, gliding up my sides. He unhooks my bra and then removes it with my shirt. I got a little too much sun today and I have tan lines from my bikini top.

He takes one nipple into his mouth and palms the other. I fist his hair in my hands, tugging the thick strands.

My body lights up as he kisses and worships each breast, then trails down my stomach. He flips us so I'm on my back, removes my shorts and panties. I groan when his mouth finds the aching spot between my legs. He sucks on my clit until I cry out, coming so hard I feel like I might die.

My hands are still in his hair, and I tug him up. His cock nudges my entrance, and my body quivers. That small movement sends me over the edge again, and I hold on to him as the second orgasm rips through me.

When I open my eyes, he's staring down at me. It isn't the cocky, *I just got you off by barely touching you*, look I expect. There's something much more in his expression.

"I have an IUD," I say when my brain functions enough to realize that expression is probably frustration. I've gotten off twice, and he's still hard and thick against my leg.

He nods but still doesn't move.

"Everything okay?"

"Yeah." He nudges just the tip inside, and we groan together. "Everything is perfect."

THE NEXT MORNING, WE PILE INTO MAVERICK'S SUV FOR THE second time in two days. He has a big smile on his face and sings quietly along with the radio. Charli's asleep in his lap. Dakota brought her class notes with her to study for a test she has tomorrow. She's studiously reading them over.

Ginny and Heath are quiet in the third-row seats, and I'm leaning against Adam, half asleep, between him and Rhett. The latter is passed out cold, arms crossed over his chest, hat covering his eyes.

The trip went too fast, but I'm glad we went. If Maverick's birthdays feel anything like my own, it was worth it.

We stop halfway to eat and stretch our legs.

"My charger's toast," Mav says. "I'm going to run into the store and grab another. I'll meet you guys at the restaurant."

We split up, the guys go with Mav, and Dakota, Ginny, and I walk down to grab a table for us. There's a fifteen-minute wait if we want to sit together, so we put our name on the list and continue down to see the little shops in the outdoor strip mall.

"I don't want to go back," I say. "Rehearsals are going to kick my ass this week."

"You've been rehearsing for weeks," Ginny says.

"Yeah, but we're completely off-book this week, and there's always at least one person who doesn't know their lines and throws us all off."

"Dr. Rossen asked me to come by tomorrow and teach the new people how to do stage makeup," Ginny says. "Do you want me to do your makeup for the show?" She's a wizard with a makeup brush and helped me, and several others, for our Christmas production. She did such a good job, they asked her to be an unofficial stage assistant this semester. She gets college credit for coming to rehearsal and making sure we're all prepared, and in turn, we all get to look fabulous.

"I would be an idiot to turn that down," I say and bump my hip against hers. "But if you'll just watch me do it once and make sure it looks okay, I think I can manage to do it for the shows."

She nods, then stops abruptly. "Oh, look, it's a wedding dress store."

The three of us turn to see the white gowns in the storefront window.

"I can't wait to get married," she says dreamily. "I want a big dress with a really long train that takes two or three people to carry it. Or maybe I want to get married on the beach with a simple dress."

"It's all about the dress," I say, looking longingly at the beautiful beadwork of one of the dresses.

"We should go in." Dakota takes a step and opens the door. Her eyes light up with mischief. "I've always wanted to try on gaudy wedding dresses. It'll be so much fun!"

Ginny and I don't move.

"Come on. You two owe me. Reagan got fake engaged, and you two kept it from me." She tilts her head to the side. "We'll be quick, and I promise to put on the most hideous one I can find."

"We're supposed to meet the guys," I say.

Ginny's switched teams, pulling out her phone. "I'll text Heath and let them know we put our name on the list and headed to look at the shops." Her thumbs tap away on the screen as she texts him, and she steps into the bridal store.

I can't think of a good excuse, so I follow them inside.

I've never given much thought to my own wedding. Things like that always led to thinking about how my mom probably wouldn't be there. No helping me get ready or walking me down the aisle. But the second I put on the beaded dress from the window, I gasp at my reflection.

"Oh my god, Reagan," Ginny says when I walk out. She's in a tulle gown with a corset-style bodice. A saleslady is fussing over her, trying to add a veil, which Ginny waves off. "No veil."

"Let's see the veil," I say.

The lady smiles at me and clips it into place.

"Definitely veil," I say.

Dakota's sitting on the bench. She put on the biggest, puffiest gown she could find and is now watching Ginny and me with rapt interest. "I agree."

Ginny sighs. "You're both right. I had this picture in my head of the gown and my look… this is none of that, but I love it all."

I smile. She'll probably be the first of us to get married. She's the youngest at nineteen, but I have no doubt that she's found her person. She and Heath are the most adorable couple I've ever known.

The saleslady moves over to me, pulling up the spaghetti straps and pinning it. I should stop her from going to all this effort since there's no chance in hell I'm going to be buying this dress, but I can't bring myself to say a word as I stare at myself in the mirror.

When she's finished, Ginny moves over, and we giggle at the sight of us.

"Turn around. I want to take a picture." Dakota holds her phone up, and we link arms and smile while she takes several.

"Those photos stay between us," I warn as I spin around to get one last look before I have to take it off. Maybe someday I'll get a chance to wear a dress like this.

"Yeah, uh Reagan, I don't think that's going to be possible."

At Dakota's words, I look up into the mirror to the front door of the store where the guys have just entered. Adam's eyes are wide as our gazes lock.

"Oh my gosh." I wrap my arms around my chest as if that could hide me. The saleslady must think I'm trying to keep the future groom from seeing my dress because she whisks past us to shoo them out of the store.

"Oh no. No, no, no, no," I mutter. This cannot be happening.

"I've got this," Dakota says. She whips off her dress, which she put on over her regular clothes, and shoves it into my hands. "Get changed. I'll wait for you two outside."

"You're fine. It's just a dress." Ginny squeezes my hand.

"You're not freaking out? Your boyfriend just caught you trying on wedding dresses."

She shrugs. "Heath and I talk about our wedding all the time. Not that we're planning on actually doing it anytime soon, but I think he's beyond freaking out."

"Well, your brother and I do not talk about it, and he's definitely freaking out." I slap a hand to my forehead. "First, I faked an engagement, and now I'm in here trying on wedding dresses. He's going to think..." I can't even finish the statement. The thoughts I imagine going through his head are too awful. We haven't even said we love each other yet, and it looks like I'm planning our happily ever after.

"Breathe, Rea. It's going to be fine."

The group's waiting outside. Adam's leaning against the

building. When he sees me approach, he pushes off and walks forward. I can't read his expression at all.

"It isn't what you think," I blurt out before he can say anything. My heart is hammering in my chest. I cannot have screwed this up over something so dumb. "I don't want to get married. I mean, maybe I do someday, but not today. Not even this year. Not even in five, probably. And we haven't even—"

He takes my hand and squeezes gently. "Relax. Dakota told me. Although for a second there, I thought you were picking out a costume for your next premed function." He interlaces our fingers, and we fall in with the group walking toward the restaurant. I search his face to see if he's being truthful or if he's sweating and swaying like he might faint. He smiles. "For the record, though, you looked beautiful."

Chapter Twenty-Five

REAGAN

YOU MAY FACE TOUGH DECISIONS TODAY. CONFUSION IS LIKELY TO REIGN. WAIT A COUPLE OF DAYS, AND THEN CONSIDER YOUR OPTIONS.

"We'll stop there for tonight," Director Hoffman calls rehearsal Tuesday night with a sigh.

Despite his continual look of irritation, the play is starting to come together. Ginny came yesterday to make sure we're all set for makeup, we've been fit for costumes, and the backdrops and props are mostly finalized and in place. It's starting to feel like we're going to pull this off.

I know we will, we do every time, but those first few run-throughs off-book always feel like we're working toward the impossible.

Mila catches my gaze and smiles as he barks out the schedule for the rest of the week. I playfully roll my eyes at him, and she holds back a laugh. It's been fun getting to know her, and she's fitting right in with everyone. We get to spend quite a bit of time together since she's my understudy. And, just as I assumed, she's memorized all of her lines with no problem.

Occasionally, Director Hoffman pulls her in so I can work on technique with Dr. Rossen. My timing is still shit, and I'm struggling with my facial expressions in a couple of scenes. Sometimes I feel like I'm the newbie instead of her.

What was I thinking going for such a different role? I will get it, though. I am nothing if not determined.

"A few of us are going out for drinks. Do you want to come?" Mila asks as we're helping clean up the stage. There's an orchestra performance tonight, and it's all hands on deck to transition the space quickly so they can set up.

"No, I can't. I have plans."

"Do they involve that cute guy that just walked in?" She nods over my head, and I turn to see Adam waiting for me.

My heart rate kicks up a notch. "They do."

Her smile is big and genuine. "Is that your boyfriend?"

"Yep, sure is." I get butterflies in my stomach just talking about him. I'm so ridiculously crazy about him. This weekend solidified that more than ever.

Now that I'm making eye contact with him, he walks toward me. "You ready?"

"Almost."

"Go," Mila says. "I'll cover for you."

"Really?"

She nods and waves me off.

"Thanks." I jump down from the stage.

Adam takes my backpack and slips it over one shoulder. "How was rehearsal?"

I kiss him hello. "Not as bad as yesterday, but not good. Your girlfriend might be the laughingstock of Valley University after this show."

"No chance." His reassurance is endearing, if not totally unfounded. "Do you want to stay and practice or rehearse, whatever you call it? I can read lines or something."

"That's sweet of you to offer, but the theater is booked tonight for an orchestra performance." I loop my arm through his. "Feed me?"

"That I can do."

AFTER DINNER, WE SHUT OURSELVES IN ADAM'S ROOM TO WORK. He's got his laptop in front of him; eyes scrunched together in hard concentration.

"How's the speech coming?" I ask.

He looks up and blows out a breath. "It's crap. I know it's crap, and I can't seem to fix it."

"Do you want me to read it and see if I can help?"

"Uh-uh." He shakes his head adamantly. "Not until it's done. It's too rough."

Adam's funny that way. Never wanting people to see his rough draft of anything. Yet, somehow he accepts me in all my unpolished glory.

He took the whole catching me in a wedding dress thing way better than I thought he would. He even made Dakota send him the picture she snapped of me in it.

Things are good with us, and that's scary. It takes a lot to trust that someone is going to be there for you no matter what. I don't have a lot of those people in my life, but I'm starting to think Adam might be one of them.

"I'm sure that you're being too hard on yourself. What would you say to the guys if you were in the locker room, down by one, going into the third period?" I ask.

"I don't even know. Words just sort of come out of my mouth without thought."

"Like…"

He thinks for a moment. When he speaks, his voice is deep and authoritative. "What d'ya say, boys? What d'ya say? Let's get that W."

"That's it?" I laugh.

He grins sheepishly and shrugs a shoulder. "I told you I wasn't really that inspiring."

I raise my arm to show him the goosebumps. "It's all in the tone, apparently."

"When I put on the uniform and step onto the ice, it's different. It's the one place I feel completely confident in my abilities."

"I get that. It's your stage."

"Yeah, I guess so. Too bad I can't give my speech there. I hate that so much is riding on this. What if I get up there and freeze or forget what I want to say?"

I climb on top of him and kiss him, hoping some of my confidence in him transfers. I have no doubt he's capable of doing anything he wants. And I highly doubt his speech is crap, even now when he claims it's rough.

"Okay," I pull back before we get carried away. "Back to work.

We'll continue this later."

Chapter Twenty-Six

ADAM

I'm sitting on my bed working on my speech while Reagan paces my room reading lines. She's been working on one scene for the better part of an hour. It sounded fine to me the first time, but what the hell do I know?

"Ugh," she groans and flops onto the bed, lying on her back and staring up at the ceiling. "I'm never going to get it right."

I abandon my work and lean over so I can kiss her. "Yes, you will. Hell, it sounds like you already know it by heart."

"I know the lines, but I'm still not getting the character right."

This is so far out of my expertise. "What can I do to help?"

"Nothing." She sighs. "Kiss me again."

I climb on top of her and kiss her until we're both breathless.

"I have an idea." I stand and adjust my dick. Down boy.

"Now?" She sits up, resting on an elbow. Her face is red, and she eyes my crotch.

"Yep. Kissing you gives me the best ideas."

"Hmmm." She hums and shoots me a playful smile that makes her dimples show. "I have a much better one."

"Later, remember?" I pull her upright. "Come on."

"ARE WE ALLOWED TO BE IN HERE?" REAGAN ASKS AS WE WALK into the arena.

"Eh… it would probably be frowned upon, but I won't tell if you don't."

She stares out at the ice. "Is now a bad time to admit I'm a terrible skater?"

"I got you."

We change into skates, and I step onto the ice. When I look back, Reagan is still clinging to the wall.

"I haven't been skating since I was five or six."

I take both her hands, and she slowly steps to me. "It's like riding a bike."

"I was never very good at that either." She wobbles and squeezes my hands in a death grip.

I'm basically pulling her along, but slowly her grasp lessens. The cool air makes her cheeks red. She's concentrating so damn hard.

I move in front of her and skate backward.

"Show off," she mutters. Her gaze lifts to me, and she loses balance. I grab her elbow before she goes down.

"Oh, baby, this isn't even close to showing off." I pull her closer to the wall so she can stop and hold on if she wants and then I take off on the ice skating hard to the other end. I jump and go side to side, backward. I even throw in a little leap.

Being on the ice makes me so ridiculously happy, but being here with Reagan is next level. It takes all of my love of skating and makes it seem more complete somehow. I want to take her skating a bunch more times until she's comfortable, although, her needing to hold on to me as we skate doesn't suck either.

She finally starts to get the hang of it after a few laps. Her arms fall to her sides, and her stride lengthens.

Together, we skate to the center of the ice.

"Thank you for this. It was good to get out of my head for a while. This play feels like it might be the end of me."

"Nah, not my girl. She's too tough to go out like that." I squeeze her hands. "You've done a whole bunch of these before. Why is this one causing you so much trouble? Or is this like your creative process?"

"Are you trying to politely ask if I turn into a drama queen, tortured artist every time?"

"Your words, baby."

"No, not usually. I love acting, and when I step on stage, it's easy. Or it used to be. Slipping into someone else is comforting in a way I can't explain."

"What's different this time?"

"Well," she starts. "I told you how I landed a part that's different for me. I'm playing the youngest of three sisters. She's carefree and fun. She's a bit silly and always doing things for a laugh."

"Sounds fun."

"It is. Turns out fun is harder to pull off. I should have stuck with something more comfortable for me."

"How come you didn't?"

"I've been trying to summon the courage for two years. Dr.

Rossen is great. I really respect her, and when I first got to Valley, I auditioned for two different roles—one serious, girl next door type, and the other was a comedic relief character. She gave me the first part, and I got such great feedback from everyone. I guess I didn't want to take a chance and fail."

"And now?"

"I'm taking all sorts of wild chances this year."

I lift her and spin around, then set her back down. "Show me."

"What?"

"Perform for me."

"Here?"

"You need a stage and an audience." I skate off to the side and pull myself up to sit on the half wall that goes around the rink.

"I can barely stand, and you want me to perform?" She looks around and pushes off one foot hesitantly.

"I had a coach once who made us run drills blindfolded."

"What?" She laughs. "That sounds really dangerous."

"Yeah, it was. My parents were pissed. But it actually worked. I had to know exactly where I was on the ice. I had to feel it. Sometimes taking away the ability to see or hear…"

"Or walk?" She screeches. "Your logic is twisted, Dr. Scott. I don't think that's going to work here."

"Either way, it should be entertaining." I cross my arms over my chest. "Let's take it from the top of scene two where you enter from stage right."

She nods, opens her mouth as if she's going to deliver her first line, and then looks straight at me. "Wait, how do you know…"

"You left a copy of the script in my room." I hop down from the wall back onto the ice and skate toward her. "It's a great part.

You're gonna kill it."

"You don't know that."

"I do. You're the most amazing and talented person I know. You can do this."

"Okay." She inhales and then lets it out slowly. "I'm ready."

I speak the first line and then watch in awe as Reagan delivers hers. Amazing isn't the half of it. When she goes into performer mode, you can't help but stop and stare.

I'm still staring when she looks at me and says, "Next line."

"Right, sorry."

From there, I manage to keep up. I haven't seen her truly perform it before now, so it's hard to say if the ice is helping or not, but I know I'm totally enthralled. She's funny. Her body language, the tone in which she speaks, the looks—it's incredible. She's incredible.

We go through the first act. I'm back sitting on the wall, and she skates over to me. She's steadier now the longer she's been out here, but she still clings to my legs for support when she reaches me.

"Thank you for this."

"Are you kidding? I feel like I just got an exclusive preview. You're going to be amazing."

"I don't know if it's the ice or maybe just you, but I feel amazing."

"We should probably go soon."

She nods. "Okay. I just want to take another lap or two."

We skate slowly. I still take her hand, even though she seems to have the hang of it now. "What made you decide to be an actress?"

"I watched a lot of TV as a kid. Mom was gone, and I was lonely."

My chest aches at her admission. "Fuck, baby. I'm sorry."

"During the day, I would go to friends' houses or play outside in the neighborhood, but at night, I was on my own a lot. I couldn't have friends stay over because I didn't want their parents to know. And I didn't want to be gone in case my mom came back or tried to call." She smiles. "TV kept me company."

"How did you end up living with Janine?"

"I told you our moms were friends, but I guess even she didn't realize how bad things were. My mom asked her to check in on me one random Saturday night. I don't know why she suddenly grew a conscience. She'd left me alone for entire weekends plenty of times before. Anyway, Janine's mom came over to see that I was doing okay." Reagan glances over shyly. "I was more than okay. I'd thrown the most epic of high school parties. Even popular kids who never talked to me showed up. I was so cool for about two hours. Alas, my popularity was cut short when Marge, Janine's mom, busted in. She was nice about it, really. It could have been worse. She made everyone leave and then told me to pack a bag."

"I'm glad she looked out for you."

"Yeah, me too. Who knows what kind of trouble I would have gotten into without her watching out for me? Popularity would have gone straight to my head."

"And your mom? She didn't care that someone else had taken you in?"

"I think she was relieved." Reagan's brows pull together. "She wasn't mean or awful to me, at least not outright. She was negligent and absent, but I think she wanted good things for me."

"And she thought that was you living with someone else?" It's hard for me to have any empathy for a woman who left her kid alone for days at a time. No matter the reason.

"Janine's family did take better care of me."

"Yeah, I guess."

"About six months after I moved to Valley, Lori started emailing me every day."

"You said you haven't talked to her."

"I haven't. I don't respond. The first few emails were apologies and promises that she was getting her life together, moving back home, getting a job that would keep her around. Now all I get is my horoscope."

"What?"

"Every morning, she emails me my horoscope. It sounds weird when I say it out loud, but it was always her thing. When she was home, she'd read them out of the paper or the magazine while we had breakfast. I knew the astrological signs before I knew my ABCs."

"You ever think about replying?"

"To say what?"

We've gone around the rink a couple of times, and we both stop near the gate where we came in.

"I don't know. Just curious if you wanted to, I guess."

"I think I'll always want to."

"You want to, but you don't?" I question, trying to make sense of it.

"I can't take her running out on me again. Even through email."

Chapter Twenty-Seven

REAGAN

SOMETIMES YOU HAVE TO DO LIKE ELSA AND LET IT GO. FORGIVENESS IS THE KEY TO HAPPINESS. PLUS, STRESS GIVES YOU WRINKLES.

The night of Adam's scholarship banquet, I get ready at my apartment with Dakota and Ginny.

"How's it look?" I ask Dakota.

Ginny has a hand at my chin and gently corrects. "Keep looking forward. I'm almost done."

It's killing me not to see what she's doing to me. Not that I doubt her. Ginny's a genius with a makeup brush.

She adds another layer of mascara and then holds two tubes of lipstick up to my face. "Dramarama or Candy Yum-Yum?"

"Dramarama," Dakota answers.

My eyes go wide at the bright red she uncaps and starts dabbing on my lips. "It's not too much?" I ask.

"Hold still." Ginny smiles as she coats my mouth and then leans back, taking in the full effect. "You look amazing. My best work yet." She looks to the bed where Dakota is sitting. "Dakota, confirm?"

My roommate's jaw is slack, and brows raised. My stomach drops. I'm already so freaking nervous, and the shocked expression on her face is not helping.

"Honey, you look..." Dakota still can't seem to find the words.

I wave her off, giving her an out, so she doesn't have to finish that statement. "I told you two I can't pull off a smoky eye. I always end up looking like a high-price escort."

I swivel in my seat to look in the mirror at the same time she says, "Beautiful. And I don't think I've ever called someone beautiful before. Like legit, I'm stunned." She points to her face. "I can't move my eyebrows down. They're stuck like this forever."

Ginny claps. "Yay! My brother's going to lose his shit."

I hardly recognize myself, and holy crap, somehow, I'm even more nervous. The alarm on my phone goes off, which means it's go time.

We head over to the guys' place. Maverick is the first to see me. He drops the controller in his hand onto his lap. "Woah, Reagan sweetheart, I think you just became the starring role in my dream later."

"Hot, right?" Ginny asks as she sits next to Heath on the couch. He gives me a thumbs up.

"*So* hot," Mav mutters and keeps staring. "You're a rocket."

Adam walks out, adjusting his tie. I think he tells Maverick to fuck off, but I'm too busy ogling my handsome boyfriend in a suit and tie.

"Hey." His gaze finally lands on me and drops slowly. "Fucking hell."

I bask in his attention, even twirling so he can get the full effect of the dress. It's long, black, and so tight I'm probably not going to be able to take a full breath all night. Totally worth the look he's giving me right now.

"You two are adorbs," Ginny says. "Let me get a picture before you leave."

"This isn't prom," Adam protests, but he wraps an arm around my waist and holds still while his sister takes a dozen photos. But when she suggests we go outside to get a few more, he guides me toward the front door. "Okay, that's enough. We have to go."

As soon as we step outside alone, Adam pins me against the building, and his mouth slams down onto mine. He sucks the remaining air from my lungs, but who needs to breathe anyway? Dying kissing this man wouldn't be a bad way to go.

"Sorry." He pulls back and adjusts his jacket. "Needed to get that out of the way. You look beautiful. Mav's right. You're a fucking rocket."

"You too." I run a hand along his chest and kiss him again quickly.

Grinning, he tucks his hair behind an ear. "Ready to do this?"

By the time we make it to the banquet (there are several more stops for kissing), the room is packed. Adam stops in the doorway and takes a deep breath. He hasn't mentioned the speech, but I know he must be nervous.

"You're going to be great," I assure him.

He brings our joined hands to his lips, and we walk in together.

Round tables are covered in white tablecloths. A single candle in a faux crystal holder sits in the center of each, water glasses are turned upside down at each place setting, and black napkins rolled up with shiny silverware gleaning out the top. Simple elegance, but not too flashy.

A low hum falls over the room as people talk. Groups stand mostly near the bar area set up near the far wall. Some guests are already sitting at the tables. There are a lot of other students here tonight with their families, which I wasn't expecting, but Adam tells me it's because they're recognizing scholarship recipients for the premed program too.

Much like the mixer weeks ago, we're swept up in conversation from the moment we have drinks in our hands. Professors and scholarship committee members want to offer their congratulations and best wishes.

Adam takes it all in stride, thanking people, answering their questions, and attentively bringing me into the fold by introducing me and talking up the show next weekend.

We're chatting with a woman who I think is a professor. I've sort of lost track of all the names and titles. She's asking me about my part in the play when Adam leans in and whispers that he's going to get us another drink.

"Be right back," he says loud enough to excuse himself from the conversation.

"It sounds wonderful," she says. "I can't wait to see it." She gives me a friendly smile. "I won't keep you talking to the old people. Go have fun. It was great to meet you, Reagan. Tell Adam good luck tonight, and you break a leg next week, okay?"

"Yes, ma'am. Thank you."

As she walks off, I sip the last of my wine and look around. Adam's at the bar. One hand in his pants pocket, waiting for his drink. He's so devastatingly handsome. I've completely fallen for him. The real him. Not the guy I built up in my mind over the years.

The one I've gotten to know this past month. The one who likes to wake me up every morning by squeezing my butt, and who owns more hairbrushes than any one person should (seriously, one in his Jeep, one in his backpack, one in his hockey bag, several stashed in his room and bathroom), and the generous and sweet man who makes the world my stage.

Someone grabs my arm, and I tear my gaze away from Adam to find Janine at my side. "Can I talk to you?"

I'd almost forgotten Janine and Sean would be here. Or maybe I was just hoping they wouldn't show. Seeing her brings back too many bad memories.

"Hi. You look great, Janine."

"Thanks," she quickly dismisses the compliment. "Lori—"

I groan. "Can't you give it a rest? Just for tonight? I don't want to get into this with you again. Not here."

I take a step, but she walks with me. "Reagan, please, you need to hear this. Lori–"

"Stop it, Janine." I keep my voice low, but I'm fuming. "I don't need to hear anything. I will not be dragged back into the past. Especially tonight."

"But—"

I shake my head and brush past her to meet Adam halfway. I press up on my toes and kiss him, trying to erase all the hurt that Janine is so insistent on bringing back up. Why can't she just let it go? It's almost as if she wants to keep hurting me by bringing up the past. But the Janine I knew wasn't vindictive. What gives?

"What was that for?" he asks.

"I…" My heart hammers in my chest. I am so in love with him. I want to tell him. I want to tell the whole world, sing it while skipping down the street and twirling—all of which he'd probably find wildly amusing. For now, I settle for another truth. "I'm really glad that I'm here with you."

His gaze roams over my face as his lips slowly pull up. "I'm glad too. Dance with me."

"No one is dancing." I scan the room to validate my claim. Light music is playing, but there's no dance floor.

"So?"

I still hesitate. A server carrying a large tray nearly hits me with it as she passes by. She mumbles an apology, and Adam tugs me toward a small area of the room that's cleared of tables.

His arms go around my back, and he brings our bodies close together. "You're in this gorgeous dress, and I want to dance with you."

More servers are bringing pitchers of water to the tables, and people are starting to take their seats.

"Looks like dinner is about to start," I say. "Maybe we should take our seats."

"In a minute. I'm enjoying this." He hums lightly as he continues to move us to the beat of the music.

"How come your parents didn't come?" I ask as I lean my head on his chest and close my eyes, letting myself relax into him. There's nowhere else I'd rather be than in his arms.

"Eh."

"You did invite them, right?"

"Nah, I wanted to spend tonight just with you."

I glance up at him. His hazel eyes are impassive. "Adam, your family would want to be here for this."

"*If* I get the scholarship. Otherwise, it would have been a long drive for nothing."

"They would have wanted to be here to support you regardless."

He shrugs. "This is more fun with just you."

I have a sliver of concern that he didn't invite them because he didn't want to introduce me to his parents. I've met them before in passing, but never as his girlfriend. Maybe we aren't at that point yet?

When the song ends, his embrace loosens, and reluctantly we pull apart. He takes my hand. I'm still dreamily leaning into him and living in our happy little bubble, when Adam says, "Dr. Salco."

A pair of reading glasses hang from her beaded necklace. "Speeches will begin right after dinner. Janine first, then you."

I feel him stiffen next to me, and I squeeze his fingers.

"I'm glad you could be here tonight, Reagan," Dr. Salco says.

"Me too." I look back to him. His nervous gaze meets mine and softens. "He's going to be great."

"You picked a good one," Dr. Salco tells him. "I'm so glad you'll have such a supportive fiancée while finishing school." She smiles. "Or maybe wife? When is the wedding?"

It takes me way longer than it should to realize she means Adam's and my wedding.

"Oh." I glance to Adam for help.

He clears his throat. "We haven't really discussed that."

If my face is as red as it is warm, then she has to know the truth. I sell it the best I can, resting my head on his shoulder and looking at him adoringly. It isn't hard to fake loving him like I think an engaged couple loves one another. In fact, it's a little too easy, and I have to remind myself we're once again playing a part.

Dr. Salco flashes me the friendliest smile I've ever seen from her. We've clearly sold her on our fake engagement, but somehow that just makes me feel worse. "Enjoy dinner and good luck tonight, Adam."

When she's gone, I turn to him and whisper, "You didn't tell her we aren't engaged?"

His brow furrows, and the corners of his mouth pull down. "I'm sorry. I meant to."

Guilt is written all over his handsome face. God, no wonder he didn't want to invite his parents. That would have been an awkward conversation. *It's a pleasure to meet you. Oh, by the way, we're just faking our engagement for everyone here. Yeah, I'm a super great influence on your son, don't worry.*

I'm peeved that he didn't come clean, which is ridiculous. I'm the one who started the lie. If anyone is to blame, it's me. Still, I can't fight the irritation I feel at him as he leads us to our table.

"I think I'm going to get some air," I say as he pulls my chair out for me.

"Now?"

"I'll only be a minute."

"I'll come with you."

"No." I place a hand out to keep him from following me. "Stay. These people came for you, not me. I'll be right back. Promise."

When I get to the hallway, I take a breath. I can't shake the awful feeling from talking with Janine earlier or the guilt of faking an engagement to a man I'm starting to be able to picture a life with. This isn't the way it's supposed to go. It all feels so wrong.

When footsteps approach, I assume it's Adam coming to check

on me. I even smile a little thinking how sweet it is that he wants to make sure I'm okay. But when I look up, it's Janine that's walking toward me.

I open my mouth to tell her to go away, but she beats me to it.

"I'm sorry," she blurts out.

"What?" I shake my head and attempt to go around her. Fleeing from Janine is the game of the night, it seems. All the air is knocked out of me when I see her. Ten feet behind Janine, her parents, Sean, and Lori stand watching us. Her hair is shorter, but otherwise, it's like no time has passed. She's exactly like I remember her. And so is the punch to the gut at seeing her.

"I tried to tell you earlier," Janine says as if that makes it okay.

"Why is she here?" I grit out.

My ears ring as she apologizes, "I'm sorry. That's what I was trying to tell you earlier. My parents called as they were leaving the house, and I wanted to warn you as soon as I found out. Lori insisted on coming. She wants to meet Adam and tell you congratulations or whatever."

"There's nothing to congratulate me for."

"I thought…" Janine trails off, her brows knit in confusion.

Of course, she believes we're really engaged, like everyone else.

"My life is none of her business."

"Janine, we should get inside," Sean speaks up but keeps his distance.

"I'm sorry," she whispers one last time before leaving me.

Their happy family all goes inside, leaving me with Lori. Slowly, she closes the distance between us.

"Reagan." The way she says my name is soft and sad. Like she's missed me—like even saying my name brings her pain.

"Hi, Mom." I don't know why I call her that. I've called her Lori since I was twelve. It must be the shock. "What are you doing here?"

"We came to support Janine, of course. And it was the only way I knew to see you."

"Maybe I don't want to see you."

"Well, you've made that clear." There's a hint of a smile on her face, which pisses me off.

"Obviously not," I mutter and walk toward the door to go back inside.

Adam's coming out. His face relaxes when he sees me, but then he must read the situation because he looks past me and comes up short.

"Are you okay?" He runs a hand down my arm from shoulder to elbow. "Speeches are starting."

I nod, not trusting what might come out of my mouth if I speak. I'm so mad. Mad that she's here and that Adam's worried about me when I'm supposed to be here taking care of him. Mad that we ever faked an engagement. Just pissed at the universe.

Applause breaks out in the room, and I glance inside in time to see Janine making her way to the front. I still can't find my voice, but I lean into him. I feel infinitely stronger with Adam by my side.

"You must be the fiancé? Janine speaks highly of you." Lori smiles and looks between us. Her gaze takes in every detail. The way he touches me and the way I let him support me. I hate that she's privy to even that much detail about my life.

"Umm." Adam's head swivels between us.

"Adam, this is Lori."

His jaw drops, and he looks at her closer. "It's nice to meet you."

As Janine starts her speech and the three of us hold our awkward standoff, I go from furious to enraged. How dare my mom show up here? After all these years? This is probably the first time she's ever shown up to a banquet or school function, and it's for Janine? Where was she my entire childhood?

I was the kid who had no one there to take pictures as I received awards, no one to take me out for ice cream after. I stopped participating in things somewhere along the way. I didn't need the looks of pity or polite applause. Why worry about perfect attendance or perform in choir if no one is going to be there to celebrate it? With theater, I could forget that no one in the audience came to see me and lose myself in the darkened room, imagining just for a minute that maybe she was there somewhere out of sight.

I can't lose myself in this situation.

"It's almost time for me to go. Do you want to go in?" Adam asks.

"Of course," I assure him. I don't want him to think about anything but killing his speech. I still haven't heard it, but I know he's been working hard on it. He deserves so much. "I can't wait to see you crush it, but can you give us a minute?"

He nods. "I'll wait at the door."

I face Lori. There's nothing that I could have done to prepare for this. Years' worth of playing this conversation over in my head, and I still don't know what to say. She's much chattier.

"He's very handsome. How long have the two of you been together?" She speaks quietly but every word slams into me with a crushing force.

I don't answer. In fact, my throat feels like I swallowed nails. Speaking to her causes me physical pain. It's why I haven't in so long.

"Okay, well, at least let me tell you congratulations. My baby's getting married."

I close my eyes and whisper, "Don't do this. Please. Just stop."

"I know that I haven't always been there for you, but you're getting married. Every girl wants her mother at her wedding. And I want to be there. I want to be in your life again. God knows I failed you, but—"

"You have no right," I say, too loudly. My cheeks heat with embarrassment, and I glance down the empty hallway.

"I know. I'm sorry, Reagan. It isn't enough, but I am. You're starting a new life. I just want you to know that I want to be a part of that."

My hands curl into fists, and my body vibrates. "We're not even really engaged, okay?" I spit the words at her. "You're off the hook. He's not my fiancé. We're not getting married. You can keep on living your life and not giving a damn about me."

I turn on my heel where Adam's waiting for me with Dr. Salco. I don't need to look at her down-turned mouth to know she heard me. Adam's face says it all.

"SO YOU JUST LEFT?" DAKOTA ASKS. I CAN READ HER JUDGMENT. I feel it deep in my soul.

"I couldn't breathe with her there."

"I can't believe the nerve, showing up like that. What was it like seeing her again?"

"Like it was just yesterday that she was running out on me. All of the anger and hurt I've tried to shove down just came right back." I snap my fingers. My body still vibrates with rage.

She squeezes my elbow. "I'm sorry, babe. And fuck her. I wish I would have been there. I've dreamed of saying that to her face for three years."

"Thank you. I love you."

"What are you going to do about Adam?"

"He had to stay for his speech, obviously." My stomach turns. "He said it was fine and that he'd come by later, but I abandoned him. He's going to hate me."

"No, he won't. It was a shitty situation without a good outcome."

But she didn't see his face. I think he was happy when I said I was leaving. Who could blame him? It was supposed to be a fun night for him. Instead, he got a dose of my crazy family drama, and I probably put his scholarship in jeopardy. Again.

I look down at my lap. "I've gotta get out of this dress. It's mocking me."

"It's going to be okay," she promises.

In my room, I take off my dress and sit on the floor. Oh, how I wish I could climb under the covers and fall right to sleep, but I know I'm in for a long, restless night, so I don't even bother getting into bed.

Long after the apartment complex has quieted, Adam still hasn't called or stopped by. I pad over to the guys' apartment and peek in.

Mav's on the couch with his phone in hand.

"Hey, Rea." He straightens.

"Is he here?" I ask.

Maverick nods toward the deck.

I mumble my thanks and head out back. My heart races as he comes into view. I see him before he sees me. Kicked back, beer dangling from his fingertips, staring out into the dark night.

He looks over as the deck creaks under my footsteps.

"Hey." He tries to hide the despair on his face, covering it with a smile like he's happy to see me. "I was just about to come check on you."

He holds an arm out, and I sit on his lap.

"How'd the rest of the banquet go?"

He runs a hand down the back of my head, and I melt into his touch. "Eh. My speech was crap, but at least it's over. We won't know which one of us got the scholarship until next week."

"I'm sure your speech wasn't that bad."

"I totally deviated from what I wrote. I'm not even sure it made sense." He makes a rough sound in his throat. "You doing okay?"

"I have had better nights." A shallow laugh escapes my lips. "My mother managed to ruin yet another school function. I'm really sorry."

"You don't have anything to apologize for."

"I cannot believe she showed up there tonight."

"Yeah, I guess our fake engagement really made the rounds. I told you, you were a good actress."

"She told me she wanted to come to our wedding. Can you imagine? The happiest day of my life, and she thinks I'd want her there?"

"But we're not really having a wedding so..."

I swallow, taking in his words. Right. "Speaking of, why didn't you tell Dr. Salco the truth before tonight?"

"I..." He stares back out in front of him and then shrugs. "I'm sorry. I should have. I started to, but I guess I was afraid of how it might impact the decision of the scholarship."

"Well, she definitely knows now. Did she say anything?"

"No, I left as soon as my speech was done. I'll talk to her and explain."

If he left as soon as he finished his speech, that means he's been home for a while. Home and avoiding me.

"Is that why you didn't invite your parents? You were afraid they'd find out we were together or think we were engaged?"

"No, of course not." His brows pull together. Then he shifts to one hip and pulls a piece of paper out of his pants pocket. "Before I forget, your mom asked me to give you this."

"You talked to her?" I don't mean it to sound like an accusation, but the thought never even occurred to me that she'd use him to get to me.

"Briefly."

I wait for him to say more. He shifts uncomfortably. "All she wants is a chance to talk."

"And you think I should?" A cool breeze stirs around us, and I cross my arms at my chest.

"I don't know. She's family. Maybe hearing her out will help."

"She's only family by blood. She was no mother to me."

"I know."

"Do you? Because you're acting like I should call her up and welcome her back into my life with open arms."

"The things she did, the way she abandoned you—it's awful. I hate her a little bit for you, but sometimes people change." He rubs my arm, but I don't feel any warmth.

"I cannot believe this. You're taking her side."

"No, definitely not. I'm on your side. Always."

"You didn't even want Rhett to talk to Carrie, and the only thing she did was boss him around for six years."

"That's not the whole story with Rhett."

"And you." I stand in front of him, a sick feeling in my stomach. "You want me to forgive my mom and hear her out. When is the last time you talked to an ex-girlfriend?"

I recognize the impassive and distant look on his face, but I can't bring myself to stop.

"Do you know there isn't a single picture of an ex-girlfriend in your room? Not the one at your parents' house either. Not in your phone. Not even on social media unless you count photos other people have tagged you in. All evidence is banished."

"Are you really pissed at me for not keeping in contact with girls I used to date?" He runs a hand through his hair. "What the hell is happening?"

"When you're done with people, you're done with them. You write them off and move on to the next. I guess I'm just wondering how much longer until my time is up?"

And there it is. All of my worst fears recognized by the look on his face. This time isn't different. It's exactly the same. And I just moved us into the final phase of the Adam Scott relationship playbook—the breakup.

"That's a really shitty thing to say."

"It's true, though, right?" My voice cracks. "When we break up, you'll take a week or maybe two to rid me from your life, and then it'll be as if I never existed. It's what you do. This time together will mean nothing."

"We're here again? Seriously? I don't know how to make my feelings for you any clearer."

I reach out for his arm, and he flinches. Small, but I catch it. "I'm sorry. I didn't mean it to sound like an attack on you. It's just, I can read you. I can see how upset you are. It's written all over your face." And I know how this goes. Someday maybe it will be different for him, but this time isn't it. "I'm tired of waiting for the other shoe to drop."

He nods, jaw flexes. "Of course, I'm fucking upset. My girlfriend is counting down the days until I break up with her. Do you know why I didn't invite my parents tonight?"

I shake my head.

"Because things are still fucked up from the divorce, and I didn't know which one to invite. If I asked one and not the other, I thought I'd hurt someone's feelings. If I invited them both and they showed up, who knows what the hell would have happened. And even worse, there was a real chance that neither one would because they're in some messed up avoiding game, so why bother?" He finishes his beer and tosses it to the ground with a clank. His voice rises, angry and sharp. "And Carrie fucking cheated on Rhett, so yeah, I didn't want him to talk to her and get sucked back in."

"I didn't know."

"No one does. That's why I didn't tell you. He doesn't even know that I know. I overheard him on the phone one day." He's agitated, angry.

Shame washes over me. I know that my anger isn't really about him, but I'm terrified that he's just one more person I'm going to lose.

"I'm sorry. Seeing my mom took me by surprise. It's not an excuse, but it reminded me how few people I have left in my life. Maybe this just wasn't meant to be. I need you in my life. Even if we're just friends." I'm not sure if I believe that or if I'm trying to convince myself because I think he does.

He stands and takes my hands, links our pinkie fingers. "You can't mean that. We're great together. I get that my track record sucks, but I'm crazy about you."

I wanna believe that. Really I do, but I'm not sure it's worth the risk. I'm not a gambler. Never have been. I learned early on that the house always wins.

"I care about you so much, Adam, but I can't do this. I'm so sorry."

His face twists with frustration and maybe even sadness.

"I should go."

He drops my hands and steps back. Jaw set in stone, mouth in a hard line, and still the most beautiful man I've ever seen.

I've watched Adam fall out of love with a lot of girls. It looks a lot like the look on his face right now.

Chapter Twenty-Eight

REAGAN

IT'S GOING TO BE A GOOD DAY, CANCER! PUT A LITTLE EXTRA PEP IN YOUR STEP, BLAST SOME TUNES, AND BE READY FOR ANYTHING.

"Reagan?" Dakota knocks on the door. "Rea, are you in there?"

I don't answer. I don't trust my voice or the tears that might follow. I'm tired of crying.

"I ordered lunch. Please open up." She waits a few seconds longer. "Okay, well, food is on the counter. I'm going to class, but if you need anything or just want to talk, text me." She waits a few seconds longer, and then I hear her footsteps down the hall, and the front door opens and shuts.

Curling up tighter and hugging a sweatshirt that Adam left in my room, I breathe in his scent. You'd think it wouldn't possibly be calming after last night, but somehow even heartbroken and angry, all I want is to be surrounded by him any way I can.

He's certainly never coming back inside my room. I was mean and accused him of awful things. I took out all of my frustrations on him. I don't blame him for not calling or texting or chasing me down and trying to win me back. No sane guy would. And maybe it's better this way.

No, I don't blame him. I blame Lori.

All night, I alternated punching my pillow and then sobbing into it. They say you can't outrun your past. I don't want to run from it. I want to move forward and erase it and all the damage and baggage that goes with it. I thought I had—stupid me.

This is for the best. All I did was beat him to the punch. Still, I sigh and wonder what if. The thing is, I may not have meant to blow up at him and say all of those things, but they were true. All of those concerns were things I was worried about even before Lori showed up. He says it's different, but is it?

When my alarm goes off an hour later, I'm in the same position. There's only one thing that could pull me out of bed today. I'm sluggish as I change clothes and splash water on my face. So sluggish that by the time I get to rehearsal, I'm late.

They've already started, and Mila is on stage for me. I get into costume for the next scene change and then watch from the wings.

Mila's come a long way from the nervous girl who walked into auditions. She's gained confidence, and that's made everything else she does better. At the end of the scene, they stop while Director Hoffman makes some adjustments to props and positioning.

"Sorry, I'm late," I say, walking out onto the stage.

Mila smiles at me, but our hard nose director does not. I know how he feels about people being late. I'd offer more than my apology, but I don't have a good reason aside from my broken heart and, I'm just guessing, but I doubt he cares.

"Everyone get set for the next scene," he says and steps up onto the stage.

Theater has always been the one place I can shut off the world and slide into someone else's skin, but today I can't summon the strength to be anyone but me. Sad, angry, heartbroken Reagan. It isn't as easy to get to that place where I block out everything else and become my character, but by the time we're done, I finally feel a little better. And I've even managed to not think about Adam for a bit.

I grab my water while we get feedback. I know my performance today was abysmal. I mean, I've been struggling to nail some of the movements and dialogue, but whatever steps I'd taken to improve over the past few weeks, I leaped twelve backward. I'm surprised when he doesn't call me out, but as we start to clean up, he calls for me and Mila.

I have an awful feeling as he regards us. He wastes no time beating around the bush. Hands on hips, he says, "Reagan, Mila is going to cover your part."

"What? Cover for me when?"

"For the duration of the play."

I laugh. He must be joking. I was expecting a lecture, but not this.

"You missed yesterday, you were late this afternoon, and the scenes you did get in today were off."

Swallowing my pride, I acknowledge that he's right. I cleared missing last night's rehearsal for the banquet, but it's obvious he's still holding it against me. "I'm sorry. I have had a lot going on this week, but I will be ready tomorrow. I promise."

"We don't have time for you to work through personal issues. The performance is in six days. I need your best now."

"I know, and I'm ready. I *will be* ready. Please?"

His mouth falls into a thin line. "I'm sorry. I think this is the best thing for the entire group."

He dismisses us with a nod and walks off.

Mila looks as if she might pass out.

"I'm so sorry," she says immediately.

My legs tremble, and my chest aches. I must have cried too much in the past twenty-four hours because I can't get past my shock to feel the really awful, soul-shattering pain I know is coming.

"I can try to talk to him," she offers.

"No," I say quickly. "He won't change his mind."

I pull at the collar of my costume dress. It has a high neck with lace trim that irritates my skin.

"Congratulations." I hope I'm smiling, but my face feels numb. "There's always next year, right?" My already broken heart smashes into a few more pieces.

I take my time going back to the apartment. I know that Dakota will want to talk to me and tell me everything is going to be okay, but I'm not ready to face her. Or Ginny. Except when I get to the apartment complex, there are very few cars in the lot, and the silence continues up to our apartment. It isn't until I'm inside that I remember there's a hockey game tonight. Everyone is there. Most of Valley. All my friends. Adam.

I drop onto the couch and turn on the TV, staring blankly. When *I Love Lucy* pops onto the screen, I burst into tears.

No play, no friends, and no Adam. It's just Lucy and me again.

Chapter Twenty-Nine

ADAM

After the game, the guys are in good spirits. It was a low-scoring game, but we were victorious, continuing our winning streak.

"Can I catch a ride to the bar?" Rhett asks.

He could easily go with someone else. Half the team is going to The Hideout to hang for a few hours. We have another game tomorrow afternoon, so most of us will call it an early night. There are a few guys on the team that can manage to party hard the night before a game and still function. Okay, not a few—there's Mav. Anyone else who tries to keep up with him tonight will be sitting their ass on the bench tomorrow or puking out their guts between periods.

"Sure, whatever. I'm not staying out long."

"You always say that, and yet you never leave until you make sure everyone else is headed home and safe." He smirks.

"Not tonight."

My head hurts. No, scratch that. My whole body hurts. Ever since last night when Reagan lashed out, kicked my fucking chest in, I feel like I can't breathe. She was waiting for me to screw up, for us to end, just like all my other relationships. I guess I can't blame her, but damn, I didn't realize she'd been holding on to it. Or that she thought so little of me. Why would she want to be with me at all if she really believed that?

Then I remember, she doesn't want to be with me anymore, so I guess that makes sense.

It still feels like a dream. What the hell happened? I mean, okay, I know what happened, but I don't understand why all of a sudden everything between us means nothing? I don't know whether or not to fight for her or back off. She's always got me second-guessing myself, and I really hate that.

That prickling sensation and nausea hit me hard. I fight it, wish it away, but it builds and builds. It's always been the same. Every relationship gets to this point where I feel sick to my stomach. Usually, it's because I've realized it won't work, but now… I'm just gutted.

I scan the bar as we enter. Ginny and a few other girlfriends of guys on the team are seated at our usual table. No Reagan. That awful feeling takes over, and I can no longer push it away, thinking that maybe it was just a stupid fight and we both needed time to cool off. Nah. It's really over. Feels like it's done before it ever really started. So many things I still want to do with her.

"Congrats on the game." Ginny stands as I get to the table and hugs me.

"Thanks."

She pulls back and searches my face. I know that look. A concerned Ginny is an unusually stubborn Ginny. "Are you okay?"

"Yup," I say. I take one of the empty glasses on the table and pour myself a beer. I nod and say hello to everyone. I make a lap around the bar. It's easier to fake quick, easy conversation than fall into something deep or meaningful with the people who know what's going on.

"Dakota's not here?" I ask Rhett as I refill my glass for the third or fourth time.

"Not that I've seen. She was at the game, though."

I nod.

"I think I'm about ready to go," he says. "You want to head out?"

I mull that over. Go back to the apartment where Reagan is ten feet away, and I might run into her or stay here where she isn't and drink? The choice is obvious. I'd rather be far away, so the physical distance matches the emotional. Being that close, knowing she's there but doesn't want to see me, makes that awful churn in my gut worse.

"No, I think I'm going to stay. You go ahead. I'm sure Heath and Ginny are headed back soon." Those two never stay out long anymore.

He looks like he might want to say something, but Rhett always chooses his words carefully—mulls them over before speaking. I take advantage of that and walk away before he figures out what he wants to say.

I find Maverick at the bar. He's got three shots in front of him. Jordan and Liam are cheering him on. Liam's got his phone out, taking video of the whole thing.

Maverick contemplates which glass to take and settles on the one in the middle. He tosses it back and then grins. "Rumple!"

He dances around playing eeny-meeny-miney-mo with the

remaining two.

"What's he doing?" I ask Liam.

"Shot roulette."

Oh fuck. "Tequila?"

"No." He chuckles, then whispers, "Cheap ass vodka."

My lip curls.

Maverick wraps his fingers around the glass on the right and closes his eyes as he takes it. "Ooooheeee," he says as he drops the empty back on the bar. "Triple Sec."

"Fuck," Jordan curses as Maverick slides the last shot to him.

"Yo, Scott." He claps me on the shoulder. "I'm unbeatable, Cap."

"Getting the team fucked up, are we?"

Jordan shoots the vodka and then gags. He shudders. "My insides are on fire."

"Another?" Mav asks him.

Jordan and Liam look to me and shake their heads.

"I'm in," I say. "But I get to pick the shots."

"Hell yeah." Maverick's excitement should tell me just how bad of an idea this is but fuck it.

Maverick goes to the bathroom while I order three shots from the bartender. "Anything else?" she asks with a smile.

"No, I think we're good after this. You can run my card."

When we're set to go again, we attract an audience. The guys on the team who are still at the bar crowd around, which pulls the attention of everyone else.

"Mav! Mav! Mav!" they chant as he selects the first shot.

It goes quiet as he brings it to his lips. He smiles and wipes the back of his mouth. "White wine. Nice, Scott. Classy choice."

I smirk.

The bar gets noisy again. Maverick eats up the attention, hopping around and making a big show out of trying to decide which shot to take next.

"Which one?" he asks the bartender.

"Oh no." She holds her hands up. "You're on your own."

"How fucked am I if I choose wrong?"

Her eyes flit to me, and she grins. "Pretty fucked. Sorry."

That makes everyone howl with laughter. He exhales a breath that puffs out his cheeks and grabs the shot glass on the left, tosses it back quickly. I don't know which shot is which at this point, so I'm waiting to see his reaction just like everyone else.

He lifts his hands overhead in victory. "Coconut vodka!"

Excited cheers ring out. A few people slap my back, commiserating. *Oh shit.*

The bartender laughs. "Looks like you're the one that's fucked."

Maverick sniffs the remaining glass before handing it over. "What is it?

"Rum and tequila," I mutter before shooting it. It burns all the way down, and I cough.

Maverick slings an arm around my neck. "You're fucking crazy, Scott."

We stay away from shots after that, but Maverick and I linger until we're the last guys on the team at the bar. Ann, the bartender, is closing out tabs, and servers are wiping tables.

"Another?" I ask him, lifting my almost empty glass.

He shakes his head. "You outdrank me. Congratulations."

"Do you guys have a ride?" Ann asks.

I feel around for my phone. I haven't touched it all night, but it's there in my front pocket. "I'll grab us an Uber."

Mav puts some cash in the tip jar and stands. "I already texted Dakota. She's coming to get us."

"Dakota?" My mouth goes dry.

"Reagan isn't with her."

"I wasn't..." I start.

Mav chuckles. "Come on, Scott. It's been a long night."

I sway on my feet. My buddy is quick to grab an arm and steady me.

"Not so sure out drinking you was a good idea."

"That's what the last guy said. Then he kissed me."

I lift my head, which has suddenly become really heavy, to check to see if he's serious. That's the thing about Maverick. He never seems serious, but I've never known him to lie or exaggerate either. He's unfiltered and honest, but the dude's fucking crazy too, so his truths always feel a little ridiculous.

"That's a story for another time," Mav says and opens the door for me.

"On a scale of one to ten, how pissed is Dakota?" I ask when I spot her car pulling into the parking lot.

He doesn't answer until she stops in front of us. "Why else do you think she'd agree to come get us?"

Pulling open the passenger side door, Mav slides into the seat. "Dakota, baby."

He rolls down the window. "You coming?"

Walking is starting to sound like a better choice. Especially when I make eye contact with Dakota and she glowers at me.

"Get in, Scott," she says, and I obey. It's a long walk to the apartment.

"Thanks for coming to get us," I say as I buckle up.

"Missed you tonight." Maverick plays with the radio until he finds a song he likes. He sits back and drums his hands on his legs. "What'd you do?"

"Oh, you know, held my best friend's hand while she cried her eyes out." Dakota's eyes find mine in the rearview mirror.

Even as the image of Reagan crying kicks me in the gut, I can't help asking for more. "How is she?"

Dakota doesn't answer.

Mav looks over his shoulder at me and then asks her again, "How is she?"

"She'll be fine, but right now, she's a mess."

I swallow thickly.

"Anything we can do?"

Dakota meets my gaze in the mirror again. "Yeah, leave her be."

I consider doing that until we get back. I linger behind Dakota as she opens her apartment door. She stops and glares at me. "She'll talk to you when she's ready."

"But—"

"Unless you're going to walk in there and tell her that she's the one and nothing is going to come between you, then walk away. She's going through some shit. She can't take any more heartbreak."

"Yeah, all right." I mumble my thanks for the ride, and she leaves me standing outside by myself. I know she's right, but I just want to see her, talk to her, comfort her any way I can. Maybe I should be angry with her, but I can't manage it.

Instead, I tuck tail and go to my place. Ginny and Heath are on the couch, lying together, watching a movie.

Ginny lifts her head from Heath's chest. "Hey."

"Hey." I go to the kitchen and grab a glass of water, chug it, and then fill another to take to my room.

Ginny steps into my room as I go to shut the door.

"I'm tired, G."

She holds out her hand. "I brought you some Tylenol. I heard you drank Maverick under the table."

I take them with a nod of thanks. "Hardly under the table. He had to help me out of the bar."

Ginny snorts and sits on my bed. I kick off my shoes and lie down. I slept like shit last night, and the exhaustion I've kept at bay all day finally starts to set in.

"Have you talked to her?"

"No. Dakota made it clear she didn't want to talk to me."

"Made it clear that Reagan didn't want to talk to you or that *she* didn't want you to?"

I shrug. "Kind of the same thing."

"What happened?"

"Do we have to talk about this now?" I rub at the ache in my chest.

"You love her. I know that you do. Whatever happened, don't give up so easily."

"She ended things with me, so maybe you should be having this conversation with her."

"Oh, I will, but something tells me that Reagan isn't going to be the one to make a move here. It's up to you."

"Up to me to what? Beg her to feel something for me that she obviously doesn't? To trust me?" The things she said, the way she looked at me… I get that she was hurting, but she took all the things I told her I didn't want to be and tossed them in my face.

"Maybe she's right. Reagan's been through some shit. We are her family. You and Dakota especially. I don't want to fuck that up for her."

"You keep saying that this time things are different, but from everything I've seen, you're doing exactly what you always do." Ginny stands. "You want to prove she's different, now is your chance."

Chapter Thirty

REAGAN

IT'S A NEW DAY, CANCER. DAB ON A LITTLE EYE CREAM AND PACK YOUR BRASS KNUCKLES. IT'S AN ANYTHING GOES TYPE OF DAY.

Dakota and Ginny are in the living room when I force myself out of bed Saturday.

"'Morning," I say.

"I think you mean afternoon." Dakota smiles sadly and holds out her arms for me to go to her, which I do happily. I sink down on the couch beside her, and she wraps me in her arms. Ginny joins us and hugs me from the other side.

"Feeling any better?" Dakota asks, still hugging me tightly against her.

"A little." I pat the bags under my eyes. The sensitive skin hurts to touch. After the game, Dakota came home and sat beside me while I blubbered for the better part of the night. Nonsensical ranting and crying.

"I brought you an iced coffee." Ginny holds out the large cup to me.

"Thank you." I set it on the coffee table.

"Has he called?" she asks.

"No."

"I saw him last night after he got home from the bar. He was in rough shape." She glances at Dakota.

I want to ask more about what that means, press her for anything he might have said. But I don't deserve to know.

"Whatever happened, you two can get through this," Ginny pleads. "I've never seen either of you so happy."

"We can't. We won't. It's over." My heart breaks a little more, saying it out loud. "And it's probably for the best."

"I refuse to believe that," Ginny says. "Kota?"

My roommate shrugs. "I don't know."

"Well, I do," I say. "You guys weren't there. It was awful. We're not coming back from that."

"People fight. Adam's crazy about you." Ginny's optimism makes my chest ache.

"I know that he's your brother, but come on, we all know that Adam doesn't do second chances. Trust me. We're over."

"What can we do? Do you want to go to the track and run it out?" Dakota asks. I find it amusing that her plan for getting over heartbreak is exercising it out of her system.

"Or we could go to the wineries. Wine and sunshine, a little fresh air." Ah, sunny Ginny.

I love these two, but there's nothing they can do to make me feel better, and I don't feel like faking it for their benefit.

"Thanks, but I have to be at rehearsal in an hour."

"Did you get your part back?" Dakota asks, a note of hope in her tone.

"No."

"Wait, what?" Ginny asks.

I shake my head. "I screwed up."

"Can't you call in sick? You look sick." Dakota smooths a hand over my hair.

"No. I need to do something. Get out of this apartment and try to function. Besides, the show is this week, and every rehearsal is crucial. Even if I'm no longer a crucial member."

I still can't believe I lost my part. There will be other shows, but it stings. I worked so hard, and I was excited about doing something different, proving I'm more than a pretty face that can recite a few lines.

"Shouldn't you be at the game, anyway?" I ask Ginny, looking at the time.

"Eh, Heath can manage one game without me."

I quirk a brow. She's wearing his jersey and has blue and yellow ribbons tied to the end of her braids.

"I wanted to make sure you were okay. I'm here for you."

"Go. I'm okay."

"Are you sure?" She uncrosses her legs to stand.

"Positive. Get out of here." I smack her on the butt as she gets to her feet. I love how excited she is to go cheer on her man. It even makes me feel the tiniest bit better.

"Text me if you need anything." She waves as she leaves the apartment.

"You're not going?" I ask Dakota after Ginny's gone.

"No. I've had enough hockey for one weekend. Do you want to order food before your rehearsal?"

"I'm not hungry. I'm going to take a long shower."

"Okay, well, I'm going to grab lunch, and then I guess maybe I'll stop by the game for a bit since you have rehearsal, but text me as soon as you're done."

"I will," I promise.

Even though I really don't want to be there, I get to rehearsal ten minutes early. I'm in the back helping pull props when Mila gets there.

"Hi," she says tentatively. "I'm so sorry."

"Don't be. You are doing a great job."

"Still." She offers me a small smile. "What if I forget all my lines and mess up the entire show?"

"You won't. I'm not going to let you. Come on, let's get you ready."

AFTER REHEARSAL, I BORROW DAKOTA'S CAR AND HEAD OUT OF town. The drive to my hometown feels like a dream. I don't remember any of it, and I don't think I even turn on the radio.

Sitting outside of my mom's house, I take in the pots of flowers on the porch and the matching white rocking chairs. The house itself looks like it's been painted recently, and the windows are open, no dark curtains pulled tight across every crack, blocking out the light and any prying eyes.

I've been sitting outside for the past ten minutes, trying to work up the courage to go inside. Maybe Adam's right, and I should talk to her. I don't know anymore. Not talking to her feels as awful as talking to her. I should have asked Dakota to come with me, but I felt like I needed to do this on my own.

Besides, I can't remember the last time I introduced someone to my mom on purpose. Not that she was around enough for that to have even been a consideration.

I don't know what I'm walking into today. Seeing her inside counting money on the kitchen table, rummaging through couch cushions, or rolling change would almost be an easier thing to see than her making home improvements or knitting. Then I could get back in the car and leave without a second's hesitation. But if she's really changed, that decision is harder.

Try as I might to push away the longing for her approval and love. I can't. I hate that about myself. I don't need her. I've proven that by basically raising myself and moving away, going to college, having as normal of a life as I can. But deep down, I can't remove that piece of me that's connected to her. If I could, I certainly already would have.

She appears at the front door, probably trying to figure out who's creeping outside. She steps out and smiles. With a lump in my throat, I get out of the car and walk toward her.

"Reagan." She smiles. "Do you want some iced tea? I just made a pitcher."

I open my mouth to say no, maybe scream how ridiculous the thought of us sitting together sipping sweet iced tea is, but I came here with a purpose, and I need to keep my composure until I say my piece.

"Sure."

I sit on the front step as she goes inside. I can't bring myself to go in. This house holds too many memories, few of them happy. A sad, lonely girl lived here, and I don't want to be reminded of her.

Lori comes back a minute later with two glasses of tea and takes a seat in one of the rocking chairs. "I'm glad you came. I was afraid I'd never see you again after the other night."

"How long have you been back?" I don't bother with pleasantries. I come out swinging. I need to know if this is another one of her month-long attempts at a normal life before she disappears again.

"Three months."

Longer than I expected.

"Janine said you're working at the elementary school."

"I am, for now. The pay is crap."

I take a sip of the tea and then put the glass down. I can't sit here and pretend to be having a lazy Saturday afternoon with my mom on the front porch.

"You can't just show up in my life like you did. It isn't fair."

"I didn't know how else to see you."

"That isn't an accident. I did what was necessary to protect myself from you constantly coming in and out of my life. Every time I think I've put it behind me, you pop up." I thought this time, the years and distance between us, it was really over, and in some ways, that was so much easier to handle. Not expecting or hoping for anything.

"I understand that."

"Do you? Do you have any idea what it was like for me?"

Her brown eyes widen and glass over like she might cry.

"You let someone else raise me."

"Marge did a much better job than I could. You were better off."

"I wasn't." Hot, angry tears fall from my eyes. I swipe at them.

"She was a better mom than you, hands down. She made me breakfast in the mornings and remembered important dates, she never asked me to give her my birthday money so she could double it, but she wasn't you. I just wanted you to get your shit together."

She closes her eyes, and the tears slide down her cheeks. "I did the best I could."

"Now you seem to be doing better, and that's great for you, but it's too late for me. I don't need you anymore."

She stands and walks over to sit beside me, pulling me into her arms. It's a foreign feeling, but not altogether terrible. Once upon a time, curling up on the couch together was a regular thing. She smells just the same, like hairspray and her floral perfume.

My shoulder shake and I sob into her. I'm still pissed, but there's something comforting that my body can't deny. I let her hold me as I cry out my frustration and hurt. When I'm done, I pull back and wipe my face.

"I didn't come here to make amends."

"Why did you come?"

"Because I need to move on." I twist my hands together in my lap. "And I guess I needed to see this place for myself to see that you were doing better. The old house looks better than I imagined."

"Doesn't it?" She beams. "I'm glad you think so. It'll go for a pretty penny."

"You're selling it?"

Her mouth opens, and she sighs, then nods. She takes my hands in hers. "Think about what we could do with the money. You could pay for school or buy yourself a new car, have a nice little nest egg for when you graduate."

"And you? Where would you live?"

Her eyes twinkle as her lips pull up into a smile. A rush of uneasiness floods my veins.

"I found a cute little apartment in Vegas."

"I don't understand. I thought you were back and working at the school."

But I do understand. I understand all too well.

"This place was never for me. Or you." She places a hand on my cheek. "You and I were made for bigger and better things."

Closing my eyes, I focus on breathing and not the shattering of my heart. "What do you need from me?"

"Nothing. Well, the house is still in your name."

"Got it. You need me to sell it for you."

"For us."

Laughter spills from my lips. For us. Right. "I should go."

"Reagan," she admonishes. "What about the house?"

"You want to sell it, fine by me."

"Great. Let me call my realtor—"

"No. I think I'll find my own. It is my house after all."

The implication of that hits her, and she looks so shocked. "After everything I've done to the place? That's rather selfish, don't you think?"

"Selfish? Ha! Don't get me started. If I'm selfish, it's because I learned from the master herself." I wave a hand at her.

"I did the best that I could. And look how great you turned out!"

"No thanks to you." I take one last look at the house and at her. I know it's the last time. She'll have no more use for me after this. "I'll make sure that you're compensated for the renovations, but after that—you and I are done. I have nothing left to say to you.

Stop contacting me. I don't want to see you or read another email. You are not my family."

Chapter Thirty-One

ADAM

"Congratulations, Adam." Dr. Salco smiles—maybe the biggest one I've ever seen from her. I can see her teeth and everything. "We're all really pleased to offer you the scholarship, and we know you're going to be a great addition to the program."

I hold the envelope with the official award letter. It feels light in my hand. Unbelievable. I was sure after everything that happened that night, there was no way I was getting the money. I don't even remember half of what I said when I gave my speech.

I obsessed over that thing for weeks, and then I got up there, and it just didn't matter. I wasn't even nervous because I wasn't there. Not really. I was a million miles away while standing in front of a group of people who mean next to nothing to me. I respect them, sure, but they aren't a part of me like Reagan is.

"I need to apologize to you." I set the envelope on her desk in case she wants to snatch it back in a moment. "I lied about being engaged. Reagan is, or she was my girlfriend, but we were never engaged. I asked her to be my date, and well, we thought it would help my chances with the committee if we exaggerated our relationship. She's a hell of an actress." I smile, thinking back to that night of the mixer. How damn convincing she was. How much I liked it. "I should have come clean immediately, but I was afraid it would cost me the scholarship."

"Anything else?"

"All things considered, I should probably tell you to give Janine the money. She played fairly, and she deserves it as much as I do. Maybe more."

"I was surprised to learn you weren't engaged, but your relationship status did not sway the committee either way. I'm sorry you felt the need to lie to better your chances. Reagan explained everything when she stopped by yesterday."

My head snaps up. "Reagan came to see you?"

She smiles. This one is definitely the biggest I've ever seen from her. It even makes her eyes twinkle a little. "Medical school is hard. It helps to have people who will be there for you. Engaged or not, it's clear you do. Anyone who would go to such lengths to help you achieve your dreams is worth keeping around." She nods toward the envelope.

I swallow thickly. I do have people like that. A lot of them. Who does Reagan have?

"Please don't let this leave the room, as I haven't talked to Janine yet, but I was able to find another scholarship for her. You both deserve to be here, and I'm doing my best to make sure that happens."

"Thank you."

Another four years of going head-to-head with Janine —yeah, that sounds about right. I leave Dr. Salco's office smiling. I did it. I really did it. My chest expands as I breathe in, and relief floods through me. I'm one step closer to getting everything I want.

Or almost everything. I pull out my phone and consider texting Reagan. A week ago, she would have been the first person I told, and now? I think it's highly likely she'd ghost me even if I did reach out. I have no idea where we stand. I miss her, but I can't shake that feeling that maybe it isn't right. Maybe we are better off ending things now and protecting whatever friendship we can salvage from here. I don't want to hurt her—that much I know.

Instead of Reagan, I text my mom and dad. One text, both parents. I'm tired of tiptoeing around their divorce. They promised us that we'd still be a family, and I'm holding them to that. If not for me, for Ginny. But, if I'm honest, mostly for me.

Their responses come almost instantly. Mom hearts my text—she just learned to do that and does it every chance she gets—and says, *Congratulations!* From my dad, I get the applause emoji, and *Way to go!*

Look at me, bringing people together. I smile, and then it falls. I pocket my phone and head to class, the gloominess I felt earlier slowly creeping back in.

WHEN I'M DONE FOR THE DAY, I HEAD BACK TO THE APARTMENT. I linger outside of Reagan and Dakota's door. Texting feels wrong, but I can't just go over there. And if I knock and Dakota answers, she's likely to slam the door in my face.

I'm standing there trying to come up with a plan when Rhett opens our door and steps out.

"She isn't there."

"Who?" I ask.

He laughs. "Reagan. That is why you're standing out here creeping in the breezeway, right? Because if you're standing out here trying to find a new girlfriend, I've scoped out our other neighbors, and you won't do any better."

Of-fucking-course I won't do any better. There is no better.

"Where are you going?"

He's in jeans and a sweater. I think he even combed his hair.

"Going out. You want to come?"

"*You're* going out? Why?"

"Carrie and I broke up. For good this time." He lifts his arms to his sides. "I'm single."

"It isn't all it's cracked up to be," I mutter and then ask, "Where are you going?"

"Does it matter?"

"No, I guess it doesn't."

Mav drives the three of us to The White House. It's Valley U's unofficial basketball house. The place is insane. When you win a national championship, I guess this is what you can expect. Here's hoping that's us this year.

There are a lot of people, as is the case any time I've ever been here. The house itself is huge and over-the-top elegance for college guys, but the backyard is where it's at. There's a keg on one side of the yard, and a folding table has been setup as a DJ stand and music pumps. It should be too cold for swimming, but their giant pool is heated, and some of the bravest are in bikinis and trunks enjoying the water with a drink in hand.

Maverick disappears, mingling as he always does, Mad Dog in

hand. Rhett and I fill our cups with beer and slowly weave through the crowd.

"Adam!" someone yells my name, and I look over the crowd until I see Sage heading toward me.

"Hey." She gives me a side hug and waves at Rhett. "I heard you and Reagan broke up." She sticks out her bottom lip.

Way to kick a guy when he's down, Sage. Fuck.

"Guess who else broke up," Rhett says, bringing the attention off me.

"No way." Her eyes light up. "Wait until I tell the girls." She claps and runs off.

When she's gone, I look to Rhett. "Thanks for that, but I don't think you know what you just got yourself into. These girls have been circling you for four years."

"That was the idea."

I don't for one second think Rhett is going to turn into the guy who sleeps with puck bunnies. It's not who he is, but far be it for me to get in the way if he needs to sleep around after dating the same chick for six years.

"What about you? How long until you get back out there?"

I glare at him.

"What? It's a valid question. Remember Montana? You broke up with her on a Sunday night, and by Monday afternoon, you were dating…" He stares up like he's trying to remember.

"Barbie," I say.

He snaps. "That's it. Barbie."

"Not the same thing. Reagan's not the type of girl you just move on from."

"Have you talked to her at all?"

"Nah. Dakota told me to leave her be. She doesn't want to talk to me."

"That's Kota talking. She's hella protective of her girl."

"Maybe, but Reagan hasn't reached out."

"All right, well, you aren't ready to move on, and you're not going to talk to Reagan. What's the plan for tonight?"

"Can't we just hang out without girls?"

He laughs. "Yeah, we could, but what fun would that be?"

"It's like I don't even know you." I shake my head. "Come on. I'm a hell of a good wingman."

And I am. It's easy to focus on Rhett when I have no interest in talking to anyone else here. It's weird seeing him flirt with girls. Or attempt to—he's real rusty. He's giving me 'save me' eyes while he talks to some chick who ran up to offer her condolences to us on our recently failed relationships. Rhett being Rhett engaged, and now she's latched onto him.

"Excuse us," I say and wrap an arm around his shoulders, pulling him away. "There's an emergency. He's the only man for the job."

Rhett hurries with me to the other side of the yard. "What's the emergency?"

"Getting you away from that chick."

"Thank you." He grins. "Nice acting skills. I think Reagan rubbed off on you."

It physically hurts every time I hear her name.

"No problem. If I'm going to be a good wingman, I'm going to need to know what your type is, though."

"I don't know." He shrugs one big shoulder. "What's your type?"

An image of Reagan flashes in my mind. Is that my type? I try to find the common thread between her and other girls I've dated. Doesn't matter. She's the only one I want back.

"Thinking about Reagan again?" he asks with a grin.

"Maybe."

"You get this look on your face. Look, I know we're different, and so any advice I give you is probably falling on deaf ears, but I think you should talk to her. Get closure or get her back, that part's up to you, but you're a real bummer to party with." He lifts both hands to his sides. "I'm finally single. You've been razzing me for years so we could pick up chicks together, let's do it!"

Shit, he's right. Many times I've wished we could do just this—party and be single at the same time.

"Okay, yeah, let's fucking do this."

For the next three hours, I am the life of the party, drinking, chatting to anyone and everyone. We play beer pong, flip cup. Hell, we even jump in the pool in our boxers. I don't even try to fake interest in the girls that blatantly hit on me, but it doesn't matter. Tonight is about Rhett and hanging with my best buddy.

Rhett's giggling like a tween girl as we leave the party to catch a ride. Mav already left. It's probably the first time ever that Rhett's stayed out later than him.

"I lost a sock somewhere," he says.

"Got a phone full of numbers, though."

"Yeah." We get in the Uber, and Rhett starts scrolling through his new contacts. "What's the likelihood I'm going to remember who Pink Shirt Hottie is tomorrow?"

"Slim, buddy, but you can always lead off with a text that says something like, 'I fat-fingered your name when I entered it into my phone, and now I can't remember it, but I really want to take you out'. In the future, have the girl enter her contact info in your phone. She'll tell you as little or as much as she wants. I once had a girl include her full name, birthday, address, and in the notes a list of her favorite color, flower, and food. You can learn a lot about a girl by what she puts in your phone."

"Wise words. Should have known you had a system."

By the time we get to the apartment a few minutes later, Rhett's so sleepy he shuffles up the stairs and into our place. He falls onto his bed facedown, fully dressed—minus one sock.

I head back out the front door, walk to Reagan and Dakota's apartment, then hesitate. I knock softly and wait. I'm about to give up, head resting on the front door when she opens it.

"Hey." I shove both hands in my jeans pockets and take a step back.

"Hi." She folds her arms at her waist and looks around. "What are you doing here?"

"I missed you." It's honest, but damn, I hadn't meant to blurt it out like that.

"I've missed you too." The words should make me feel better, but she says it like it's a real inconvenience.

"I started to text, but I wasn't sure you'd answer."

No response.

"Listen, I'm sorry about the other night. I can't imagine what that was like for you having your mom show up. I should have gone with you, and I never should have let her use me as a messenger."

"She would have found another way. She's amazingly resourceful when she needs something. I went to see her today."

"You did?"

Reagan nods. "I thought maybe she really had changed." She

huffs a laugh. "Lori wants to sell the house, but it's in my name. She didn't come to Valley to reconnect or because she thought I was engaged, she needed money. Like always."

"I'm sorry." Damn, I hate that woman.

"It's okay. I feel like maybe I've finally made peace with it. Or I'm working on it." She rubs her upper arms and shrugs. "She is who she is, and I have to accept that."

"You shouldn't have to accept that. You deserve so much better."

She nods. Her brown eyes are haunted, and I want nothing more than to chase away the ghosts of her past.

"Can I come in? We could watch TV, talk some more. I just want to be near you. I've missed you so damn much. I got the scholarship, and all I could think about was calling you up and telling you."

"You did?" She sounds as shocked as I felt.

"Yeah. Thanks to you. I appreciate what you did. All of it."

"I should have done it sooner. I'm sorry that I almost cost you the scholarship. I bet Janine's bummed."

"Actually, it sounds like they found another scholarship for her too."

"Congratulations. That's amazing. Truly. I'm really happy for both of you."

"We could celebrate. I think I've got a bottle of red." I jab a thumb back toward my apartment. Standing here talking to her is the best I've felt all week, and I don't want to leave.

"I don't think that's a good idea. It's late."

"Okay. Can I see you tomorrow? This weekend?"

"The play is this weekend, so I'm going to be pretty busy. Even though I lost my part."

"I heard. I'm sorry."

"I still have to be there. The show must go on and all that."

"Well, how about next week? You name the time and place." I consider throwing in next month, but she looks like a startled horse about to bolt.

"I need you and me to be okay. Just about the worst thing I can imagine is the two of us not being able to be in the same room together. You mean too much to me. You, Dakota, Ginny, the guys—you're my family, and I can't risk losing the only family I have left."

"Never. You have us. Always. That doesn't change whether or not we're together."

"Doesn't it, though? This is the first time we've spoken in days." She shakes her head. "I should go. It's late. It was really good to see you, Adam."

My fingers itch to touch her, pull her to me, kiss her, but instead, I back away, slowly watching until she shuts the door.

With a sigh, I head back inside. I sink onto the couch. Ginny's in the kitchen getting a glass of water.

"Hey," she says, voice deep from sleep. "Where've you been?"

"Outside talking to Reagan."

"Yeah?" Ginny looks hopeful.

"I don't know what to do. I miss her, and I want to be with her, but maybe it just isn't meant to be."

"Why do you say that?"

"I always thought when I found the right girl, I'd just know. That things would click into place. That it would be easy. Mom and Dad always made it look that way." I realize what I've said and add, "And look how well that worked out. Fuck. I don't know."

"You're a guy who likes facts and certainties. I get that. I can't tell you if it's right or not with Reagan, but I know that this is the first time you've ever acted like you cared when a relationship ended."

"That's because I didn't want it to end."

"No?" Ginny's brows pinch together. "Then why did it?"

"Reagan said she could read it on my face—that we were done, and we weren't meant to be or whatever. That she was tired of waiting for the other shoe to drop." I rough a hand through my hair. "I hesitated. I thought maybe she was right."

"But you don't think that now?"

"I can't stop thinking about her."

Ginny looks at me with big, sappy eyes.

"I don't want to lose Reagan because I gave up too soon, but I know that she's been hurt, and I can't add to that—even unintentionally. What if I'm wrong?"

"You could start by telling her all that."

"I did." I think back. "Okay, I didn't use those words."

Ginny rolls her eyes. "Try using the words you mean, bro."

I chuckle. "Yeah, I guess you're right."

"Also, if you're going to win her back, you should do it not reeking of alcohol or wearing jeans with a wet crotch."

I glance down. My boxers were still damp when I pulled on my pants, and sure enough, there are weird wet spots all over the front. Fuck me.

"Go to bed," Ginny says. "We'll figure it out in the morning."

Chapter Thirty-Two

REAGAN

I walk to campus and head to University Hall. Janine's waiting for me at one of the tables.

I drop into a chair across from her, and she slides a cup across the table. "Light cream, half sugar."

"Thank you." I wrap my hands around it but don't drink. "And thanks for meeting me here. I wasn't sure you'd show."

"Figured it must be important. You haven't called me in years."

I nod. "I wanted to apologize for the way I've acted."

"No, Reagan, you don't need to apologize. When I found out that Lori was coming to the banquet, I should have told my parents to turn the car around. I know how crazy she's made your life."

"She wouldn't have listened."

"My mom told me she's leaving. I'm sorry. I really thought this time was different."

"You couldn't have known." I shake my head. "What I wanted to apologize for is avoiding you these past few years."

"Oh." Janine leans forward, and a hint of a smile spreads on her face. "Go on."

"When we got to Valley, I was so eager to start fresh. You were a reminder of the past. You knew all the awful, embarrassing things that I wanted to forget. I felt like I couldn't really have a new life as long as anyone around me knew about my messed up childhood."

"I get it." Her smile is small and sad.

"You were always great to me. I don't know where I would be today without you or your family."

"Something tells me you would have done okay on your own. Just like you've done these past three years."

I think about Dakota, Ginny, the guys. I've never been on my own. Not really, but I appreciate her words.

"You deserve to be happy, Rea. It's all I ever wanted and if being friends with me complicates that, I get it."

"I'm stronger now. Just promise me we never have to mention Lori again."

"Deal."

I lean back in my chair. "So, tell me everything that's been going on with you."

"What do you want to know?"

"Everything that I missed the past three years. I did think about you often, for what it's worth."

"You haven't missed much. I have been so focused on school. I kind of forgot that this is the time I'm supposed to have fun."

"You want to stop focusing on school and have fun?"

"Well, no, let's not talk crazy. School is still my priority, but I let Sean talk me into only taking one class this summer."

"Such a slacker," I tease.

"How's Adam? Is he gloating over the scholarship?"

"He's okay. Excited, I think. We actually decided to end things."

"Seriously?"

"Are you really that surprised?"

She shrugs. "Sure, Adam's dated a lot of girls, but you two seemed so great together."

"We were faking an engagement around you, so I'm not sure you saw the most authentic version of us."

"Maybe, but I did read his speech."

I'm quiet, and she checks my expression.

"You didn't see it, did you?"

"No, I left before he gave it." I hate that I wasn't there for him. Maybe if I'd stayed, things would have gone down differently. If I believed that, it might be easier without him. We were always going to end.

"Not the speech he gave, the one he wrote." She pulls out her phone and slides it across the table. "He sent this to me the day before. Read it."

"I'M SO NERVOUS. I DON'T THINK I CAN DO THIS." MILA HOLDS A hand to her sternum and breathes deeply.

"Relax. You're going to be great. As soon as you get out there, you'll forget all about being nervous."

"No, I don't think so. I'm going to be sick." She rushes out of the dressing room and runs toward the bathroom. I follow, entering as she slams a stall door shut and heaves.

Eww.

"I'm just going to wait out here in case you need anything," I say as she heaves again.

Our costume designer walks into the bathroom. She has Mila's dress in one hand, standing in the doorway holding it open. "Have you seen Mila?"

"She'll be right out."

"She's late. Director Hoffman wants to see everyone in two minutes."

"We'll be there," I assure her.

Once the door shuts behind her, I ask Mila, "Are you okay?"

"No." Her voice trembles.

"Come on. Let's get you in your costume. Then you'll feel ready." I have no idea if that's true, but I sure hope so.

She steps out of the stall, looking a little green.

In the dressing room, she gets into her first costume, and we touch up her makeup.

"There. You look perfect." And it's a good thing because I can hear Director Hoffman's voice outside in the hallway calling for everyone to gather around.

We join the rest of the cast as he gives his usual pep talk, which includes no less than five reminders, all worded slightly differently to stay alert backstage and be ready to go when it's our turn on stage. We've never had an issue with someone sitting backstage not paying attention. We're all anxiously and acutely aware of every second of the show until the curtain drops, but we listen to his reminders anyway.

Mila grabs my hand and squeezes. I try to think back to my first show at Valley in front of a larger stage than I was used to in high school or community theater. I'm sure I was nervous, but all I can remember is how excited I was.

My heart aches that today I won't be the one out there.

When he dismisses us, someone else yells that we have five minutes before the house lights drop.

"Director Hoffman," Mila says, still holding my hand. "I don't think I can go on." She presses her free hand to her stomach. "I think I have food poisoning."

"Are you sick or nervous?" he asks, with no hint of compassion in his voice or eyes.

"Both, but I'm throwing up every few minutes." She winces like she's about to again.

He takes a step back, and his gaze moves to me. "Looks like you're up."

Butterflies swarm in my belly.

"Quickly now, we don't have a lot of time," he grumbles.

Mila drags me into the dressing room. She takes off her dress and hands it to me. I pull it on in a daze. My hair and makeup are already done, but she smooths a few wisps back.

I meet her gaze. She's beaming, and she looks far less green.

"You aren't sick, are you?"

She shakes her head and speaks quietly, "This is your part. I'll get my chance."

"Mila, no."

"Yes." She grins. "It's already done. Now go break a leg."

WHEN THE CURTAIN FALLS, I CLOSE MY EYES AND SOAK UP THE applause. My heart only now starts racing as if all the adrenaline and nerves are finally hitting me. The lights come up, and we go out in groups to take our bows. From the wings, I can see out into the audience. I scan, like I always do, seeing faces I don't recognize and searching for the one that's never there.

Sometimes I like to pretend my mom is here, and I just don't see her, or maybe she snuck out early to keep it a secret that she came. It's a fantasy I don't truly believe, but I indulge in it. One last time.

When it's my turn, I walk out to cheers and yells. I wave and then bow. The applause seems to get louder and louder, and I let it fill me up, soothing the pain. Here I make a difference to many. I'm all of their daughters, all of their friends. I'm family, if only for tonight.

The entire cast joins hands, and we take one last bow together. As I stand and we start off stage, I get one last glimpse out into the audience. I know she isn't here, but maybe I'll always look for her.

Mila is waiting for me backstage. She squeals and practically tackles me with a running hug. "You were amazing."

"Thank you," I say. "For letting me go on tonight. It was everything."

She nods. "Welcome. Now go back out there and let your fans squeal at you."

I accept congratulations and other encouragement from people as I walk out in front of the theater. I stop and chat, smile for pictures, and accept hugs from strangers.

"Reagan," someone calls, and I glance up to see Dakota, Ginny, and the guys. Even Adam. Especially Adam.

"What are you doing here? I told you, you guys didn't need to come. I wasn't even supposed to go on."

"Good thing we didn't listen," Dakota says and gives me a one-armed hug.

Adam hangs at the back of our friends. After everyone else has hugged me, he steps forward. "Congratulations. You were amazing. I am in awe of you."

"Thank you."

They keep fawning over me, and I absorb it all. After this past week, I will never take for granted these moments or these people.

"I should mingle and get changed," I say after a few more minutes talking with my friends.

Everyone else offers one last congrats and hug, then Adam smiles tentatively. "Can we talk real quick?"

People are coming up, standing by to talk to me. One person taps me on the shoulder. I smile at them and then glance back to Adam. "Sorry. I need to–"

"Yeah, of course." His brow furrows. "Of course. Congrats again."

"Thanks for coming." I hug Dakota again because I can't help myself. I'm so glad that she's so stubborn. "I'll see you guys later."

It feels like an hour goes by, and the theater is still packed with people, cast members who haven't been able to escape, as well as families and friends that are lingering to talk.

My hand goes to my throat, and I apologize to the nice couple I'm talking to, citing needing a drink of water. It's true. My throat is dry and scratchy, but I am ready to retreat back to the dressing room, change back into my normal clothes, wipe off my makeup and go home.

I'm almost to the door that leads backstage when a deep voice crackles over the speaker, "Hey, everyone. Sorry to interrupt."

Chapter Thirty-Three

ADAM

I've had worse ideas, but as I start talking and every head in the theater snaps up to look at me, giving me their undivided attention, I can't think of a single one that could have ended with this level of humiliation. I can usually talk myself out of bad ideas. I'm good at weighing the pros and cons and deciding against whatever stupid notions pop into my brain.

Not tonight. I'd do anything to prove to her that I'm not going anywhere. That I'm either going to fail spectacularly loving her or be the best friend she's ever had. Still, I hope I don't pass out or get booed off stage before I can force the words out.

I make the mistake of looking at Rhett and the guys grinning from the back of the theater. I appreciate their support, but I can barely look at them without wanting to hop off this stage and tell them all to fuck off.

"I'm looking for Reagan," I say to the crowd. I was waiting for her to finish talking to her fans, but at some point, I lost track of her. It was somewhere between hearing my buddies' suggestions for winning her back and deciding myself that she deserved nothing less than seeing me lay it all on the line for her. Now, here I am.

Everyone looks around for her. I might have just made an ass of myself for nothing. She's on her way back to the apartment, and I'm still here standing on stage making a fool of myself.

"There she is." A guy in front of the stage points, and I follow the line to where Reagan is slowly walking toward me with a confused look.

The spotlight comes on, blinding me. Well, that feels unnecessary. I glower in the general direction of whoever turned it on but can't see shit.

"What are you doing?" Reagan asks quietly.

"You missed my speech last week. I think you should hear it."

"Here?" She glances around, smiling politely and waving at the crowd.

I almost jump down and beg her to hear me out anywhere else but here, but I need her to listen—really listen. "Here."

She nods. Then I start to get really nervous. What the hell was I thinking? I should have gone with one of Maverick's ideas. They were bold and ridiculous, but they didn't include public speaking.

"Umm…" I sweep the crowd and swallow down my nerves. "When I was eight, I broke my arm playing hockey on the street with some friends. My mom drove me to the hospital, bone sticking out of my arm. I didn't even cry. I was shocked, terrified, really. All I could think was that they were going to have to amputate my arm." I chuckle and swallow down the lump in my throat. "I was so scared I'd never play hockey again. When the doctor came into the room and told me I could keep my arm and I'd just have to wear a cast for a while, I was so happy I cried."

I continue on with the story, telling them how the doctor

talked me through the entire process, taking extra time to make sure a kid my age understood every single thing. I gloss over some of that this time I tell the story because this audience doesn't care about how fascinated I was with the process or how it made me want to be a doctor. But the procedure for setting a broken arm wasn't all I learned that day.

Reagan smiles. Her body language relaxes with every word pushing me to continue.

"It's just one of many times I was awed by the impact one person could have on my life. There's a study out there that estimates the average person meets ten thousand people in their lifetime. *Ten thousand.* Yet, the ones we remember, the ones who change the very core of who we are is a much smaller number."

"I've been lucky. So many people have touched my life. Most of them in a good way. Family who guided me to be a better man, friends who make me crazy but that always have my back."

There's a "Hell yeah!" from the back that I think comes from Maverick.

"Professors who have helped prepare me for the future, peers who push me to work harder in school, so they don't make me look bad, and a girlfriend that reminds me every single day what real bravery looks like. I will be a good doctor not because I want to change the world but because I want to make a positive impact on every single person I meet. I want to take their pain or confusion and ease it, help them get back to what's important—living life.

"I always thought that nothing could be more important than that – helping other people." I shake my head. "And I don't want to trivialize what it means to heal someone. I long held on to the doctor who fixed my arm as my ultimate hero. I thought it was his skills as a medical professional that I admired, but it wasn't—it was the hope he instilled. He made me feel like everything was still possible. Like the world was at my feet if I was just brave enough to get back out there and try.

"A scared kid afraid of never playing his favorite sport isn't high on the list of traumatic events, but it didn't matter to him. He treated me like nothing was more important. His affection and compassion changed my life. A million other doctors could have healed my arm, but if it had been anyone else, I might not be standing up here.

"I think the way that we impact people, wherever we stumble upon them, is far more profound than whatever we choose to do. Doctor, hockey player, actress, they're empty titles that come alive with the people who claim them.

"I just started seeing this girl." I meet Reagan's eyes. "A talented, beautiful actress. She couldn't fix a broken arm or do anything that she'd think is heroic, but she is the single bravest person I know. The core of who she is reminds me a lot of that doctor from long ago. She inspires me every day to pay it forward. Ten thousand people, but none of them have made me feel like her." I lock my gaze on hers. "I love you, Reagan. I have fallen in love with you. Ten thousand people, but I just want you."

I step away from the microphone. The place booms with applause and cheers. I almost forgot we had an audience. That prick of nerves is back, and I start to sweat at the nape of my neck.

She comes to me, smiling, tears in her eyes. I'm fresh out of words, so I kiss her instead. I don't know if I believe there's one right person for everyone, but I believe in her.

"That was a pretty good speech," she says, pulling back and

staring up into my eyes. "Did you mean it?"

"Every word. I'm not going anywhere. No matter what."

"Even the ones you left out? There was that whole section where you compared love to school. The importance of choosing the right one and working hard. I liked that analogy."

"How do you…"

"Janine showed me." She lifts her hand. Her fingers are curled around her phone. "I was just about to text you."

"Yeah?"

"The speech I had prepared wasn't nearly as good as yours, though, so I'm glad you went first."

"Still want to hear it."

"You stole the show and my line. I love you too, Adam. You're worth risk. *We're* worth it."

I chuckle and wrap my arms around her waist. Feels so good to be near her again. My lips are millimeters from hers when Rhett comes out of nowhere and hugs us around the neck.

"That was epic," he says. "So much better than those weak-ass pep talks you give us."

"Saved the good stuff for her," I say.

I hold on to Reagan as the rest of our friends join us.

"You're back together?" Ginny asks, voice about five pitches higher than normal.

"Yes," Reagan answers for us and leans up on her toes to kiss me. *Fucking finally.* "I should warn you, though. I've fallen so deeply in love with you. You're not getting rid of me now."

I swear my heart fucking leaps for joy. Like I'd ever try.

Chapter Thirty-Four

REAGAN

THINGS ARE LOOKING UP, CANCER. ESPECIALLY IN THE BEDROOM. EXPECT MIND-BLOWING ORGASMS ON THE REGULAR.

Did you write this?" I ask as I reread Adam's text with what I can only guess is my daily horoscope.

"Of course, I did. A lot more where that came from too. Every day, baby."

Since I saw Lori and told her I was done, she's stopped emailing my horoscopes each morning. There's a finality in that somehow. It was the one thing that tied us together all these years.

"You know she didn't write the horoscopes, right? She just pulled them from some website and emailed them."

"Well, how very unoriginal of her. Besides, it isn't a horoscope so much as it's a mantra for the day. And I'd say I already fulfilled today's." He winks.

Yes, yes, he did.

"Can you grab my ChapStick in that top drawer?" I ask Adam.

He's lying closest to my nightstand.

He tosses it to me and then asks, "What's this?"

"Hmmm?" I slather my dry lips. There was a lot of kissing last night and this morning. I look over to see a piece of red paper folded up into a small square. "Oh no, give that to me."

"What is it?!" He's smiling now, more determined to see it. He's unfolding it while I tackle him, trying to pull it free. He stands on the bed and holds it up high so I can't reach it. Stupid height.

"Dear Adam," he says and then falls quiet.

I sit on the bed and cover my face. Oh, god. Why didn't I burn the thing?

"Wait, wait, wait..." He looks down at me. "Is this what I think it is?"

"If what you think it is, is the most embarrassing moment of my life, then yes. Seriously, give it to me." I try sticking my bottom lip out. He is not moved by my pouty face.

"You put this in my room that night?" he asks and keeps reading.

"Yeah, I slid it under your door after a bad date and a bottle of wine. When I woke up the next morning, I knew I had to get it back."

"Why?"

"I'm sorry. Did you get to the line about holding my heart in your hands?"

He chuckles and joins me sitting on the bed. "This is one of the nicest things anyone's ever done for me."

"Almost done. And, if you would have woken up and found that, we would never have gotten together."

"You don't know that."

I stare at him disbelievingly.

"Okay, I probably would have thought it was a little over the top for a girl I'd barely talked to." He pulls me onto his lap. "But I love that you had a bad day, got drunk, and your thoughts went to me. Do you promise to always think of me when you're drunk?"

I think for a moment. "I do."

"There was this one time..." he starts. "Right before spring break last year."

I know which time he means immediately. It was just the two of us at his apartment while the rest of the group went to get food. I hung back that night just to spend more time with him. "I almost told you the night before you left, but I chickened out. Then you came back and started dating Maria."

"Man, what an idiot I was," he says, and then he more than makes up for it by kissing me until my alarm goes off. There goes my ChapStick.

"I have to go," I say reluctantly.

"Five more minutes."

"Can't," I say. "You said that at my last alarm, and this time I really do have to go."

He loosens his hold. "Fine. I gotta get to the rink anyway. Will you come out with us after your show?"

"Yep. Also, you have glitter all over your face," I tell him with a smirk and attempt to wipe it away. It's hopeless.

He gets up, pulls on his jeans, and tucks the heart into his back pocket. "I'm keeping this."

"No, it should be burned."

"Too late. It has my name on it, and I want to frame it."

I groan. He drops one more kiss on my lips. "See you after the game. Break a leg today."

"Good luck," I call after him.

"Don't need luck. I've got your heart in my hands," he says, voice fading as he walks out of my room.

Today's final show is a matinee. There's a difference in the air from just yesterday. Nerves are calmed, and all of those worst-case scenarios we all worried about have been thwarted temporarily. Ten minutes before showtime, we'll all feel it again, but nothing is as terrifying as opening night.

Director Hoffman looks up as I walk backstage. "Reagan, good morning. You're early."

"I wanted to talk to you before everyone else got here."

"Sure. Shoot." He drops his clipboard to his side and opens his stance to me.

"I'm sorry that I missed a rehearsal and that I was late, but I worked hard for that part. Mila's fantastic, but I want to finish out the show today."

The lines around his mouth pull up as he smiles. "It's yours. Mila called out sick. I think she's actually sick today. That's karma for you."

"Wait, you knew that she was faking?"

"Please." he scoffs. "This may be my first time directing, but I've seen it all before. You wouldn't believe what kids will say to get out of class."

"I'll bet."

"You did a great job yesterday. You found your fire. I know that I've been hard on you, but it's because I know you can do better. You just need to believe in yourself. Not the character. You."

"I think I'm starting to."

"Good. Go get ready."

I start toward the dressing room, and he calls my name.

"Yeah?"

"You're a good mentor to Mila. I know she appreciates it, and so do I."

"Thank you."

Since the hockey team has a game today, the guys won't be in attendance. Ginny comes before the show to make sure I'm set with makeup, then wishes me luck and heads out.

The matinee audience doesn't have the same energy as the night show, but when we take our final bow, it's to the same enthusiastic applause. Dakota's in the front row cheering and clapping with a huge, proud grin on her face. I don't think she's ever missed a performance now that I think of it.

I scan the crowd out of habit, and my breath catches when I see her. Lori is on her feet, clapping with everyone else. My knees buckle, but I'm held up by the people on either side of me. We exit, and the curtain falls for the final time.

I grab water and then head out front. I look for Lori, sure I imagined her, but there she is in the same spot, clutching her purse to her side, looking more than a little nervous. She gives me the briefest nod and then disappears into the crowd exiting through the back doors. I let her go. Maybe she needed her own closure. I have mine.

"You were amazing." Dakota hugs me. "Someday when you're a big star do you promise to still be my best friend?"

"Please. I'm going to need a personal assistant." I slip my arm through hers.

"And a personal trainer." She runs in place.

A groan escapes from my lips, but she laughs it off. "Come on. If we hurry, we can make the end of the game."

Chapter Thirty-Five

ADAM

"Great game, son." My dad hugs me, and then my mom takes her turn.

I look between them. "You both came."

"Of course." They look at me like I'm the crazy one, and they haven't been absent from all of my games for the past two months. I let it slide.

I don't know how comfortable they are being together, and I decide that tonight I don't care. "Let me grab Reagan, and let's go out to dinner. Heath and Ginny, too. Shit, let me just grab all the guys." They promised we'd be a family still, and families go to dinner after the game with their friends.

We head to The Hideout and span two tables that they've pulled together for us. I don't have any delusions that my parents are going to decide to get back together or that things will be easy from here on out. I'm sure there are lots of things I haven't even considered yet that will pop up and remind me that we're no longer the same family we once were. But for tonight, this is just about perfect.

"Is this okay?" I whisper to Reagan. It hadn't occurred to me until now that being around my family might be like rubbing salt in an open wound.

"Yeah, it's great. I'm glad to see you and Ginny both smiling so much."

I bring our fingers up to my lips and kiss the back of her hand. "You're pretty great."

She leans into me and presses a quick kiss to my lips. My mom doesn't miss a thing. She's smiling as she watches me and Reagan interact. I'm definitely going to get some phone calls about us. I introduced her as my girlfriend, but if the way I feel is projected in my actions even a fraction, then they'll know how special she is.

The conversation is light and fun. Mav is good at injecting humor into any situation. I can see my parents relax at their opposite sides of the table, and that makes me take a deep breath and sit back too. Dad asks me about our upcoming games. We're down to only a few games in the regular season, so the guys are quick to jump in with their excitement and hopes for regionals.

The only awkwardness comes as we're saying goodbye and my parents get in their separate cars. That's going to take some getting used to, but they came, and I feel like maybe we're gonna be okay—a new normal. Not the way I would have pictured it, but what is? Life has a way of taking whatever you think you know and flipping it upside down—testing your faith in people, love, and even family.

Back at the apartment, we all file out to the deck.

"Should we play sardines?" Dakota asks.

"I'm pretty cozy right here." Reagan snuggles into my side. I hear that.

"Yeah, and I'm tired of having to be a trio with those two." Rhett tips his beer toward us. "It's a real bummer."

I flip him off and pull Reagan closer.

"I took care of that and called in a backup," Dakota says. "Come on. It's so nice out, and sitting here with these happy couples makes me feel like I'm on a bad episode of *Bachelor in Paradise*."

"I would totally pick you if we were stranded on an island," Mav tells her.

"Who says I'd pick you?" She smiles at him, though.

It is a nice night. The late February weather promises spring is near. Warm enough to skip the layers but cold enough Reagan still sticks close for warmth.

"Where's this backup, Kota?" Maverick slings an arm around her shoulders as we get close to campus.

She points, and we all look ahead where Liam is walking toward us.

"Dreamboat?" Mav asks. "Whose team is he on?"

"Not it," Rhett calls quickly.

"What's up, guys?" Liam says.

"Hey," I say. "Ever play sardines?"

"Not outside," he says, looking around.

Rhett and Maverick argue over who has to pair up with him.

"I'll be on his team," Dakota says and rolls her eyes. "You guys are ridiculous. We need another person now that Adam started dating in the family."

Ginny giggles. "That sounds so wrong."

"If I'm dating in the family, so are you," I tell my sister. Heath's arms snake around her waist.

"But he might wrinkle his jeans," Mav says, motioning toward

Liam's pants. They are impeccably wrinkle-free. "Man, this sucks. Rhett needs a girlfriend. I want my partner back," he yells at Liam.

"Then maybe that should be the rule for the night," Dakota says and looks at Liam. "Take off your pants."

"No pants?" Rhett barks a laugh. His gaze rakes over Dakota's legs.

"Just for the boys," she clarifies.

"Aww, come on," Heath complains. "Tomorrow's laundry day."

"So?" Dakota lifts her hands in exasperation.

Ginny's laughter echoes into the night, and pretty soon, there are tears in her eyes. "Oh my gosh, again?"

Heath's starting to blush.

"What the hell?" I ask.

He turns to the side and pulls his jeans down enough that I get an eyeful of bare ass.

"Dude." I put up a hand to block my vision.

"Are you going commando, bro?" Mav asks.

Reagan laughs, and I pull her tight against me and duck down. "Shield me."

"Okay, wow. Well, that's unexpected." Dakota smirks. "I guess the guys can keep their pants on."

"Thank you," Rhett says and shakes his head. "There are some things you just can't unsee."

Reagan turns in my arms and looks up at me. "How come you never go commando?"

"I prefer not to chafe my dick on my jeans." Just the thought makes me shift uncomfortably.

"Fair point, but think how easy it'd be to cop a good feel if I could just slip my hand down," she says as she does just that—

slides her hand down the front of my jeans over my boxers.

I chuckle and groan, glance up and suck in to give her more room.

"Hey, hey, you two." Rhett kicks a rock at us that hits my hip.

"Dude, you could have hit her."

"But I didn't because I was aiming for you. No getting it on out here. Reminds me I'm going home by myself tonight."

"Gonna touch base with yourself?" Mav asks him, then laughs at his own joke.

Rhett nods enthusiastically. "Absolutely. A strategy session, if you will. Plan out all our goals for the coming year."

"Oh geez." Dakota shakes her head and gives Liam an apologetic smile. "You still want to be a part of this? I won't blame you for bowing out now."

"He's used to us," Mav says. "And he's gonna do the same thing later. Aren't you Dreamboat?"

Liam turns a bright shade of red.

"All right. Let's get this thing started." It's clear I'm going to have to be the one to take control of their ridiculousness, per the usual.

But tonight, I'm feeling pretty ridiculous too. Ridiculously lucky, ridiculously happy, and absolutely, ridiculously in love. Anything's possible. It's a one and a million kind of night.

Epilogue

ADAM

Four Months Later

"What could you possibly own that is this heavy?" I ask Ginny as I carry a cardboard box up the stairs to the girls' new apartment. She's moving in with Reagan and Dakota into a three-bedroom a floor up from their old place.

"I think you have the box with the sex swing," she says casually over her shoulder.

I stop, and Heath runs into me from behind with another box.

"Chill, dude, she's kidding. I think, anyway." His voice raises. "Did you buy us a sex swing, baby doll?"

Ginny laughs. "Who needs a sex swing, when you—"

"Okay, all right." I wince, ears bleeding, and mind going places no man's mind should go about their sister's sex life. "We've heard enough."

With all of us helping, it only takes one trip to get Ginny's stuff from my Jeep to the third floor, and then I'm free to grab Reagan and pull her into her new room.

It's a replica of mine, right up to the sliding door that goes out to the deck. It's open, letting in a nice breeze.

"Looks good. You got a lot done since this morning," I say, walking around to inspect all the details. Pictures are taped up on the wall above her bed—her with Dakota or Ginny, some with the entire group, and lots of the two of us.

"When was this one taken?" I ask, pointing to a picture of us sitting side by side at a party. There's a ton of people around, and we aren't paying any attention to the other. It's the old Reagan—the one who barely talked to me. I can tell by her posture and the reserved look on her face. And I guess it's the old Adam too because there's no way I could sit next to her now, reserved or not, and not notice her.

She laughs. "I found it in some of Ginny's photos. It's a picture of us, but it isn't really a picture of us. See Heath in the corner? I'm pretty sure she was trying to sneak a picture of him, but instead, she got me freaking out because I was sitting next to you."

I frame her face with my hands and kiss her. I hate that I can't spend all day every day kissing her and making up for all the missed opportunities.

"Ouch. It's going to take some getting used to all this." She tugs on my beard.

"I'm a college graduate now. Mature and wise. Gotta look the part."

She scrapes her nails along my cheek. Damn, that feels good.

I groan and pull back. "I have a meeting with my advisor. Hang later?"

"We're having a girls' night to celebrate our new apartment. Wine, junk food, The Notebook, face masks."

I smile, thinking of the last time I stopped in on their face mask party. My adorable llama girl. "Can I crash again?"

"Any time." She glides her hands over my stomach. "But maybe not until after midnight. Why don't you grab the guys and do something? Otherwise, Heath is going to show up here. He and Ginny are inseparable. Do you think it's possible they are more in love now than a year ago?" She shakes her head at the notion. "Crazy."

"I'd like to be inseparable," I say and kiss her again. I don't think I'll ever get enough. And yeah, I think it's real fucking possible I'll be even crazier about Reagan in a year. Time doesn't seem to do anything but make it more obvious how damn lucky I am. "How long is your lease?"

"A year. I graduate next May, remember?"

"Oh, I remember. You're going to graduate and move to New York or Hollywood to blow up the stage." She talked about it often when we first started dating. I don't doubt for a second she'll do it. She's so freaking talented.

"Actually, I've been thinking I'd like to open a community theater. Something for kids." She looks down. "A place they can come after school and learn acting, singing, dancing. A safe place to be creative and silly."

"Yeah?" I ask. I hate that she needed a place and didn't always have one as a kid, but I love her so much for wanting to make a difference for others like her.

She nods. "Does it sound crazy? I haven't told anyone else yet, but since the house sold, I have enough to pay off my student loans and even a little extra."

"Not crazy at all. You wouldn't miss performing?"

"I'm not sure. I could always do local theater if I do. I don't really care about the size of the audience."

"You're pretty amazing. You know that?"

Her grin hits me right in the chest. "I do."

"Move in with me."

"What?" Her face pales. "But we just signed a lease. Ginny and Dakota have been so looking forward to the three of us living together."

"Not this year." Although the idea of having her in my space all the time sounds pretty great. "After graduation. Stay in Valley and move in with me. We'll figure out how to open your theater together."

"I probably have to get some experience first. I don't know anything about teaching kids."

"Can you do that here?" I ask hopefully.

"You're serious?"

"Completely."

Her smile is slow, but soon she's ear-to-ear grinning, dimples lighting up her face. "You want to live together?"

"Mhmm."

"What if you change your mind? A year is a long way off."

"I'm not going to change my mind, but if you want to think about it or decide later, that's fine."

"I don't need to think about it. Yes!" She bounces. "Yes! Yes, to all of it." She jumps into my arms, attacking my mouth. It's a welcome invasion. I forget all about my meeting. What can I say? I've got it bad.

Her fingers slide through my hair, holding my head in place, and I walk her backward to the wall so I can pin her against it.

When her back hits the glass, I adjust my grip and slide my hands under her shirt. Then dive back in, kissing her, savoring every stroke of her tongue, living for the way she nips and tugs at my lower lip.

She goes for the button of my jeans, and we maneuver around, mouths still joined, trying to get our clothes off. Not an easy feat. We slide along the door, fumbling and grinding into one another. Lifting her, I switch us so that I can lean against the door long enough to get her naked, but I take one step too many and free-fall backward.

"Oh shit," I yelp, knowing I'm about to slam into the ground. I hold tight to Reagan so that I'll take the brunt of it.

My tailbone hits first, then my shoulder and my head. The wood deck has no give, and I grunt as all the air's knocked out of my lungs.

"Are you okay?" I ask. Pain shoots through my ass, and I think I took a knee to a vital organ.

Heath comes running outside at the commotion.

"What the hell?" He sounds concerned at first, but then he bursts into laughter at the sight of us sprawled out on the deck.

My pants are down to my ankles, and Reagan's missing a shirt.

I don't answer him because I still don't know if Reagan's alright. I lift my head. Yeah, definitely going to have a bump on the back of my noggin, but it's the least of my worries. Reagan's curled up on top of me, and her face is buried in my armpit. Her back shakes, and I freeze. Oh shit.

"Reagan, baby." I lift her chin. Tears stream down her face, but her lips are curved up, and those shakes are from laughter.

"Oh my god, are you okay?" That's all she manages to get out before she starts laughing again.

"And you say we're bad?" Ginny stands next to Heath, smiling at the scene in front of her.

"Yeah, yeah. Glad we all think this is funny. Oh damn, that's gonna leave a mark," I say and rub my ass. "Gonna need to see if Coach will let me borrow some padding next time."

Reagan tries to make a pouty face, but she can't keep from laughing. "I'm sorry."

I get my pants up. Bending over hurts, but I'm distracted by Reagan's cleavage because she's still topless. She doesn't seem bothered by it, but I pull off my shirt and then bring it down over her head to cover her boobs from prying eyes. Just in time, too, because Mav, Rhett, and Dakota make their way outside.

"Great. Wonderful. Let's all enjoy this moment together." Damn, it hurts to talk.

They're laughing their asses off at the situation.

"Bet you wish you had a sex swing now," Ginny says.

She pushes the guys back inside, leaving Reagan and me alone.

Reagan jumps to her feet, looking far more spry than I'm feeling capable of.

"Come on, big guy." She takes both hands and helps me to my feet, leads me inside to her bed, and as soon as she starts kissing me again, the pain magically disappears.

Out of nowhere, she starts giggling again. Her brown eyes twinkle and soften. "I can't believe that just happened. Are you okay, really?"

"Never been better."

And that's the damn truth.

Epilogue

REAGAN

Two Years Later

TODAY IS THE START OF SOMETHING BIG, CANCER.

The Valley Children's Theater ends the summer session with a performance of Alice in Wonderland. Adam's in the front row, clapping and smiling as the kids take their bows. I watch him from the wings, heart bursting with how proud he looks of them. He should be. With the amount of talking and obsessing I did over my first assistant director job, he probably knows these children and their struggles as well as I do.

When Director Martinez calls me to the stage, Adam gets to his feet with the rest of the audience. I wave, not quite as at home on stage in this role yet, but getting there. We all take one last bow before the curtain falls.

I have to see to the kids backstage, make sure they get changed and find their parents before I can meet him out front. He's leaning against the wall with a dozen roses in hand.

"Happy Birthday, baby," he says, kissing me and wrapping me in his arms. "And congratulations. They were great."

"Thank you." I lift the roses to my nose and inhale. "Aside from the white rabbit forgetting his watch backstage for his first scene, it went pretty smoothly."

"Kid looked panicked there for a second," Adam says with a smile. "I was ready to hand over my own watch, but he rolled with it. He did well. So did you."

We head out of the theater and start the walk home, hand in hand.

"Now I can catch up on sleep, read a book or two, maybe reorganize the closet, get a manicure." I lean into him. "I'm not leaving the house for a week."

The theater is closed for two weeks before the fall session starts up, and I'm glad for the break to get in some late summer relaxing and tackling the things around our house that I've neglected over the past month.

"You could do that, or you could ignore all of your responsibilities completely and let me take you on vacation somewhere to celebrate."

"We do not need to go on vacation to celebrate my birthday," I insist. Last year he gave me a gift every hour, on the hour, all day long. I think it's sweet how he wants to pamper me on my birthday as if he's trying to make up for the fact the woman who brought me into this world doesn't, but it's totally unnecessary. Adam's love shines through every single day in a million different small, seemingly insignificant ways that mean everything to me. And that's all I could ever ask for.

"Not just for your birthday." He fights off a grin.

"Oh my gosh." I search his face. "Did you get your test results back?"

He nods. "Two hundred and forty-eight."

"Adam, that's amazing!" I throw my arms around him. He's been seriously stressing the results of his step one test. He and Janine spent months studying for it. Med school is not for the faint of heart. "Did Janine get hers back?"

"Yeah."

"And?"

"Two hundred and fifty." He rolls his eyes.

"Oh, she's never going to let you live that down."

"No kidding. She keeps sending me silver medal GIFs and memes."

"Ah, what an amazing day. Did you already know this morning with the horoscope?" He still sends them to me every morning, and it's my favorite part of the day. Sometimes they're silly, or sweet, sexy, but they always bring a smile to my face.

"No, uh, actually, I didn't."

"Must be fate." I rest my head on his arm as we walk up the sidewalk in front of our house. It's just a rental, halfway between campus and the theater, and within walking distance of both, but I love it.

My phone rings in my pocket, and I take it out. "Dakota's calling. She probably wants to make sure I didn't blow my first assistant directing job. I threatened to eat my way through the entire ice cream aisle if I did. I should answer and let her know I survived."

"She'll call back." He plucks it from my hand and puts it in his back pocket, then takes my hands. "We're having a moment here celebrating us."

His mouth slants over mine, and I lift up on my toes to thread my fingers through his hair. He breaks the kiss and rests his forehead against mine. Those stunning hazel eyes pierce right through me. I don't think I'll ever look at this man and not feel like the world is standing still.

"I almost forgot to give you your birthday card." He reaches into his back pocket and pulls out a red piece of paper.

"You made it?" I ask as I take it from him. The construction paper is cut into a perfect heart shape.

He grins as I unfold it.

REAGAN,
MY HEART IS YOURS. MARRY ME?
ADAM

The words register slowly. I read it twice, tears blurring my vision.

"I love you. I want you to be my wife. I want to send you horoscopes every day for the rest of my life and celebrate your birthday big every year. I'll be in the audience every single time you're on stage, whether it's acting or directing. I'll cheer you on or wait with a tub of ice cream. I want all of it. Marry me, Reagan?" He pulls the ring box out of his pocket and gets down on one knee. It's straight out of a fairy tale – no, it's straight out of my dreams.

"Yes. Oh my gosh, yes!"

He slides the ring onto my finger. I toss the roses to the ground, jump into his arms, and kiss him with everything I have. He spins us around, laughing into my mouth. My heart is so full and complete, all because of this man. The past two years have been the best of my life. And now, he's promising me more.

My phone rings again. The melody starts softly and gets louder.

"She'll call back," I say, knowing it's Dakota again. I was a tad dramatic when I called her this morning freaking out about tonight, so I know that she'll keep right on calling until she knows I'm okay.

Adam places me on the ground and hands me my phone.

"Answer it." He grins and then kisses me on the forehead. "She wants to tell you congratulations."

It dawns on me that she already knew he was going to propose tonight.

Today is the start of something big.

Of course, she knew because Adam thinks of everything, and if he were going to ask anyone for permission to marry me, it'd be her. She's my family.

And now he is too.

Epilogue

REAGAN

Four Years Ago

KEEP YOUR EYES OPEN TODAY, CANCER! SOMETHING GOOD IS COMING YOUR WAY.

I can't believe it! Our own place." I drop the first box onto the empty living room floor.

Dakota pulls her hair back into a ponytail and fans her face. "I should have waited to break up with Miller until after we moved in. Could have really used a hand carrying all this."

"Who needs boys?" I ask. I'm feeling too excited to care about the sweat dripping down my back. "There's just one more box. I'll get it."

I head back out and lift the box from Dakota's trunk. It's so hot. I'm exhausted, arms quivering from carrying all of our belongings up a flight of stairs, but nothing is going to make this day less awesome. For the first time in my life, I'm living in a place I picked out all by myself. Nothing but good things to look forward to.

I maneuver awkwardly, closing the trunk with a foot and holding tight to the box. When it slams shut, I breathe out a sigh of relief. I did it! Wow. I might need to start exercising again because I am weak.

I come up short when I spot him. He's getting out of a black Jeep. The white T-shirt he's wearing clings to his upper body like Rose holding on to that door in *Titanic*. Sweet, sweet mercy.

My heart races as his gaze slowly lands on me. A small smile tugs at the corner of his lips, and he lifts a hand in a quick wave. I look around to make sure he's waving at me. I don't understand. Why is he waving at me? Probably because I'm staring. But I can't seem to stop.

Awkwardly and about three seconds too late, I return the gesture, carefully lifting my fingers from one side of the box. He heads toward me, and it feels like a dream.

"Hey." He tips his head in greeting.

He's even more gorgeous up close. Sandy blond hair that falls past his ears. Hazel eyes and a hint of a smile that comes off somewhere between cocky and genuine.

"Can I give you a hand?"

"With what?" I'm staring up at him dumbly.

He laughs quietly, and holy smokes, that sound—I feel it all the way to my toes. He steps forward, and I hold my breath as his hands brush mine. He gets a grip on the box and steps back.

"Oh right. Thank you." I tuck a wisp of hair behind one ear. Getting air to my lungs has never felt like such a chore.

"Moving day, huh? Coming from the dorms?"

"Yeah. You? I mean, do you live here too?"

"Yeah." He motions with his head. "You wanna lead the way?"

I'm sweating through my shirt, and I think it has little to do with the blazing sun sitting high in the late afternoon sky. Walking feels like a major feat as I move toward my new apartment. It's a big complex, and all the units look alike. I scan the numbers on the buildings until I find it and then manage to lead us up the stairs without tripping.

"You live here?" he asks, staring at the only door behind me.

"Umm… yeah." I double-check the number to be sure.

He shifts the box to one hand and jabs a thumb behind him. "I live just there. We're neighbors."

"No way." My heart flutters.

"I'm Adam, by the way."

"Reagan."

He grins. "This is awesome. I'd invite you over to meet the guys, but we've got training in thirty minutes."

"Training?"

"Hockey."

Also known as my new favorite sport. What I wouldn't give to see him slam someone into the boards. My sex clenches. Woah. Yeah, okay, maybe that's me I just pictured being slammed up against a wall by this guy. Any old wall will do.

"We're having a party at our place tonight. You should come."

"I wish I could."

"Hot date?" he asks.

I've never regretted having plans more in my entire life.

"Got it. Of course. Makes sense."

"Another time. You can meet my roommate Dakota, too."

"Can't wait." He hands the box back to me and then reaches

around to open the door for me. "Guess I'll be seeing you."

He looks over his shoulder once more before he goes into the apartment across from ours.

I let out a long breath, walk inside, and drop the box on the floor.

"Oh, good. I hope that one has toilet paper in it." Dakota lifts the flaps and rummages around until she pulls out some of our bathroom supplies.

I stare back toward the doorway.

"Reagan? Hello? Are you okay? Did you get too hot? I turned the air conditioning on, but it's going to take a few minutes to cool down in here. One hundred and ten degrees. Ugh." She's going on and on, and I'm still standing staring toward my new hot neighbor's apartment, a little stunned.

"Rea? Can you shut the door? Otherwise, the AC is kind of pointless."

"Sorry." I shake my head.

"Take a seat and cool off. I got it."

I'm burning from the inside. Holy hell. My heart's racing, and I can't seem to catch my breath.

"Rea? You're scaring me." Dakota steps in front of me and places a hand on either shoulder. "Did something happen?"

I nod.

"Whose ass do I need to kick?" She glances back at the doorway and then to me again.

Opening my mouth, I can't find words.

She gives my shoulders a shake. "Call the cops or grab my switchblade? What kind of situation are we dealing with?"

Well, that snaps me out of it. "You have a switchblade?"

"Focus." Another gentle shake.

"I'm fine. Don't cut anyone and definitely don't call the cops." I fan my shirt away from my chest. Sweat trickles down in between my boobs.

"You scared the crap out of me. Did you get too hot or what?"

"No. I met a boy. A very cute one."

"Already?" She glances toward the still open door, walks to it, and looks out. "No one. I see no one. Hot boys!" She holds her hand up to her mouth and calls. "Where are you?"

"Shh." I pull her inside and shut the door. "Oh my gosh, quiet. The neighbors will think we're crazy."

"I swear, wherever you go hot boys manifest in front of you. Poof! Hot attracting hot or something."

"Please, you're hot too."

"Yeah, I'm okay. You look like you belong on the freaking cover of a magazine. Even sweaty." She looks me over. "It's really not fair."

"I don't have your winning personality, though," I say sarcastically.

"True." She smiles. "So, tell me about the boy. Hot enough to invite in and christen your new room or just average, hope you'll bump into him again hot?"

"Neither."

Her brows scrunch together.

There are no words to describe the man I just talked to. I feel warm all over again just knowing he's ten feet away. Maybe naked. He said they had training. Is he in there changing?

Dakota snaps. "I need details."

"Way hotter. Hot like I think I just found the man I'm going to marry."

ACKNOWLEDGMENTS

Thank you to my family and friends who continue to support me, ask about my books, and even read them. I'm so grateful to have so many people cheering me on.

Thanks to my beta readers Amber, Amy, Anelise, and Katie, and to my editors Becca and Ellie. You ladies make my books so much better with your insight and eagle eyes! Special shout out to Anelise for letting me ask her husband eight million questions about medical school. And to Joe for answering them.

Thank you to my readers. Your messages and emails mean more to me than you know.

And lastly, thanks to my husband and kids for being the loves of my life.

ABOUT THE AUTHOR

Rebecca Jenshak is A new adult romance author, caffeine-addict, and lover of all sports.

Be sure not to miss new releases and sales from Rebecca – sign up to receive her newsletter *www.subscribepage.com/rebeccajenshaknewsletter*

www.rebeccajenshak.com

Made in the USA
Las Vegas, NV
11 August 2023

75971960R00181